GUILTY

RUBY SPEECHLEY

Boldwood

In memory of Lucy Fassett

First published in Great Britain in 2024 by Boldwood Books Ltd.

Copyright © Ruby Speechley, 2024

Cover Design by 12 Orchards Ltd

Cover Photography: Shutterstock

A CIP catalogue record for this book is available from the British Library.

Paperback ISBN 978-1-83751-398-7

Large Print ISBN 978-1-83751-399-4

Hardback ISBN 978-1-83751-397-0

Ebook ISBN 978-1-83751-400-7

Kindle ISBN 978-1-83751-401-4

Audio CD ISBN 978-1-83751-392-5

MP3 CD ISBN 978-1-83751-393-2

Digital audio download ISBN 978-1-83751-395-6

Boldwood Books Ltd
23 Bowerdean Street
London SW6 3TN
www.boldwoodbooks.com

PROLOGUE

The crisp air pinched their cheeks as they trudged up the steps, expelling white streams of morning breath as they went. The dull clang of shoes on metal echoed across the otherwise peaceful lane of gently swaying trees.

When they reached the top, they struggled to hold their chosen heavy lump steady, the roughness of the gravelly surface digging into their gloved hands. They leaned against the railings as they lifted it up high.

The thud, like a gunshot from a cannon, was louder than any of them could have imagined. It sent a dark cloud of startled birds up from the trees. They ran away laughing wildly, then, at a second, different kind of bang, they stole a glance at each other. But they didn't stop, didn't look back to see what they had done.

1

After receiving the news yesterday morning, my mind has shattered into tiny pieces. But I need to carry on.

'Come along Milo, let's take you to your room for the week, shall we?' I slip the lead from Mrs Wilkins' pale hand. She says a teary goodbye to her fourteen-year-old Cocker Spaniel who's been coming to our kennels since he was ten months old. He's slower than he was last year, but still has a spring in his step and bright eyes when he wants to play with a ball. 'I know how you feel, boy,' I tell him as I trudge down the path with him plodding by my side.

'Do you want me to take him for you so you can go and have a nap?' Lisa rushes up to me from the stables after dropping off three Yorkies. Her wellies are caked in mud and her fair cheeks are ruddy like the colour of her hair. She's wearing Martyn's old green quilted gilet from the boot room, which is far too big for her. I've told her to buy a new one and stop wearing that old thing, but she says she doesn't mind. Only her trained eye can see I'm struggling. I mentioned to her earlier that my head is thumping and I hardly slept.

'If you don't mind settling him in for me. See if he wants feeding too, I forgot to ask if he'd eaten.'

I'm not myself today at all. I'm completely hollowed out. I hate to leave it all to Lisa, but now I know I'm not going to be around much longer, there's no point clinging on. I'm tempted to tell her before the others get here, but I want to give her a few extra hours of *not* knowing. I hope she doesn't feel like I'm abandoning her.

'Will do. Now go and have a sleep,' she says.

I step into the kitchen and check the time then pour myself a large glass of water and drink down a couple of tablets. Thirsty work running the kennels in this mild end of August weather and a busy time of the year, apart from Easter and Christmas. We might have to start winding down bookings sooner than I thought; it's fast becoming too much for us to cope with. I gaze out of the window at the lush green lawn and the path that leads down to the old stable buildings I had converted into dog kennels. I never imagined it would come to this.

I kick off my boots and slowly climb the stairs. My legs are heavy with tiredness and my hip bones are screaming at me to lie down. As soon as I'm undressed, I fall into bed, shutting my sore eyes.

Martyn wakes me two hours later.

'Lisa's gone home to get changed,' he whispers, kneeling on the floor next to me. 'She'll be back a bit later.'

I open my eyes and smile at him. He's still wearing his suit and tie.

'The others will be here in about an hour. I thought you might want to start getting ready.'

I nod and he helps me sit up.

'I've ordered the usual Chinese. It'll be here at 7.30 p.m.'

'Thank you.' My voice is croaky, but I feel so much better. I take a minute then he helps me stand up. In the shower I rehearse what I'm going to say.

An hour later, I'm dressed and ready, thanks to Martyn hanging my clothes on the wardrobe handle to save me having to reach up to the rail for them. I finish my make-up and open my jewellery box. I pick up my favourite interlinked heart necklace, which

Martyn bought for my birthday seven years ago, just after we came back into each other's lives.

Cathy and Robbie are the first to arrive. She's wearing a buttercup-yellow strappy dress and sandals I've not seen before, which complements her auburn hair, and Robbie is in his usual designer jeans and navy polo top combo, bottle of prosecco in one hand, red wine in the other. Martyn and I kiss them on both cheeks.

'This is so nice; we're not used to going out in the middle of the week. Special occasion? Not forgotten a birthday, have I?' Cathy laughs, knowing full well she hasn't. She's not forgotten my birthday in thirty years.

'Nothing special, just a bit of news,' I say quietly and take champagne flutes out of the cupboard.

'Ooh that sounds mysterious.' She grabs the bottles from Robbie and hands one to me and the other to Martyn.

'What would you like?' I ask, even though I know what she'll say.

'Prosecco, please.' She turns to Robbie and straightens his collar even though it doesn't need it.

I try to open the bottle then pass it to Martyn who's ready at my side to take it from me.

'How about you, Robbie?' Martyn asks.

Cathy's only been with Robbie two years, and he

doesn't say much. Being so quiet and moody, we wonder what she sees in him, apart from the obvious – his Porsche and the expensive holidays he takes her on.

'A glass of red for me, thanks,' he says.

The doorbell rings and Cathy rushes to open it. It's Lisa. I silently expel a sigh of relief. I'm not sure I can deal with Cathy and Robbie on their own today. She's got far too much energy and tends to go over the top about everything. Robbie seems to be the complete opposite, but what they do have in common is neither of them seem capable of reading other people's moods or feelings. Lisa and I hug, as though we've not seen each other for days. I've come to rely on her so much recently. She's a good friend as well as my business partner. The rest of our close friends arrive and everyone is buzzing with energy and good vibes as though they're anticipating good news. It's lovely to see everyone dressed up so smartly. I hope I'm not going to let them down.

All through dinner I try to work out in my head how I'm going to word it – going away or leaving? I've been dreading this. I thought I knew how I was going to say it, but now I'm not sure at all. I push my food away. My stomach is a bag of snakes and I hope to God I'm not going to be sick. Kill or cure, I swallow down the feeling with a glass of prosecco which goes straight to my head. Now I've got a piercing pain above my eye.

'So, come on Heather, what's the great mystery? Why have you gathered us all here tonight?' Cathy spreads out her hands and laughs, as though we're about to have a seance. She glances around the table to garner everyone's backing of her stupid joke, but they are all beaming at me expectantly. Martyn tips his head as if to say, over to you. I blink and give him a barely detectable nod.

Guilt floods through me as I gaze around the table at all the happy but puzzled faces in the candle-light, chatting and laughing until a moment ago. Apart from my boys, these are the people I cherish the most.

But now I'm about to blow their world apart.

2

I place my hands on the table and push myself up. I need to be on my feet to break my news. I will not sink into my chair and become invisible; there'll be plenty of time for that down the line. This is my moment and I'm going to grab it by the throat.

'There's no easy way to tell you this.' I hang my head and shut my eyes, picturing the boys' faces when I told them last night.

'Take your time, Heather.' Martyn touches my arm and the warmth from his hand steadies me, which I need right now but try not to let on. I smile weakly at him, acknowledging the pain etched around his eyes. Part of me wants to push him away.

Maybe it wouldn't hurt so much if I hadn't let him back into my life. All I ever wished for our lives together has vanished. I clear my throat in the silence. Except it's not completely silent. The ticking wall clock is suddenly loud and cruel, reminding me how little time is left. But I'm learning how to slow down time, by not rushing about, enjoying the moment. Being present.

Morris and Monty are lying at my feet. Morris lets out a loud satisfying yawn making everyone laugh nervously. Monty licks my hand.

I'm a dog person through and through, from when I was a little girl. Anyone who knows me well knows that. Sometimes I wonder if dogs are more loyal than humans. I smile sadly and lean down to stroke their soft chins. They gaze at me with loving eyes. I take a deep breath and stand up straight.

'Right, I'm just going to come out and say it.' My stomach clenches as I gaze at their slightly concerned but expectant faces. I didn't think it would be this hard, but words have the power to change everything.

'The doctors say I haven't got long. The treatment's not working.' I take in the shocked gasps. 'It was always going to be a long shot, and well, it's not gone my way.'

My knees buckle but I manage to hold myself up – with Martyn's help. He puts his hand on mine, and I nod that I'm okay.

'Do you mean you're dying?' Cathy stands up, sending her seat falling backwards, her hands either side of her face. She's always been dramatic and clumsy. I picture a pot of red paint landing upside down on our classroom floor when we were eleven, and the look on Miss Tate's face as though she'd walked into a crime scene.

'Please don't be sad, Cathy, or any of you.' We reach across the table and hold hands. 'I actually think I'm lucky. I mean, we're all going to die some time aren't we? None of us gets out of this alive.'

My attempt at a joke is met with shocked faces.

'We don't usually know how long we've got, so I'm grateful I've been given notice so to speak, and I want to use the time I have left wisely. Especially while I still feel reasonably okay. I'm tired sometimes admittedly, and I'm getting slower moving about, but hopefully I'll have time to put my affairs in order, do some things I enjoy, be with the people I love.'

I open my hands out to them all and cast my gaze around each person. Not one dry eye. A pang of guilt reverberates through my body, but for once I have to accept that this is all about me. I can't deflect it on to someone else.

I wish someone would say something.

'Oh Heather, I'm so sorry,' Lisa says, wiping her tears on her napkin.

'I wanted to tell you this morning so we could discuss how the kennels will function without me, but I didn't think it would be fair on the others.'

She shakes her head. 'No it's fine, I understand.'

I look around the table at the rest of my closest friends. I've lived in Dunstable my whole life. It's part of who I am. Most of my family and friends still live near the town centre or around and about. A few have moved away, but their parents are still nearby so I see them when they come to visit. Tom and I bought this farmhouse a few months before Ben was born. It was in disrepair but buying a house to do it up was all the rage back then. Once we'd finished the house, I knew what I wanted to do with the barn and stables and half an acre of land. Converting it to kennels became our next big project, but by the time it was finished, Tom and I were over, and he'd moved out.

I want to put Lisa in full charge, do a handover while I still can. The thought of leaving my beloved animals and my dearest sons, Ben and Scott, hurts beyond comprehension, although thankfully they're old enough to look after themselves. They've grown up and left home and have their own lives now. I reach down and ruffle Monty's ear. How will I help the dogs understand I'm not going to be around for them? What if they think I've abandoned them? The thought of it sends an ache through my chest. They rely on me for everything. Old Morris is a bit deaf now and his joints play him up no end. Lisa's the only one who has enough patience for him. I straighten up again and my gaze lands on Cathy who is wiping her eyes with a napkin. I seem to have vacuumed the joy out of the room.

'I'm so sorry to drop this on you. You're the few most important people I wanted to tell straight away. Please keep it amongst yourselves. You know I don't like a fuss or sympathy, so please just treat me as you normally would.'

'There must be some new medicine they've not tried yet?' Cathy's tears track down her cheeks. 'They can't just give up on you.'

Her bottom lip sticks out when she's upset, and her voice becomes whiny like a child's.

I slowly shake my head and swallow the lump in my throat. 'The treatment hasn't even touched the sides. It was a long shot, I knew that, but it really is too late, it's too far advanced. There's nothing else they can do.' I flop back down into my chair as if a huge wave has knocked me off my feet and swallowed me up inside it.

It's barely a year since my diagnosis and it's taking every ounce of courage and strength to come to terms with the news. I blame myself for not going to the doctor sooner, but they say it probably wouldn't have made any difference because it's such an aggressive strain. I'm trying not to let myself plan too far ahead because it could be a matter of weeks not months that I have left. It's hard not to constantly go over the past though. My head won't stop digging up every little thing that's happened in my life, making it almost impossible to sleep through the night. Nobody warns you when you're given a terminal diagnosis, how regrets you'd buried and tried so hard to forget about rise up to the surface to torment you.

Robbie frowns at each of us in turn.

'Have you looked online to see if there's some other treatment they offer abroad?' he asks. 'A friend at work has taken his sister to America on some new trial. We could crowdfund it for you; it's sure to cost a fortune, but if it gives you longer.'

I shake my head. I understand Robbie wants to help. Being told nothing can be done is not always acceptable to people. It's only natural to want to try to find solutions. Everyone thinks they have the answer, have heard of someone who found a miracle cure. It's sweet of him. And it's the most he's ever said to me in one go. He's not that bad after all, I think. And he's clearly besotted with Cathy. I hope he looks after her.

Martyn has that same vacant look on his face as when I first told him. I squeeze his hand, urging him to answer for me.

'We've looked online at the various treatments and trials here and overseas, asked all the questions, of course we have, believe me. Every single night since Heather's diagnosis. But there's nothing. The illness is advancing too rapidly. We knew this was the likeliest outcome.' He draws the back of his hand across his forehead. 'Accepting there's nothing more that can be done has been so incredibly tough.' He looks at everyone then down at the table.

'Shit.' Lisa buries her head in her hands. Cathy is silent. She looks at us one at a time and when her gaze hovers on Martyn then back at me, I guess what she's thinking, probably what they're all thinking, desperate to ask.

I take a deep sigh and just say it. 'They don't know how long I've got exactly. A few months at the very most.'

'Oh Heather.' Cathy stifles a sob. Robbie pulls her to him.

Lisa is crying. She gets up and hugs me. Then everyone stands up and one by one they take turns holding me in their arms and hugging me tightly. I'm going to miss our little group. I picture them a year from now when my chair is empty.

'I hope you'll all help me organise a party to celebrate my life. I think I need to hold it in the next couple of weeks, while I'm still feeling well enough. I'd like to say my final farewells to everyone I've ever known. It'll give me the chance to tell people all in one go, otherwise it's going to be quite a task.'

'That's such a lovely idea,' Lisa says. 'I'm sure we'll all be more than happy to do our bit.'

Everyone nods as they dab their eyes.

'Of course. We'll all muck in.' Cathy's gaze lands with sympathy on Martyn. She probably feels sorry that our great romance is going to end so soon.

Shock is still registering on everyone's faces.

I let out a long breath and shut my eyes. A final party will give me the perfect chance to say goodbye, as I will not have the time or the energy to meet up with people individually. I want to thank everyone I've known for being part of my life, the good *and* the bad, because I can't pretend everyone has had a positive impact on me.

I need to unburden myself and leave this world with a clear conscience, which will mean revealing secrets, especially the biggest one that's been burning a hole in my heart for the last twenty-seven years.

It's time to tell the truth.

3

THREE WEEKS LATER

'Are you sure you still want to do this, Heather?' Martyn stands behind me in front of the mirror, his eyes drooped with sadness, locked onto mine.

I nod. 'I've never been more sure of anything.'

His warm hands smooth down my arms.

'I'm just saying, there's still time to cancel if you want to change your mind.'

We don't look like we're getting ready for the party to end all parties, me in my fluffy old dressing gown and hair towel, him in a T-shirt and shorts. How many more times will we stand here together? It shocks me that he has more white hairs in his stubble than brown. When did that happen? And the irony that I've finally reached my ideal weight isn't lost on me. Still, I have to find humour in the darkest corners.

'I want to enjoy myself one more time and it's the best way to tell everyone all in one go. I don't want friends and old neighbours and colleagues finding out in the local newspaper that I've died and wondering why I didn't say anything to them.'

'I just hope people understand why you've chosen to tell them like this. It's not easy news to take. But I know, it's your decision, your life; you're entitled to do whatever you want.' He kisses my neck.

I nod and press my lips together tightly. I don't really have a choice. I don't know how much time I have left. I could say nothing and slip away virtually unnoticed. I've considered it. I'd rather not have to do any of this. I'd rather be curled up under a blanket in the conservatory with a good book, Morris and Monty lying either side of me, with not a care in the world. But this party is for me as much as it is for my friends and family. I've told the most important people in my life, and this is my chance to tell everyone else face to face, then I can relax and really enjoy myself, for one evening at least. Maybe I'll use the opportunity to say a few home truths.

Perhaps I should have travelled more or tried living in a different county, or country come to

that? What if I'd married Martyn straight out of
school and never met Tom? My life would have
been so different. Our little gang all went to the
same upper school in Dunstable. It's where my love
for Martyn Dunn blossomed and the innocence of
our childhoods faded forever. I haven't told any of
them what I intend to say at the party tonight, because I know they'll try to stop me. Everyone who
knows the truth swore to secrecy. But living with a
secret as big as that, has been like dragging a
weight around with me everywhere. The truth is
crying out to be released. I can't leave this world
without speaking *my* truth. That's what they call it
now, isn't it? Thank goodness for the younger gen-
eration.

There are bound to be some who won't approve of
the way I make the big announcement, but I want to
be true to myself. Do things my way, even if that
seems selfish. I don't think I've ever put myself first, so
it does feel strange, but I need to. I can imagine some
of the oldies like Aunty Joyce, whispering behind her
hand about how undignified it all is celebrating such
a thing, and how it would never have happened in
her day. Yet she's always been quite happy to take advantage of my good nature and has never paid a
penny for Bonny to stay in the cattery. Well, she'll

have to dig her hand in her pocket next time or find other suitable lodgings.

I've invited just about everyone I could think of that I consider to be a friend or family, going right back to people like Aunty Joyce, who was there the day I was born. I've even invited people who used to be my friends but for one reason or another we fell out or lost touch. Martyn thinks it's a step too far, especially when he saw Dan's name on the list.

'We've not been in contact with him for decades.'

'I can't not invite him. He's one of us.'

He was even less enamoured that I'd invited a small cluster of our so-called enemies.

'Tell me you're joking,' he said.

'Why not? I want to look them straight in the eye, let them know there's no hard feelings on my part.'

I'm not sure if he thought I was going a bit mad or if he simply thought forgive and forget was impossible in some cases.

'But Dan, seriously?' He frowned.

'I need to see him, just one last time. Please try to find him. We don't even know if he's okay.'

If he does turn up, it will be strange for all of us, I know that, but I'm not going to apologise. I won't get another chance. I can't miss this opportunity to celebrate with *everyone* I've known, all 190 or so people.

And it will give me the size of audience I could only dream of.

It seems like nearly everyone is coming too. The invitations went out two weeks ago, but within a day half of the guests had clicked yes, and by the third day, over 90 per cent said they'd be here to see me off. They only know 'I'm leaving'. Some probably think I'm going on a round-the-world cruise or I've decided to live somewhere like America or Australia. There was a time when I wanted to do those things, but I never did. I met Tom, had the kids and settled here. A few would be glad to see the back of me, I'm sure, but that's okay, they're the ones who'll have to live with their mean selves.

I glance up at my red velvet dress hanging over the wardrobe door. The old me would have chosen to wear something even more daring without a second thought, and I hope to capture a little of my fierce younger spirit. I hate how diminished I've become in the last few months. How reliant I am on everyone.

In the mirror, I see Martyn follow my line of vision. He reaches up and touches the velvet cloth between his thumb and forefinger before unhooking it from the door and handing it to me.

'See how it made better sense to hire outfits,' I tell him wistfully. For once, being right feels bittersweet because I threw out all my party clothes after my last prognosis. In fact, I only kept things I knew I'd be wearing over the coming weeks, and none of those are remotely glamourous. It was a hard process, wrenching away part of me, mourning who I used to be. Every skirt, every dress reminding me of nights out and events where I was sexy, confident and fierce. Facing up to who I am now and the short life ahead of me, in touching distance, has sometimes been harder than the physical pain.

Martyn looks away, still finding our circumstances hard to process. He can't really argue with me I suppose, and he probably wouldn't want to. He's seen me deteriorate and he feels helpless, as all my family do. He constantly laments the years we've wasted being married to other people. I don't see it like that, otherwise I wouldn't have had my two beautiful boys, and the truth is, I loved their father. But I admit, when I bumped into Martyn in Spain seven years ago, I felt the same flutter in my chest I'd felt at our first school disco. I remember the glittering light sparkling above us as we moved towards each other on the dance floor, our hands outstretched.

The doorbell rings, interrupting my thoughts.

'I'll get it.' Martyn kisses my cheek and hurries along the landing. It's probably Lisa.

I glance at my mobile phone and tap open a notification. It's from a number I don't recognise. I let out a small gasp at the short message, blink at it a few times then stab it shut.

I check the time on my bedside clock: 5.33 p.m. I pick up my box of tablets from the dressing table, pop two out and knock them back with the glass of water Martyn brought up for me earlier. I'm feeling so much brighter after my nap and shower.

Only two hours to go until my party kicks off. I've always been a people pleaser but for once I'm putting myself first, because this old lioness still has some fight left in her, and after tonight, nothing will ever be the same again.

4

There's a light tap on the door. Lisa pops her head round. Her new honey highlights brighten up her red hair.

'Come in, come in. You look gorgeous. Love the curls on you.' I greet her in a hug.

'Thank you. Thought I'd ask my own hairdresser to freshen up my look for this evening. How are you feeling?' She takes my hands in hers and scans my face, her brows knitted with concern.

'I don't feel too bad. I had a good sleep, took my medication, and had a lovely shower. I'm ready for this.' I swing our joined hands in resolve.

'I want you to enjoy every second of your evening and the pampering, okay?'

I nod, tears in my eyes. She's always so kind to me. It's embarrassing how everything is making me cry these days. I've never been one of those women who cries easily.

Lisa does most of the dog walking and mucking out of the kennels now, but I'm still able to help with the feeds. It's almost three weeks since we cut down the number of bookings, and it's still busy. I enjoy the day-to-day routine and will miss it when I become frail. How I've taken the simple things for granted. I craved stability for the business for so long, and when I met Lisa and she started working at the kennels and cattery, I knew straight away I'd found it. The dogs and cats are my life now the boys are grown up and have left home. It took me ten solid years to build up the business from scratch, and I'm sorrier than I'll admit to anyone to be leaving it. If I could take my two spaniels, Morris and Monty with me, I'd be happy, but it would hardly be fair on them. 'This is probably going to be the last time I get dolled up and look remotely human and dare I say it, attractive.'

'No, that's not true. You always look attractive, and there'll be other celebrations, I'm sure.' She smiles but it's tinged with sadness and a doubt that it's true, but I appreciate she's being kind and hopeful so I don't correct her. Sometimes I think it would be better not knowing I only have a short time left to live. But some days I feel so ill, the uncertainty of not feeling better would have made me worry anyway. Lately I've tormented myself thinking about all the 'last times' of things I'm going through. Such as driving my car, going to the cash and carry to do a big shop and taking the dogs for a long walk across the Dunstable Downs on my own.

Then there's the ones I hadn't realised *were* final until long afterwards. Like the last time I was at my parents' house at Christmas, when they were both still alive and happy many years ago. Before Alex died. Before everything. My heart aches with longing to be there with them all again, to hear them laughing, the four of us together as a family. Alex sitting with us round the kitchen table playing Mouse Trap, eating orange smarties from a giant tube he received in his Christmas stocking. Mum and Dad eating Grandma's Christmas cake. Both sipping dainty glasses of sherry. I long for that carefree hustle and bustle of the whole family, gathered together. And now there's just me and my children left.

'Right, let's get your hair and make-up done. Cathy will be here soon to do your nails.' Lisa's carry case is open in front of her, hairdryer and tongs already plugged in, and brushes laid out on the table. I must have zoned out for a few minutes. Lisa was a freelance hairdresser before she came to help run the kennels, and she's still often called on to do people's hair for special occasions. 'Right, what am I doing for you today?'

She carefully eases the turban towel off my head and my wet hair tumbles out. She dabs any excess moisture from the ends.

'I know exactly how I want it – soft curls. I think it frames my face well and Martyn says he loves it like that. I want to get at least one last "wow" out of him.'

'We can definitely manage that.' Lisa smiles as she combs my hair through gently with a wide-toothed comb. The thick locks I once had are now thin and weak, but I try not to let it bother me.

We talk about this evening, and who is coming.

'There'll be loads of Martyn's and my old school friends there, including a few exes of ours, and some that we fell out with at one time or another or didn't particularly get on with. But I didn't want to leave anyone out. The idea was to invite everyone I've ever known, as far as that's possible. It's up to them if they want to come. Quite a few have replied to say they are so at least I won't be in a big hall on my own.' I laugh and Lisa laughs with me.

'I'm sure whoever you fell out with has put it all

behind them. Be a bit sad to be holding grudges for this long, wouldn't it?' she says, concentrating on untangling a knot.

'That's what I told Martyn, but he thinks I'm mad inviting "frenemies" as he calls them.'

'I can't imagine anyone not liking you, Heather. You're such a kind, generous person.' She puts the comb down and our eyes meet in the mirror. I smile at her. I've been so lucky finding a friend like her. She's the one who's kind. There isn't a thing she won't do for me, and she never complains.

'Thank you, that's so sweet of you, although I'm not sure that's entirely true.' I laugh nervously.

She dabs the ends of my hair again with the towel.

'For example, don't you think it's selfish of me to not want Martyn to meet someone new? You know, after I've gone.'

'No, not at all.' Her slightly higher pitch tells me she's saying what I want to hear. But I can't help the way I feel.

'I want him to be happy, of course I do, and I know we're not married but... marrying again, I don't know. I feel sick at the thought of it. I suppose I'm worried he'll forget me, love someone else more.' Even as I speak, I can sense the tentacles of jealousy sliding around my heart. I hate the thought of him being in love with another woman, laughing and enjoying life with her, growing old with her, like we were meant to. Rationally it's ridiculous. It's not like I'll know he's met someone else. But still.

'How could he ever forget you? It's impossible. You're the love of his life.'

'I know. I'm being silly and childish, but I can't help it.'

'Do you love Ben more than Scott?'

'Of course not!' The thought of loving one son more than the other is impossible.

'There you are then.' Lisa squirts a ball of mousse into her hand and when it's fully expanded, she gently distributes it through the lengths of my hair.

'Maybe it's because we've lost years of being together. I just wish we could have longer.'

Part of me wants to know why I'm the one who has to die young. Much as I also feel 'why not' me, I secretly can't stop this aspect of dying eating away at me. In a strange way, the sour, rotten jealousy curdling in my stomach is partly what keeps me feeling alive, wanting to make the effort to look good and try to keep Martyn with me, carry on as normal.

'You're entitled to feel like that, because honestly,

what you're going through is so awful, you wouldn't wish it on your worst enemy would you?'

I shake my head and bite my lip, trying to keep the building tears at bay.

'What time will your boys be here?'

I check my watch. 'Anytime from now.'

Lisa sprays heat protector onto my damp hair and switches on the hairdryer. She runs her hands through and lifts sections up so she can blast the hot air underneath. My hair used to be so thick and bouncy. I was known for my shiny dark brown locks. It had been the one thing I would spend time on to get just right. I never needed much make-up, I'd been blessed with clear skin and a good bone structure so too much would have distorted my natural features. But now my hair is so much thinner and breaks easily. Even my skin has changed. I need a richer moisturiser and a thick foundation to cover the dryness and redness on my cheeks. The illness on top of early morning feeds at the kennels in cold and windy weather have taken their toll. If only I could be a younger version of myself just for today. A final flourish. But I have to make do as I am and accept that the doctors can't keep me alive for any longer. I won't have the privilege of growing old.

'So do you think you'll go through with... this big

announcement tonight?' Lisa asks quietly when she finishes the rough blow-dry and switches the hairdryer off. I'm mindful not to reply when it's quiet, in case Martyn or the boys are in earshot. I've not heard them arrive yet, but I wouldn't if they came round the back door, which is usually unlocked when we're in. Lisa clips up sections of my hair then picks up the round brush and switches the hairdryer back on.

I catch her eye in the mirror. 'I'm going to bite the bullet and do it. It's been playing on my mind for so long. It's now or never.'

5

'Have you ever thought about telling people before?' Lisa asks me in the mirror.

'Often. Ever since I was first pregnant, more than twenty years ago.'

'I don't know how you've managed to live with a secret for so long. Aren't you worried about the repercussions?' She pauses a moment and the heat from the hairdryer burns my head. I flinch. 'Oh gosh, sorry,' she says and switches the heat setting down.

'I probably won't be here to worry about that.' I plaster on a temporary smile, but a chill runs through me. 'I have considered the fallout, but I've been so determined to go ahead, I've told myself it will be fine, but maybe it is a bit dangerous outing people.'

'People? Sounds serious.'

I'm careful not to give any details, even to someone as trustworthy as Lisa.

'It is. Someone died.' I glance at her in the mirror.

'Oh, goodness.' She pauses then finishes blow-drying the last section of hair. She's concentrating on what she's doing so I'm not sure how closely she's really listening. Like all hairdressers, she has this knack of getting her clients to talk and talk and she just nods along, not necessarily taking it all in.

'Yeah, but I think it's time they faced what they did. Can you imagine not getting justice for a loved one?'

'It must be really awful.' Lisa turns away and switches on the curling tongs. 'But isn't what you're going to do a bit risky? Wouldn't it be better for you to leave things be?'

'Probably, yes, but what happened was a terrible thing and I've really tried to make peace with it. Kids can do stupid, impulsive things when they're angry. But I can't leave this world knowing what I do. It's been killing me slowly having this hanging over me more than half my life. It's been hard living with it through the years. If it was my brother or son, I'd want to know who was responsible.'

'I understand, I do. But maybe you should just go

to the police, tell them everything you know, let them deal with it?' She wraps a section of my hair around the tongs. It's unnerving to see wisps of smoke rise as she holds it steady for a few seconds, then releases a perfect curl.

I shake my head. 'I need to tell people. Everyone thinks I'm such a saint running the boarding kennels, but I've been holding back this terrible truth. I can't keep this lie any longer. It's exhausting. It's like my card was marked that day and this illness is my come-uppance.'

I show her how I can reach around part of my arm with my thumb and forefinger until they touch. I'm already so much thinner than I was one or two months ago.

'I'm so sorry.' Lisa puts the tongs down and hugs me. Tears prick my eyes.

'I have to go ahead with this. I can't let people find out that I kept this terrible secret after I've gone. They'd feel betrayed and wonder if they really knew me. I just hope I'm brave enough to tell them now while I'm still alive, while I still have the chance to explain myself... and perhaps they'll for-give me.'

'It is brave of you.' Lisa nods and touches the top of my hair with her fingertips. 'As long as you're sure.'

'Thank you. I'm sorry I've not told you any of the details, but I know you understand why.'

'Of course, please don't feel bad. Secrets can be powerful and dangerous. You'll know when you're standing up there in the moment if you're ready to tell.'

'You're so right. And if I'm not ready, then I'm not. It's entirely up to me.' My stomach flutters just thinking about saying it out loud. I take in a breath and let it out slowly to calm myself. 'I appreciate everything you've done over these past three weeks.'

'You don't have to thank me. I'm just so sorry this is happening to you.' Lisa sniffs and presses the back of her hand to her nose. I reach up and squeeze her wrist.

'Look at the state of me.' She dabs the corners of her eyes with her knuckles. 'The others will be here soon. Let's finish your hair then I'll do your make-up. Have you thought about how you'd like it?'

'Natural, soft, but with my signature red lipstick.'

'Always.' Lisa laughs as she releases the last curl.

'And now I have something for you.' I reach across to my bedside drawer and take out a small glossy black gift bag.

'What's that?' She looks at me in the mirror in surprise.

'Didn't I tell you I've made family and close friends a party bag each?'

'No, you kept that quiet.' She crosses her arms but she's smiling.

'I've chosen a piece of my favourite jewellery from my collection to give to a select few, together with a personal note inside each bag, just to say thank you for being there. So, here's yours.' I hand the gift bag to her.

'My goodness, how lovely of you. Can I open it now?'

'Of course, please do.'

Lisa pushes open the top of the bag and takes out a small jewellery box and envelope. She looks at it in wonder, not sure which to open first.

'Open the box,' I suggest.

She gently prises it open with her thumb and forefinger. Inside is a gold dog-shaped broach of a Golden Retriever with sapphire blue eyes and a diamond encrusted collar.

'Oh Heather, it's absolutely beautiful.' Lisa's hand hovers across her mouth, her eyes wide.

'It's one of my most treasured items and I'm so happy it's going to you. I've hardly worn it in years, truth be told. Only because it's not the sort of thing you wear to go and feed the animals. But when I worked at a solicitor's, before I had the kids, I wore it all the time.'

'It must be worth a fortune. Are you sure you don't want one of your boys to have it?'

'God no. They'd never wear it and I want it to be worn, not stuffed in a drawer, and I know you will.'

'But you're already signing the kennels over to me.'

'Yes, because you deserve it. You helped me expand the business, so don't let anyone tell you that you shouldn't have it, okay? I've made it all perfectly clear in my will if there's any dispute when I'm gone.'

'Christ, Heather, this is really happening to you, isn't it?' She blinks at me, hands cupping the sides of her head. 'I don't want you to die. I'd give anything for you to beat this.' Tears roll down her face. 'Don't you cry too,' she sniffs at me, 'or I won't be able to do your make-up.' We both half-laugh, half-cry.

I reach for a box of tissues before we're an irretrievable mess. 'I'll tell you what though,' I say, 'there's an upside to being ill. I'm finding out who people really are.'

6

'Why do you say you're finding out what people are really like? Has someone upset you?' Lisa wipes her nose.

'Don't worry, just me getting emotional.' I brush my comment away.

She tips her head to one side and frowns at me, then lets her fringe fall over her eyes, but I shake my head. There are some secrets I can't share right now.

A long blast of hairspray finishes my hair and hopefully ensures it will stay looking this glamorous all evening. She shows me the back with a small mirror. I only give a cursory glance then nod my approval. I've seen enough to know that Lisa has spun her magic, making it look fuller and glossier again.

'It's lovely, thank you.'

There's a beat of silence before Lisa speaks.

'It's not me who's upset you, is it?' Her face pinches with worry.

'Of course not. It's never you, it's just me feeling maudlin.' I pat her arm. Lisa couldn't harm anyone even if she wanted to.

I click the radio on, and we listen to some nineties tunes while Lisa starts applying my make-up. I'm trying my hardest to live in the moment, enjoy every second, as my family keeps telling me I should, but it's difficult for me not to look back on happier times when I didn't have this darkness looming over me. Sometimes I picture an oversized clock above my head, counting down the seconds I have left on earth.

When she's finished my face, Lisa nips off to the bathroom to wash the make-up and hair mousse off her hands.

My mobile beeps, making me jump. I pick it up, tap open the message and draw in a breath.

'Everything okay?' she asks, coming back in a few moments later.

'Yeah.' I look up. 'Yeah, it's nothing.' I turn the phone face down and fake a smile at her in the mirror. I can hardly tell her it's the second threatening message I've received today.

'If you ever need to confide in anyone, outside of your family, you know you can talk to me, don't you?' Lisa looks concerned.

I nod, grateful for the offer, but she'll find out the big secret soon enough at the party. Sharing anything else would be passing the burden on and I'm not prepared to put Lisa in that position when I'm not going to be around to protect her from the fallout.

Martyn knocks on the door just as Lisa is applying setting powder to my face. She went for false eyelashes in the end as I don't have many of my own left. I've not worn falsies before. I quite like how they sweep down when I blink. I glimpse the younger-looking, healthier me in the mirror. It's been a while. It's the version of me that's stuck in my head. The one I instantly conjure up when I think of myself dressed smartly to go out, forgetting how my face and body have aged. Although forty-three isn't what I think of as old. How lucky I was to have those years, when some have their lives cut so much shorter.

Like Alex.

'Come in!' Lisa and I call together like we're fourteen years old. I catch another glimpse of my face from a different angle and the younger me has vanished. Perhaps she was never there; I just imagined her. Now I'm older, the finishing powder cruelly emphasises my lines in the bright light. My sickly pallor is carefully hidden under the layers of foundation, but there's no natural rosy glow as there once was, only the orangey pink powder applied to try to restore it.

'Woah, look at you.' Martyn wolf whistles. I smile, but my lips barely move. In my mind's eye I see myself as Aunt Sally and the thought of *Worzel Gummidge* brings a genuine smile to my lips. Martyn's being kind. He doesn't have to be. He hands us both a glass of champagne. 'Thought you might like a little tipple before the others arrive.'

And as if on cue, the doorbell rings and Martyn rushes off to answer it.

Cathy walks into the bedroom a few moments later looking immaculate and sassy as always in an elegant navy sleeveless dress, holding her nail technician box. She's a legal secretary by day and runs her own little nail business in the evenings and at weekends. She's closely followed by Martyn with another flute glass and the opened bottle of champagne.

'Look at you, you look amazing.' Cathy puts her box down and hugs me. Martyn hands her the glass and fills it with champagne. She smiles at him as she takes a sip. The front door slams and Ben calls out asking where everyone is.

Martyn opens the door and shouts down over the banister, 'Up here. Grab yourselves a glass each and come up.'

Moments later, Ben and Scott come bowling in and make a beeline for me. One, then the other, lean down to kiss my cheek and wrap their arms around me. Ben's girlfriend, Emma, strolls in after them, hand on her neat bump. I stand up and kiss her cheek, then she opens her arms, and we hug. I remember how uncomfortable and almost impossible it is to bend down when the baby starts to get bigger. There's only eight weeks until the due date, so I'm hoping I'm still well enough to meet my first grandchild. I try not to think about it too much though, because the thought of being so ill or not being here at all is too overwhelming. As it is, I'm going to be absent for most of their life. I'll be that grandparent Ben and Emma tell them about when they're older, the one who *died before you were born* or just after. I picture a time I sat with Ben at the park eating ice-cream when he was little. He'd fallen over and grazed his knee and I was trying to make him feel better with a treat. Scott was just a baby, asleep in his pram. If only I'd understood then how precious my time with them was, even doing seemingly simple things like that. Now I've learnt that all I have is this moment, and maybe the next if I'm lucky. I have no control over anything beyond that.

'You all right, Mum?' Ben asks, holding out three glasses to Martyn. I nod and smile, dabbing my wet eyes with my fingers.

'You look great, Mum.' Scott's eyelids flutter and he sniffs. A tear rolls down his cheek. I reach for his hand and squeeze it three times, looking into his eyes. He squeezes back. Our little signal from when he first started primary school and became too self-conscious to say he loved me in front of everyone. He's two and a half years younger than Ben and has always been the more sensitive.

Martyn fills Scott and Ben's glasses with champagne and Emma's glass with sparkling water. Ben finishes his drink in two gulps and pushes it towards Martyn for a refill. Martyn pretends not to notice for a few seconds then probably thinks better of it and tops up his glass. Today is not the day to rile each other up.

'Here's a toast to my dearest, beautiful Heather. Wishing you the best party and the happiest night of your life. Cheers, everyone.' Martyn raises his glass, smiling down at me.

'To Heather,' they all say together.

'The best mum ever,' Ben and Scott add. I watch

everyone raise their glasses. Their smiles tinged with sadness. These are the people I love most in the world. I try to picture them drinking together like this after I've gone and the empty space where I'd normally be standing. It's hard to envisage... *not being here*. Ben and Emma's baby being born, growing up, his or her age marking the years since I died as a simple visual reminder to everyone.

For a moment I zone out of the chatter about the party arrangements and listen to the comforting ordinariness of sounds outside the window. The drone of distant traffic. A dog barks, and another yaps back. An airplane engine buzzes somewhere up in the clouds and a bird I've not heard before starts singing its little heart out in a tree. Life's wonders will continue, but my tiny place in it is ending.

'We'll wait downstairs, Mum,' the boys say. Ben takes Emma's hand. She glances over her shoulder with a sympathetic frown.

They are so natural together. I'm glad they've found each other. Ben will need her when I'm gone. I'm not sure if they'll get married. Ben said once that neither of them mind either way. It seems to matter less these days and I'm not going to push them. Having a baby together is a bigger commitment. They don't need pressure to conform, least of all from me.

As long as they're happy and kind to each other. That's what counts. But I can't help adding one of my children getting married to the list of life events I will never see. And after that, probably the most important of all is possibly not seeing them become parents.

I started writing letters to Ben and Scott when I was first diagnosed. I've written cards for their birthdays for the next ten years too. Each with a piece of advice I think they'll find useful. They're here, in this room, in a locked box under the bed for them to open after I die. No one knows about them, but I hope they bring them solace when I'm gone. I wanted to tell them what I was like when I was a child growing up. The sorts of things I worried about and how I got through it. How I met Tom, their dad. How I felt about him and what went wrong, which was no one's fault. They know snippets, of course they do. I've told the highlights hundreds of times. If they stitched them all together it would become the story of my life.

But there's so much more they don't know about me.

7

'Are you okay?' Martyn touches my shoulder, bringing me back into the room.

'Yeah, you know. I'm going to miss the simple things. Corny, I know. But all the things we take for granted, like birds singing, dogs barking and even the pesky traffic. There's beauty in everything if we stop and look and listen. I just wish I could have longer with you all. I don't want to leave yet. I'm not ready.'

A familiar ache bubbles up in my chest and wedges itself there. I can't control what my body does; I want to scream at everyone, including the universe. My life wasn't meant to be this way. I didn't plan this. I didn't see it coming. It's like some nasty trick or prank has been played on me and it's not funny because I can't hit reset. I'm slowly falling into a black hole of nothingness, and I can't stop myself.

'I know, darling. I'm sorry. I wish I could do something to slow it down or better still, find a cure.' He pulls me into his arms. 'What am I going to do without you?' he says. I let him hug me, but really, he has no idea what he's talking about. No idea at all what it's like for me, what I'm really going through. Being as ill as I am, is the loneliest place to be. Everyone is looking at me with their sympathy and kind words, but the truth is they'll all go home tonight and carry on their normal lives with barely a thought of what I'm going through. And when I'm gone, my mark in the world will gradually vanish. Most of my clothes and possessions will go to the charity shop. Over the coming months and years, photos of me will be taken down and replaced with ones of a new partner, grandchildren I'll never get to hold or know, special days out and holidays I'll never experience. Eventually I might still be represented around the place by one or two things, like the patchwork quilt I made, tucked away in a drawer, or the ceramic double picture frame on the bookshelf of Ben and Scott when they were babies. But when the house is sold, other people will live here, and they'll not know anything about my life here before them.

They'll not know that my dear Labrador Lola was put to sleep on her favourite blanket in the conservatory, or that Maud had her puppies in the bay window in the living room. Or that I woke up in our bed and found my waters had broken when I was expecting Scott. Huge milestones in my life will all be forgotten. *I* will be forgotten.

Lisa and Cathy have stopped talking and are watching us. I pull away from Martyn.

'We'll look after him, don't worry. Won't we, Lisa?' Cathy sips her drink, peering at us over the edge of the glass.

'He'll need someone looking out for him for sure. But to be honest, I don't know what any of us are going to do without you here organising us,' Lisa says, half laughing as she struggles to hold in her tears. We all laugh with her.

'Thank you both. Until then, Martyn's all mine.' I smile and pull him close to me and snog his face off in front of them, just like we're sixteen years old again.

'You'll smudge all your make-up,' Cathy tuts, but she's smiling as she turns to her case and takes out her nail kit.

I pull away from Martyn. 'It's worth smudging for this one, believe me.' I tug playfully at his collar. 'By the way, I've got a little thank-you present for you, Cathy.'

I untangle myself from Martyn and take a gift bag out of the bedside cupboard. 'Here, I hope you like it.'

Cathy takes it somewhat hesitantly.

'Open it,' I tell her.

She unties the satin ribbon and eases open the velvet gift bag. Her hand reaches in and takes out a small cardboard cake box, a square jewellery box and an envelope. She looks up at me in mock alarm then tears off the round cake lid.

'Oh my God, my absolute favourite,' she squeals and sniffs the stack of double chocolate cookies so they're practically touching the end of her nose. She sinks her teeth into one with a big bite. Shutting her eyes, she chews slowly, the ecstasy of the taste playing out on her face. We all laugh. It's so Cathy. We'd have been disappointed if she'd reacted any other way.

'I made this batch just for you.'

She swallows and suddenly she's stooped over and tears are dropping from her eyes.

'What's wrong?' Martyn says, but Lisa and I are already on it; both of us take one of her hands each.

'I'm never going to eat your cookies again, am I?'

Lisa and I look at each other with shocked faces. 'Yes, you will,' I say quickly. 'I've put the recipe in the envelope for you.' We all laugh because otherwise we're all going to burst into tears.

'Oh my God. Have you really? You absolute darling. Not that they will ever be the same if they're not made by you.'

Lisa shakes her head. Martyn's smile is upside down now in a sad face. I hand her the jewellery box and try not to cry again.

'This too?' She takes it from me.

'I'd like to see you open it,' I encourage her.

She peels the lid off and takes out a gold ring studded with diamonds and sapphires.

'What is this, Heather?' She frowns at me.

'It's for you. I want you to have it.'

'Really? But I love this ring.'

'I know you do, you've told me a thousand times,' I laugh, 'and that's why I want it to be yours so you can think of me every time you wear it. I can't take it with me.' I laugh again, but there are tears in my eyes. 'It's the friendship ring Martyn gave me soon after we first got back together.'

Martyn raises his eyebrows and keeps them there.

'You don't mind, do you?' I ask him.

'No.' He looks somewhat bewildered.

'You'll have everything else, apart from what's

going to the boys, if that's what you're worried about.'
I pat his arm.

'I'm not,' he says immediately, eyes darting over
my face. Now he's frowning. I've upset him talking
like this. But making a joke of it is the only way I'll get
through it.

'I'm really touched, thank you.' Cathy leans forward and hugs me. 'Can I wear it now?'

'Of course, why not.' I smile. She opens the card
and moments later she's dabbing her eyes again.

'That's so lovely, thank you. I'm lucky to have you
as a friend too.' She hugs me again just as the ethe-
real tones of Jennifer Warnes singing start on the radio, accompanied by the smoky voice of Joe Cocker
about love lifting us up where we belong, and
without planning to we all join in and it's as if we're
nearing the end of a sad movie. When the song finishes, none of us says anything. Martyn tops up our
glasses and says he's taking the boys ahead to the
venue to make sure everything is in place.

Cathy sits down and makes a start on my nails.
Lisa finishes her drink and takes her kit out to
her car.

'You will keep an eye on Martyn, won't you? I'm
worried about him,' I say to Cathy, trying to catch her

eye but she's concentrating on applying cuticle remover to my nails.

'Of course I will, what are friends for?' She pauses and tilts her head at me.

'I can tell he's putting on a brave face for me, but I sense he's struggling.'

'I've noticed it too and I promise I won't let him suffer on his own.'

'You don't think he's already met someone else, do you?'

'Why do you ask that?' She doesn't look up.

'He seems... distant, distracted. I can't get close to him like we used to. He doesn't confide in me about how he's feeling.'

'It's probably a normal reaction to your situation, self-preservation, cruel as that is, because he knows he's losing you and he has no control over it.'

'Maybe you're right.' I swap hands in the warm bowl of water.

'Anyway, he'll have me, Lisa and Robbie, and all the others looking out for him.'

'I know you say that, but the reality when someone dies is that people fade into the background, even the ones who promised they'd call you or say you can call them whenever, then don't answer the phone. It happened after Alex passed away. Then my parents.'

'I hear you, and I promise.' Cathy lays her hand on top of mine and looks me in the eyes.

'Thank you.'

'Now tell me what colour I'm painting your nails.'

'Red please, to match my lipstick if you can.'

'Of course.' She starts pushing back my cuticles. 'You may as well know now, I've decided to end it with Robbie. Tonight,' she says without looking up.

'Oh,' I exclaim. I didn't see that coming.

'It's not working for me any more, but I'm worried how he'll react, so I'd rather tell him in a public place.' She glances at me briefly to gauge my reaction.

'At my party?' I raise my eyebrows. She looks down again and concentrates on scraping the gunk from my nail bed and wiping it on a tissue.

'It's just that he's less likely to kick off with everyone around.'

'Are you worried he'll hurt you?' I try to catch her eye.

'No, but he does scare me sometimes.'

'Christ, Cathy. Look, if you want me or Martyn to be with you when you tell him, please just say.'

'Thanks.' She glances at me as she washes off the cuticle cream then dries my hands and applies a bottom coat to my nails. I leave the silence to expand for a few moments before I broach the question that's been niggling at me.

'Do you ever think about... that day?' I try to say casually.

Cathy's head jerks up. Of all the days we've spent together, she knows exactly which one I'm talking about.

'No. Never; why?'

'I do. It's been bothering me a lot lately.'

'Why let it?' She frowns.

'I can't help it.'

'Do you think they ever gave a toss about you?' She stops what she's doing to look at me.

'I don't suppose so.'

'There you are then.'

'But don't you think the truth always has a way of coming out?' I try to catch her eye.

'Maybe.' She keeps her head down.

'And when it does, what then?'

8

At 6.45 p.m., there's a knock at the front door. Cathy helps me downstairs in my low heels as Lisa trots ahead and opens it. A chauffeur is standing there in a smart suit and peaked cap.

'What's this?' I frown at Lisa then Cathy, a big grin on my face.

'A little surprise,' Cathy says. 'We're getting a lift to the venue in style. Are we all ready to go?'

Cathy leads me outside and Lisa follows, locking up for me. Parked on the drive is a shiny vintage car, the sort you see trimmed with ribbons for a wedding. After we'd written a list of what we'd need for the party, Lisa suggested I write a bucket list of ten things I'd love to experience, and this was one of them.

'It's so lovely, thank you,' I squeal. 'Honestly, you two!'

'It wasn't just us. It was Martyn, Ben and Scott too.'

The driver opens the passenger door for me, and I climb in. Lisa and Cathy join me in the backseat.

When we pull up at the hotel, Martyn and the boys are waiting for us outside. I thank the driver and he doffs his cap at me.

'That was wonderful, thank you all.' I hug Cathy and Lisa, Ben, Scott and Martyn.

'Glad you enjoyed it. Welcome to your party.' Martyn sweeps his hand towards the entrance and leads the way into the Mansion House, the lakeside venue we picked on the Luton Hoo estate. Two waiters approach us on the red carpet, holding silver trays. They offer us a glass of pink champagne. We all take one and Martyn directs us further along, to a 'living' wall packed with fresh rose heads of all different shades of pink, cream and lilac.

It's so beautiful and the scent is unbelievable. My name is fixed in gold lettering in the message at the top: *Welcome to Heather's Farewell Party*. It's another surprise I knew nothing about. There are a variety of gold picture frames for people to hold up and take selfies against the floral backdrop. Martyn chooses the largest, most ornate one, and asks Cathy, Robbie, Lisa, Ben and Scott to stand with me. A photographer I hadn't noticed before steps forward, shakes hands with Martyn and with me and takes a few photos of us all together and a couple with me on my own, my leg playfully kicked up behind me. It's such fun, almost like I'm a star at a film premiere.

'Shall we go in?' Martyn puts his arm around my waist as we walk through an archway of roses into the main hall as the Pet Shop Boys' 'Love Comes Quickly' starts to play. Tears instantly fill my eyes. I don't know if Martyn's aware but it's the song I first kissed my ex-husband Tom to.

'You've probably guessed; Tom's already here.' Martyn points to the DJ at the far end of the hall. 'He's been setting up. I'm sure he'll be over shortly to say hello.' Tom looks up from the decks and nods. I wave back. We had such a great evening coming up with my ultimate playlist; it turned into quite a session of reminiscing about the old days. All those eighties and nineties tunes I love, the soundtrack to my youth and much of our time together.

Tom and I met at a Pet Shop Boys gig about fifteen months after Martyn and I split up. I was coming up to eighteen and cynically didn't think I'd ever fall in love again. But we stayed up all night talking about music and what we wanted from life. I felt so comfortable with him. I thought he was the one. Looking back, I'm not sure when it went wrong. After getting married and having two children, the lust and love gradually faded I suppose. Thankfully we realised we were still good friends and decided to part amicably. We parented the boys together before co-parenting was even a thing. Of all the achievements in my life, that's up there as one of the ones I'm most proud of, and the boys have said how much they appreciate that we still get on so well.

Near the bar is a huge twelve-foot Christmas tree decorated with pink and silver baubles, even though it's late August. It's something I really wanted to have for one last time because I probably won't make it to December. I love the magic of Christmas, especially when the children were small.

On the left is a smaller wire-framed Christmas tree on a table and next to it is a pile of glitter-edged card shapes threaded with string.

'I hope you like it, Mum,' Scott says. 'I thought people could write a personal message of hope to you, then hang it on a branch.'

'That's such a thoughtful idea, thank you, Scott. I

look forward to reading them.' I gently squeeze his arm. His eyes are red and wet. I wish I didn't have to cause my children any pain. Leaving them will be the hardest thing I'll ever have to do.

'Also, there's this guest book that will be going around the tables for people to write longer notes to you,' says Ben.

'Thank you. I love that as well.'

By the side of the Christmas tree, a film starts to flicker on the wall. My mouth opens in awe. It's a home video projected onto a large blank space behind the low stage, of me with the children when they were little, Scott and Ben opening presents by our Christmas tree. Tom is behind the camera, his new toy, zooming in and out on each of our faces and the boys are giggling like mad. Then Tom props the camera on the dining table and comes and scoops the boys up, one under each arm. I watch mesmerised, my heart swelling with love for them all.

'I haven't seen this for so long. I didn't know we still had it.' I twist round. Cathy points to Tom, who smiles as he dips his head down to his decks for some last-minute check. I should have guessed. Scott stands beside me and slips his hand into mine. On the other side, Ben links arms with me and leans his head on my shoulder.

'It's not long now before I'll be standing up there delivering my speech,' I say to them.

Ben lifts his head. 'Do you want to have a go, see how it feels standing, or you might prefer to sit?'

I hesitate a moment. 'Yes. Go on then.' I step up to the stage and Ben moves the microphone and stand in front of me. I imagine everyone's reaction when I tell them my news. Haddaway's 'What is Love' starts playing and makes me think of the day that everything changed, because it was playing on the radio early that morning when I woke up. I'm lost in the moment and step forward without thinking, losing my footing. It feels like I'm stepping into a chasm. In slow motion, Cathy, Lisa and Robbie reach forward, their faces distorted with panic. Martyn opens his arms and I fall into them, narrowly stopping me careering off the edge of the stage.

'I've got you,' he says close to my face. I didn't realise how shaky and nervous I am about tonight. But it's hardly surprising really. I'll be seeing people I've not seen since I was a teenager. And I'm planning to say things that have been kept a close secret for almost thirty years. It's bound to upset a few people.

Martyn didn't want to contact Dan, and he won't tell me if he did or not, or even if he tried to find him. None of us has seen him since that day. We don't know what he thinks of us for what we did or even what he's like now.

Maybe inviting him wasn't such a good idea, because Dan knows *everything*.

9

When the first guests start to trickle in, I head over to greet them, taking up to a couple of minutes with each person. The waiters do an excellent job of supplying drinks as people arrive, as well as circulating with trays of canapes amongst the growing crowd.

Lots of people have dressed up in holiday and beachwear as it's August. I asked them to on the invitation, and I'm keenly aware from people's questions that the consensus is that I've won a competition prize and they're sending me off on a luxury holiday to the Caribbean. All I tell them is they'll find out soon when I make my speech. But those who know me well will surely wonder how I can do such a thing, abandoning the dogs and cats I care for in the kennels and cattery. Maybe the more astute among them will guess something is wrong simply from my weight loss.

A group of my old secondary school friends arrive. I recognise Lucy straight away, wearing a navy pencil skirt and a floaty blouse in various shades of aqua. We used to sit together in drama and were close friends in years seven and eight.

'My goodness Heather, look at you. You look am-a-zing! How is it you've not changed a bit? Tell me your secret, how have you stayed so slim? Honestly, since becoming perimenopausal, I can't even look at bread without piling on the pounds.'

'Aw, thank you. You look fantastic too. It's really good to see you. Thanks for coming.' We hug and I wonder why I didn't keep in touch with her and so many other people. Life took us in different directions I suppose. Isn't that what people say? How ridiculous we humans are. Why did it take a death sentence to realise my priorities should have been with people I liked and cared about? I want to scream at myself sometimes for all the wasted hours I've spent on stupid pointless things like waiting in queues or watching rubbish reality TV shows.

'So, come on, what's this party for? You're moving overseas, aren't you? You can tell me,' she whispers.

'Not LA is it? I've always wanted to go. If it is, can I be your first visitor? Please say yes!'

'Sorry, it's not America. Or any kind of travel.' I smile, holding in my pain, wishing with every fibre in my body that she was right. I want to keep it vague for now but also, I don't think it's fair to be misleading. What I really want to say is: *For goodness' sake, if you want to go there, just go. Save the money, do whatever it takes. Why wait? Go as soon as you can, because you never know when your time is up, and your chance has passed you by.* I wish I'd gone a few years ago. I could have taken the boys. But other priorities came first, a new bathroom being one of them. How utterly ridiculous that seems now. What good is a luxury bathroom to me? Yes, the toilet and sink were in desperate need of repair or replacement, but it could have been done much cheaper, and with the other few thousand pounds we spent on the steam shower and whirlpool bath, we could have had wonderful memories of a holiday of a lifetime instead.

There are a hundred places I'd love to have travelled to. The plan was to sell up the kennels in eight to ten years' time and travel the world. What an idiot I was waiting for the perfect time. The perfect age. I am the perfect age *now*. I want to scream at myself for my shortsightedness.

Lucy's face drops. 'That's a shame. Well, whatever it is, it's all very mysterious, sending out invitations saying you've got a big announcement to make but not giving us any clues. You're keeping us all in suspense. I cannot wait to find out what it is.'

My smile fades a touch and I force myself to plaster it back on. I wish I was going somewhere glamorous. Anywhere would be better than my destination. 'I can't say any more, but you'll find out soon, I promise.'

I raise a hand to greet Jane and Marcus behind her and once I've chatted with them, I point them to a corner of the hall where the others from school have gravitated to in their own mini reunion. There are one or two who I didn't get on with particularly well, but they were friendly enough towards me when they arrived and I'm not holding anything against them.

'Life's too short for grudges, isn't it?' I said to Martyn when he questioned again why I'd invited people like the Morley twins, notorious thugs from our school. 'They're family men now with good jobs, so who am I to judge them for what they did when they were fifteen? We all did stupid things for money or love, didn't we?'

Martyn raised an eyebrow, and I flicked my hair

over my shoulder in annoyance. I go and say hello to Tom.

'Thanks again, I appreciate you doing this.' I hand my ex a glass of champagne.

'Cheers. I'm glad to help, you know that.' He takes the glass and clinks it against mine. We both have a quick slug then he opens his arms and gives me a warm bear hug. We keep it brief and pull away at the same time. 'Silly question I know, but how are you feeling today?'

'A bit weak, but high on adrenaline at the moment. It's so good to see everyone and to feel a party vibe. It's been so long. I should have had more parties. They make you feel young and carefree again, don't they?'

'That's why I like my job, I guess.' He smiles, lining up the next song.

'I'll probably crash out later, so I'm not sure I'll last until the end.'

'I'll keep the tunes coming, don't you worry. This is a party no one will forget.'

'Thank you.' I touch his arm with my fingers, not sure if I'm allowed.

'It's honestly the least I could do.' He tips his head back and drains his glass.

'And I love the video compilations. Thanks for

doing that. I could watch it for hours. In fact, I hope you'll let me have a copy so I can watch it again when I'm... less mobile and stuck for things to do.'

'Of course, of course.' He nods and looks down at his Converse trainers.

'I know it's difficult to accept I'm going to get that bad. It's hard enough for me to imagine, but I must face reality.'

'Sure.' He nods, still looking down.

'Anyway, it's a real shot of nostalgia seeing our home movies again. I'd forgotten all about them. How I wish for those days again... didn't we make the most gorgeous children?'

'Yeah, yeah we did.' He looks directly at me and smiles but his lips quiver. His eyes crease up and glisten, and even in the dim room of flashing bright lights it's clear how upset he is. He looks down at his trainers again, and my heart cracks.

'How have the boys been? They've not said much to me about how they're coping with it all.' I worry about Tom being left to parent on his own. Even though Ben and Scott are grown up, they still need both of us. They still ask our advice and like to be reminded of our family days out, holidays, dens they used to build in the garden, all the fun and stupid things we got up to as a family, everything that made them who they are today.

'You know what they're like, they don't say much because they don't want you to feel worse than you already do.' He pauses and swallows before looking up at me. 'The truth is it's all happening way too fast. For any of us. They're hurting like hell. We all are.' His mouth crumples, and he looks away again. In the silence that follows, the chatter of the room comes back into focus.

Everyone seems to be having a great time. Perhaps I should slip away now, go home and not say anything. Why not leave them to enjoy themselves? Why spoil their fun by telling them my bad news?

'It's a long goodbye, that's for sure.' Tom sniffs and wipes his hand over his mouth, pressing hard. His eyelashes flutter and I'm stunned that he's crying. He never cries. I reach my arm around his broad shoulders, and he swipes away the tears with his fingers.

'Although to me that's lucky because it gives me time to have this party and say goodbye to loads of people I'll never see again. Losing someone suddenly is much more traumatic.'

'Oh course, of course. I'm sorry. I didn't think. What happened to Alex was... unforgiveable.'

'Don't be sorry. I'm only saying that's what I think in my experience.'

'But that's the thing, you know, don't you. I mean with Alex, it must have been... horrific.'

'Yeah.' I swallow down the pain. 'But I'm not trying to diminish your impending loss. I mean, I'm guessing you're going to miss me a lot; you'll be left to parent solo for a start. Did you ever see that coming?' I laugh because dark humour is one way I've found to stop me crying all the time, and he can't help laughing with me too.

'Never in a trillion, zillion years. I'm going to say as much in my speech. I take it you've got yours all sorted?' He wipes his face with his hand.

'I think so. I'm seeing it as a unique opportunity to say whatever I want, because hey, why not? It's my party and a chance to put things right. Something that should have been done long ago.'

'What do you mean?' He squints at me, lips pursed.

I sip my drink.

'Straighten a few things out. A few home truths maybe.' I flash a teasing smile. 'Maybe a confession or two. But mainly thanking people.'

I dip my head a bit, embarrassed, then glance up to gauge his reaction.

'So I'm guessing this lot are in the dark about why they're here? Because to be honest, they all look too damn happy.'

'I'll break it to them in a minute. I thought about going home and not spoiling their fun. But I think they'll appreciate the truth coming straight from me rather than hearing it later on the grapevine. And they're having a pretty good evening so far. I guess it's up to me to spoil it.' I grin.

'I suppose so. Are you going to say what your illness is?'

'They don't need to know. I wouldn't be able to bear all the questions, or worse, the suggestions for treatment or a cure. *Have you tried this, my auntie Maureen swears by it and lived to 100.*'

'I don't blame you.' Tom laughs and I see a glimpse of the young man he once was. We always could make each other laugh. I miss that. Martyn's much more serious and doesn't always get my stupid jokes. Although he was the one all the girls fancied at school for his moody good looks and playing hard to get, he was always a bit lacking a sense of humour. When he chose me, I'd never felt so special. But after what happened, we broke up. He moved away with his family, and I didn't see him again until seven years ago.

'What is there to confess anyway?' Tom asks, pulling me out of my daydream. 'Nothing to do with me I hope?'

It's sweet that he actually looks worried.

'No, it's not about you, Tom. You'll have to wait and see.'

10

I point to the film projected on the wall as it flickers to another reel, this time of me aged about twenty, standing against my dad's red Ford Escort outside our family home. 'Look at my frizz-ball hair, what on earth did you see in me?' I laugh.

Tom smiles and blinks slowly. 'I was mad about you from the moment I clapped eyes on you. Mad to let you go too.'

He looks away, towards Ben and Scott. It's easy to long for the old days, but it wasn't perfect. We didn't have much money and were always arguing about it. He worked as much overtime as he could, so the boys and I didn't see him as much as we'd have liked.

'Hey, hang on, you didn't let me go. I wasn't your

pet.' I raise an eyebrow. 'We agreed to go our separate ways, remember?'

'I know that. All I mean is, I shouldn't have let things slide. I should have worked harder to keep us all together.'

'It wasn't your fault. It was a joint decision. Something in me always wants to cut and run when the going gets tough. Even with this illness I'm following the same pattern.' I let out a peel of laughter, but he doesn't join in.

'I still can't believe this is happening to you, Heather.' He gazes into my eyes and for a millisecond I'm transported back to the day we broke up.

I take in a long breath. 'I know. Neither can I most of the time.'

We move towards each other and hug tightly and somehow my body still fits with his. I feel a dozen sets of eyes boring into my back, but maybe that's just because of the guilty thought running through my head about spending one last night with him. A last hurrah. Luckily the idea evaporates as quickly as it appeared, as most bad ideas do. Tom pulls away and scratches his head.

'I don't know when's a good time to ask you this, but I'm pretty skint at the moment and the landlord is putting the rent up again.'

'What is it, Tom?' I cross my arms.

'I don't know. Maybe this is not the time or the place, but then I don't know when will be.'

'Go on.'

'I've been wondering what the arrangement is with the house, if it'll be sold, if I'll be getting my half when... you're gone? Now that Scott's turned nineteen.' He pauses and I say nothing, so continues. 'We agreed to the sale in the divorce settlement.'

I grind my teeth together. I wondered when this would come up. Sometimes I think people can't wait for me to die.

'Yes, I'm aware of our agreement. It will be sold after I've... passed on. The house is now a separate plot from the kennels which, as you know, is going to Lisa, and you will get your half of the house and the boys will get my half. It's all in my will.'

He nods and smiles awkwardly. 'For what it's worth, I strongly believe you should leave the kennels to the boys too.'

'I see. Why's that?'

'I don't think you should be giving their inheritance away to someone outside the family.'

'But it's my choice. Lisa has helped me build the business up.' I cross my arms tighter. 'She's my friend.'

'No disrespect, but I helped you convert the stables and barns. By rights half should be mine as it was part of the original plot. I didn't exactly agree to you giving it away. Lisa gets a generous wage from what you've told me, and she could stay on as manager, take all the profits from the business if you like, but I don't understand why you insist on *giving* it to her?'

'Because I want to, and I believe it's the right thing to do.'

'I'm sorry but I think you're cheating the boys out of what is rightfully theirs. When we come to sell the house, it'll put most buyers off having a kennels practically at the bottom of the garden, whereas if the house and the business were being sold together, someone who wants to keep things going could buy the whole lot.'

'Nice try. So you want me to put Lisa out of a job as well, after all her hard work and loyalty?'

'Whoever buys it might want to keep her on as manager.'

'It's unlikely. Anyway, I've thought it through. It's all drawn up in my will.' I'm about to walk away but he carries on talking.

'I guess it's up to you, but our boys could really do with the extra money right now.'

'How come?' I can't think what he means, they'd have told me if money was tight, wouldn't they?

Tom dips his head down before he speaks. 'Scott's rent keeps going up and he'd really like to put a deposit down for his first house. As for Ben and Emma, with the baby on the way, they'd really love for Emma to go freelance so she can work from home while the baby is growing up.'

'Why don't I know about any of this?' My face heats up with embarrassment. Why haven't they come to me with their worries?

'They didn't want to add to your stress. They've only just told me, and it got me thinking about the house and how we could make that money stretch a bit further. I know you think a lot of Lisa, but I'm sure she's not expecting you to put her above your sons.'

I'm silent for a few seconds. 'I don't agree that I shouldn't leave the kennels to Lisa, but I promise I will think about it.'

He nods and touches my arm before heading off to grab another drink. I look over at Ben and Emma laughing with some of our old neighbours, the baby bump the centre of attention. I'm grateful they're enjoying a straightforward pregnancy. The birth can be traumatic and the early days of their new lives in a crazy routine of feeding, changing nappies and lack of sleep can be so hard and such a shock. I wish I could be there for them. Maybe there is more I can do to make things easier for their lives going forward.

It's not long before the waiters and waitresses parade out one after the other holding large platters of finger food and lay them out on four long tables. I go back to Tom and ask him to announce over the microphone that the buffet is open. He tells everyone to tuck in and puts on a song from the eighties, Sade's 'Smooth Operator', which is suitably low tempo to encourage people to stop dancing and fill their plates with food. I mingle around the cluster of tables, chatting to people. My mobile phone beeps. I glance at who it's from and a bolt of adrenaline stabs my chest. Unknown number *again*. Who is this? I excuse myself and make my way to the ladies. I lock the cubicle door behind me and sit on the closed seat, staring at the text message. Swallowing hard, I consider the consequences if I don't go ahead with what I plan to say. It's not just about me getting things off my chest any more. It's become bigger than that.

Cathy is standing at the mirror preening herself when I come out. She's the picture of health. Her mid-length auburn hair is curled to perfection. I despise the stab of jealousy in my chest. But maybe it's because Cathy always seems to have everything easy.

She never appears to suffer from lack of confidence, lack of boyfriends or lack of anything, come to think of it. But I know it's all a front. She's trying to make up for the hard start she had in life.

'Are you feeling okay? You look nervous, understandably,' she says, leaning forward on the sink surround, lipstick in hand. Her nails are a deep glittery purple. Too gaudy for me, but Cathy always likes her over-the-top bling. At school she sprayed glitter in her hair. She saw herself as a bit of a comedian. We'd ask a question like, how far did you go with your boyfriend? And she would say, all the way to White City on the bus.

'I am a bit nervous,' I whisper. One of the toilet cubicles is locked and we don't know who might be in there listening. 'I keep meaning to ask you, do you know if Martyn managed to get in touch with Dan?'

'I asked him earlier, but if he did, he's not saying. Didn't even give me a hint.' She finishes applying her lipstick and smudges her lips together. 'It's left me feeling so on edge.'

'Maybe he got hold of him but didn't get a clear reply or perhaps his arrival is meant to be a surprise.'

'Do you think so?' Her face in the mirror is the picture of alarm but with a mischievous half smile.

'What will you do if he does come?'

'I don't know.' She pauses. 'I suppose it would give me the chance to say sorry to him.' She tucks her lipstick back in her clutch bag and snaps it shut.

'Do you think he holds a grudge? All these years I've never understood why he left so suddenly that night... without saying anything.'

'Maybe he does. What else should I say to him, except sorry?'

I shake my head. We turn to each other and hug, then she follows me back out.

Everyone is gathered around the stage. My blood pressure bumps up and my stomach and chest are all aflutter thinking about the text, what I've been told to do. Tom must have announced I'm about to make my speech because there's an air of excited anticipation, yet I'm about to bring the mood crashing down. I need this out in the open for my own peace of mind and now this threat leaves me with no choice.

I have to do this.

'Are you ready?' Martyn takes my arm in his. Ben and Scott flank me on the other side. I look away from the spotlights.

'As I'll ever be.'

11

Tom passes me the microphone and I take a moment to look around at everyone's beaming faces. The hairs on the back of my neck prickle. There's a quietness in the room, as people wait for me to begin, punctuated with enthusiastic whistles from the back of the room.

'Good evening, everyone, thank you all for coming at such short notice, and for dressing up so beautifully in your beach clothes, without questioning the reason. It's lovely seeing so many familiar faces from the past and present, from every area of my life over the last forty-three years. Many of you won't have met my sons, Scott and Ben.' I gesture to them, standing either side of me. 'They are the biggest joy of my life. And this is Emma, Ben's girlfriend, who is expecting my first grandchild in October.'

I sweep my hand across to her, kiss my fingertips and blow her and her bump kisses.

'Probably not many of you will be aware that Martyn Dunn came back into my life seven years ago. We were once teenage sweethearts but went our separate ways and married other people. My ex-husband Tom is here, supporting me and our boys as he always does. I don't regret a moment of our years together, because although it's a terrible cliché, without you I wouldn't have my beautiful sons.' I turn to Tom as I say it. Scott and Ben touch my hands either side of me. Scott holds my free hand in his and Ben rubs my arm.

I take a deep breath. 'I know you're wondering why I've brought you all together like this and kept you in the dark about the reason for the party and frankly I've loved hearing all your theories as I've circulated around the room. It's been worth it just for that. But no, sadly I'm not getting married again, moving overseas or going to the Arctic as I think I said I would one day at school when my ambition was to film polar bears.' Everyone laughs. I cough as my voice deserts me. Sweat drips down my back. 'And no, I haven't won a holiday in a competition. The reason isn't something I could be blasé about and write in an invitation. The truth is, I have to go away... and I'm so sad to tell you that my departure is permanent.'

A rumble of surprise and comments ripple through the room, none of which are audible to me.

'Are you going to prison... for life?' someone shouts in a jokey voice and a few of my old school mates giggle, including me, because it's a preposterous suggestion, but one I'd almost welcome as an alternative.

'Sadly, it's more permanent than that.' I stop and swallow, giving everyone another couple of seconds to let it sink in while I wrestle with myself again about whether it's a good idea to leave out the details of my symptoms and not specifically mention the C word. 'I won't go into the exact nature of my illness,' I hesitate, 'but I haven't got long left. This is my final goodbye to you all.'

The mixture of stunned silence is peppered with small gasps as realisation sets in. Sitting at the front, a couple of my old work friends from the travel agent's start crying. They hug each other as I continue.

'Please don't be sad for me. I feel lucky I get this

chance to gather you all together and say farewell. I
know some of you will be thinking this is a bit weird,
having a party – isn't that what the funeral is for – but
I wanted to be here with you. Not everyone gets the
opportunity to know how long they have left, but I
have, so I want to use the time wisely, and of course
that includes saying a personal so-long to you all. I
particularly want to thank Martyn, Cathy, Robbie,
Tom and Lisa for helping me pull this evening together in three short weeks.'

Someone claps and everyone joins in. It gives me
a breather to have a sip of my drink.

'Some of you will know that I was diagnosed
about a year ago and over the past few months I've
been having treatment, which the doctors weren't
sure would work.' My breathing becomes shallow as
my emotions take over. I swallow and take a deep
breath. My heart is pounding out of my chest. 'I was
told a few weeks ago... that the treatment hasn't done
what they hoped it would do.' Scott squeezes my
hand. 'There's nothing more that will make me better
unfortunately. They've given me at most a few
months, possibly only weeks left.'

Ben passes me the glass of water and I take a sip.
Everyone is hushed, stunned, mouths open, staring at
me and at each other.

'It's devastating to hear your doctor say those words, of course it is and you may think me selfish telling you in this way, but please take a second to consider it from my point of view, how much worse it would be for me to have to repeat over and over to each and every one of you, that this is it, I'm nearing the end, I am dying. I think this in itself would finish me off!' I swallow and steady my voice. 'Like I said, please don't be sad for me. I've brought you all to-gether to celebrate my life, to celebrate our friendship and the time we spent together, whether that was forty years ago or last week. You know me, I'd rather go out with a bang than slip away quietly. And that's what this party is for, so that I can see you all at least one more time and say a proper goodbye – to as many of you as possible who I've known over my lifetime, whether that's a small or large part you've played in my life, it's meant the world to me to know you, and I thank you from the bottom of my heart.'

I take a deep breath. 'My sons would like to say a few words, then Tom and Martyn, and I'll finish off.' I pass the microphone to Ben. Scott helps me into a chair behind where I was standing.

'I want to thank all of you for coming to celebrate Mum's life. She's always made us feel special and ca-pable and has been fierce in being there for us, standing up for us, caring for our every need, but encouraging us to do things for ourselves, to not be afraid.'

A low murmur passes around the room. Near the back, I spot Cathy talking to a man with blond spiky hair. She's almost touching his face with hers. He nods and says something back and she laughs. Ben continues. 'What I'm trying to say is, she is the wisest person I know. Losing you Mum is going to be the hardest thing I've ever had to deal with. I love you more than words can say.' Ben's voice breaks up. He bows his head and wipes his eyes as he passes the microphone to Scott. I stand and put my arm around Ben's shoulders, pulling him to me to kiss his cheek.

'Thanks Ben, how am I supposed to top that?' Scott dabs his fingers at the corners of his eyes. 'Mum, what can I say? You are without doubt the best of the best, and really there are no words to properly express that.' He sniffs, and I reach for his hand and squeeze it tight. 'Can I just say it's so unfair that you're being ripped away from us like this. I know people get ill all the time but why does it have to be you?' Scott thumps his hand on his chest over his heart and sniffs back his tears. 'I love you, Mum.' The lights come up as Scott turns to me and falls into my arms, crying his eyes out. We hug each other tight.

He pulls back and kisses my cheek, passes the microphone to Tom, and joins his brother beside me. Cathy is still speaking to the blond man. It seems intense. They're not paying attention to the speeches at all. I wish I knew what she was saying.

'Erm, this is completely surreal, I had what I was going to say all prepared and now it's gone.' He presses his fingers to his head and looks at me. 'As you know, Heather has always been the driving force in this family. Even though we're not together as a couple any more, we still very much see ourselves as a family with the boys and now Martyn. I'm grateful to her for not shutting the door on me after we split. She asked me if I ever thought I'd be a solo parent and to be honest, it never crossed my mind.' His voice breaks up. Ben passes him a glass of water. The room is silent as he drinks it down and clears his throat. 'I'm just glad the boys are not little any more. I'm not sure how I'm going to cope without her.' He turns away, rubbing his eyes with his fingers, holding the microphone out to Ben.

I follow Tom to the side of the stage and put my arm around him. Ben announces a short break. He and Scott help me comfort their dad and after a few minutes I leave them to it.

'Who's Cathy talking to?' Martyn whispers in my

ear as the lights go up. Cathy is holding a blue drink in a cocktail glass, still chatting to the man with blond spiky hair.

'No idea. I don't recognise him,' I say.

12

After a short break, Tom hands Martyn the microphone and the lights around the room go down again.

'When I first saw Heather at school, she pretended not to notice me. It was a ploy, she told me later, not to look too keen. But I knew once I'd seen her, she wasn't someone I'd ever forget. Not just for her striking good looks, but the aura of quiet confidence, the sunny disposition. She oozed charisma. It took a while before she agreed to go out with me. Heather was never into casual dating, not like some of you girls who had a different boyfriend every couple of weeks.'

He laughs waving a hand in the direction of our old school friends, who let out a cheer. Cathy barks a laugh which carries to the front of the room. There's no doubt he's referring to her in particular because they dated briefly before he asked me out. He dumped her after two weeks. Said he only went out with her because I took no notice of him.

'No, Heather was looking for a certain level of commitment from the start. And once I'd passed all the tests... I'm not sure exactly what the tests were, but I'm glad I did so well' – he pauses while everyone laughs – 'she agreed to let me take her to the cinema. We ended up going out for about eighteen months. She was the love of my life. Unfortunately, certain events got in the way, and we went our separate ways then lost touch completely after I moved away.'

Someone shouts out, *What about Simon?*

Martyn twists round and frowns at me as though being heckled is my fault, but I can't respond, I'm frozen to the spot. A rumble of voices rises from the crowd, heads turning to see who spoke. Many of them knew who Simon was, but some don't have a clue.

Martyn sweeps his hand through his hair. 'Yes. That dreadful incident marred all our lives, and I like to think that I was there for Heather through all of it, because it understandably brought everything back for her about her brother's death.'

Who killed Simon? the same voice shouts. A shiver runs through me. The crowd's chatter is louder now, more highly charged. I press my fingers to my lips, eyes darting about, trying to see who spoke.

Martyn turns to me, his eyes widening. I raise then drop my shoulders.

'It's too dark at the back to see who it was,' I whisper to him. We're both staring ahead to where Cathy was talking to the blond man, but neither of them are there.

'That question remains a mystery. The police failed to find out who was responsible. I can tell you this has hung heavily over Heather. The loss of little Alex tore her family apart, but none of them ever asked for any kind of rough justice.'

Ben passes Martyn a pint of beer and he drinks half of it back. His hands are trembling as Ben takes the glass from him again. I swallow and feel myself swaying as my head swims with a sudden rush of blood. Martyn clears his throat and tries to continue his speech about how we met, but his voice is flat, all the energy and exuberance has gone. He stutters and can't seem to get back to where he was, what he wanted to say.

The room is hushed as if everyone is holding their breath. Faces are blank, not knowing what's going to happen next. People look around at each other bewildered, as though nothing awkward has just happened to sour the atmosphere. No one seems to know what to do or say. Martyn attempts to raise a smile, but it falters. I try to follow his eyeline. He seems to be looking at someone in the crowd. Has he spotted who shouted out?

He looks at me again. 'Can everyone please raise their glasses to the one and only, Heather. It's truly an honour to be part of your life.' Everyone does as he asks. Glasses are lifted high, and my name is repeated with a little less gusto than we hoped for. I lay my hand across my heart, hearing my name chanted with love.

'Now I'll hand back to you.' Martyn passes me the microphone. Again, he's distracted by someone standing at the back. I try to see who he's spotted. He steps down from the stage and strides towards them. He stops midway and speaks to Cathy who is holding another blue cocktail. She's shaking her head. Does he think the man she was speaking to is the one who shouted out Simon's name? If it was, he's nowhere to be seen.

I wait for Martyn to come back and for the noise to die down, because no one will want to miss what I've got to say next.

It's time to tell everyone the secret I've been keeping for twenty-seven years.

13

I thank everyone who's made a speech for their kind and thoughtful words.

'And now on a more serious note, I've been thinking a lot about my parents lately; I miss them every day. As many of you know, they never got over losing Alex, which from my perspective now as a mum, is even more understandable. Dad took to drink, and Mum locked herself away then took her own life. There's not one day I don't wish they and my brother were still here. Sometimes I picture what Alex would be like now at thirty-seven, and I often imagine him standing by my side. So, I suppose part of accepting that I don't have long is thinking that I'm going to be reunited with them again. I don't particularly believe in an after-world and I've never been religious, but Ben and Scott bought me a beautiful white carved stone angel with a crystal embedded in it and I've had it next to my bed ever since. It brings me comfort and strength in my darkest moments. When I hold it in my hands, I can feel its energy passing through me. I believe my parents and Alex are somehow with me, protecting me on my final journey.' A trickle of applause goes round the room.

But what about Simon? It's the same voice as before, shouting from the back of the room. Lots of people turn around to tut and shush him, fed up at the repeated interruptions ruining the mood.

'Hello, whoever you are. I will come to that, I promise.'

I look over my shoulder at Martyn and can see him stretching his head up high, trying to see who spoke. I catch a glimpse of the slide show on the wall behind me. Giant, almost ghostly images of me throughout my life, from a baby in my mother's arms to growing up, playing with our dogs in the garden, then Alex being born and me holding him as a proud big sister, then later getting married to Tom, and having my sons. One of Alex appears where he's holding my hand. He must have been six, only months before he died. He has the biggest smile on his sweet face, standing in front of the Chinese Pagoda at Kew Gardens. If only I could have kept him safe. I take a deep breath, determined to carry on.

'Now for my confessions.' I smile as I scan the room, trying to hold my nerve. My head starts thumping. Can I actually do this? I swallow and think of something else to say first. 'Who remembers the sleepover at Perri Cassady's house in year ten?' A few hands shoot up and shouts of yes. 'And do you remember the ghostly happenings that night?'

'We still talk about it!' one school friend calls out.

I tell everyone how Perri's parents were renting a house that was meant to be haunted. We witnessed some strange goings on that night, such as books flying off a shelf, but now I confess to everyone that Perri and I were behind it all. Roars of laughter ripple around the crowd.

'I can't believe you did that,' someone says, in between laughing. I'm laughing too but at the same time my insides are flipping over at what I really want to tell them. I stall again with another harmless story.

'And you remember our missing cat, Doctor Jones?' As I'm talking I'm squeezing and twisting my hands together. I take my time recounting the different ways we searched for him. How we discovered that an old guy down our road was feeding him as a way of keeping him there for company. Everyone says 'ah' at the same time.

Scott passes me my drink and I take a good glug. My face is hot and sweaty. I'll need to rest soon. But right now, the room is quiet, everyone is listening, waiting for me to speak. I'm never going to get this opportunity again.

'When I first found out I didn't have long left, all the wrongs I've ever done or witnessed plagued my mind. I've barely been able to sleep at night for stressing about them. Silly things some of them, like the ones I've just told you, although they seemed a big deal at the time, like breaking Mum's favourite teapot and hiding it with all the broken pieces in the bottom drawer of the Welsh dresser. It took her a few weeks to find it, but she immediately knew it was me, so I don't know why I didn't just come clean straight away.' A few people laugh. 'And at school, it was me who wrote, *Everyone hates Sarah-Jane* on the blackboard, so when Miss Norton spun it round, the whole class could read it.' I hear a couple of *oh my God* comments. 'I was a silly jealous girl and I've always regretted upsetting her. I understand she lives in Canada now, and I've tried to email her to apologise. In my defence it was only a few weeks after Alex died, so I'd somewhat gone off the rails. But one of the worst things I did was when I was working my first job in the estate agents and found a letter on the printer from my manager to HR, asking how they could legally sack a colleague of mine. I took it, photocopied it and put a copy on everyone's desk to show them what an arsehole he really was. Then I went out one lunchtime with a bundle of their confidential papers about a competitor they'd been spying on, posted it through their door and never went back. By the way, my colleague went to a tribunal and won.'

Everyone cheers and starts clapping and whistling. Martyn passes me a glass of champagne and I glug it down. I'm buzzing, and I'm just getting started.

'I feel strongly that I need to come clean about everything before I die. Like I said, I'm not religious but I believe in angels looking over us and something in me won't let me leave this world with guilt, regret, or wrongs on my conscience. I don't mean to get anyone in trouble or do any harm, but this is something I need to do, so please forgive me.'

I try not to look at anyone in particular.

'I think one of the worst things we do as humans is keep secrets from our loved ones, our friends, people we know. And I'm as guilty as anyone. I've been sitting on a huge secret for the whole of my adult life. If anyone else has done this, you'll know how it eats away at you. It's always there, like a dagger wedged in your ribs. A perpetual pain that never eases. The guilt and the shame of it has dragged me down, swallowed me up like a black hole. I read somewhere not long ago that secrets as big as this *make* you ill and can mean that you live a shorter life. So if this illness is my punishment for staying silent, perhaps I deserve it.

'Now I've been told I haven't got long left, you'll hopefully understand the whole concept of keeping things quiet and secret "forever" seems utterly ridiculous to me. Because suddenly, "forever" isn't very long at all. I mean I'm probably not going to see the final series of *The Crown* for starters.' A low-level laugh filters through the room. 'This new perspective on life is sometimes incredibly crippling and on the other hand, it's powerful. Time is of the essence for me, of course, suddenly everything comes into sharp focus, but it is for all of you too, it's just that you don't realise it yet, you're still blissfully happy in your little bubbles, living your lives. Which is as it should be. You've not had the shock I've had. But you will. One day. Because it comes sooner than you think – none of us knows how long we've got. None of us is ready for this. We always think we have longer. We plan what we're going to do with our lives, months, and years ahead, assuming we'll be around to live our dreams, carry out our wishes. But it's worth remembering, there are no guarantees as to how long we have. Any of us.'

I take a breath and another sip of a new glass of champagne. If I get drunk tonight, it will be my last chance to do so, so sod it. I glance at my trembling hand. Come on. I need to do this.

'Most of you will be aware that my little brother Alex was killed when he was almost seven years old by a man named Bob Eyre. He ran him over backing his van out of a space in the leisure centre car park at speed. An eyewitness said Mr Eyre didn't even look before he reversed the vehicle but just put his foot down. Alex was rushed to hospital but died two hours later. Mr Eyre served just two years nine months for dangerous driving. A few weeks after he came out of prison, someone going by the name of Mr Eyre was killed. Except it wasn't Bob. It was his twenty-two-year-old son, Simon. His killer has never been found.'

A murmur flies around the room.

'What I need to tell you is, I know who killed Simon Eyre.'

14

Martyn steps in front of me and tries to prise the microphone from my hands.

'Are you crazy?' he whispers. 'Think about what you're doing, how much danger you'll be putting people in.' His words are loud and clear over the microphone. The noise in the room rises as people react by standing up and talking to each other. Martyn and I stare into each other's eyes, but I won't let go.

You can't prove who killed Simon, a different voice from before shouts from the crowd. We both look around to see who spoke. Do I know that voice? If I do, I can't place it. Distracted, my hold loosens, and Martyn snatches the microphone from me. I almost lose my balance, but Scott leaps over and grabs my arm, steadying me.

'What are you doing?' I shout at Martyn.

'Sorry about that, folks,' he says into the microphone, still looking at me, then into the crowd. 'It's the heavy medication Heather is on, she didn't mean what she said.'

'Don't apologise for me!' I yell, but my voice is too small without the microphone, and he ignores me.

'As the man over there alluded to, we can't be throwing accusations around when there's no evidence, it will just stir up trouble.'

I turn away and storm off the stage. Both my boys catch me as I stumble again. They help me to a back room and sit me down in a chair. Ben dispenses a drink of water from a jug on a nearby table and hands it to me.

'What's got into Martyn?' Scott asks, crouching beside me as I sip the water. My hands are shaking. I put the plastic cup down on the table. I don't trust myself not to spill it. It's only now that I realise how woozy my head feels. I'm quite drunk. I shouldn't be drinking alcohol with my medication.

'Mum, who is Simon Eyre?' Ben asks.

I swallow. I've been waiting for my boys to ask this and I'm well prepared. The answer trips off my tongue. 'He was a young man who died in a terrible accident a long time ago.'

'But you said someone killed him?'

'Yes they did, except they said his death was... a mistake.'

Ben frowns at me, probably hoping I'll explain what this is all about.

'But why? I don't understand.'

'People said his father Bob was the intended victim because he killed my little brother, your uncle Alex.' I cup Ben's face. Tears fill my eyes. Sometimes I look at my boys and I see Alex. Simon should never have died. He was the same age as Ben is now. Twenty-two. My head swims remembering that day. The thought of losing one of my boys brings fresh tears to my eyes. Could I be putting them in danger by outing the killer? I try to suppress the urge to retch by pressing my fist to my mouth, but a second later I rush to the toilet and throw up.

I lean back from the bowl and wipe my mouth on toilet paper. What am I doing to myself? I should never have drunk so much. I should have kept quiet.

When I come out of the bathroom, Martyn is waiting with Ben and Scott by the door. I quietly ask the boys to leave us a minute.

'Are you okay?' Martyn strides over and wraps his arms around me. 'Is it something you ate?'

'I think I've drunk too much, that's all. Not a good idea with these tablets I'm on.'

'I'm sorry about...'

I nod, reluctant to admit he's probably right. It's not a good idea to drop people in it. The compulsion to tell everyone who was behind Simon's death has been growing stronger in the buildup to the party. I was so sure it was the right thing to do. But now I think it's a mistake. I shuffle back into the chair.

'I know you said you want to clear your conscience, but if you say publicly who the culprit is, I think it's going to create some serious problems. It really is better to take it to the grave with you because, well, without concrete evidence, I don't see the point—'

'Maybe you're right,' I interrupt. 'It was a crazy thing to say. This damn medication is sending my head all over the place. I thought it would help me find peace. I've carried it around for so long. I became so desperate to unload the burden onto someone else, which is selfish I know.'

'It's not and you're not selfish at all. Don't you think I feel the same?'

I blink up at his face, at the pain he's letting show through for the first time.

'But no one can change what happened, so there's no point going over it. Nothing will bring him back.'

He seems relieved to hear he was right to stop me. I nod and lean my head against him. I doubt if he's the only one who doesn't want the truth to get out, especially in front of all these people.

'Let's go and enjoy the party,' I say. 'It's my last one after all. We shouldn't spoil it. I'll say something about my outburst, make an excuse about drinking too much.'

'Are you sure?' Martyn looks surprised.

'Yes, we should leave the ghosts behind.'

Martyn threads his arm through mine and leads me back to the hall and onto the stage. Ben passes me the microphone.

'Well, that was a bit too public for a domestic, especially when I've had a few drinks and then some.' I laugh, fixing my eyes on Martyn but he's only pretending to smile. I can tell he's still nervous I'm going to blab. Everyone else joins in laughing. 'Seriously though, Martyn's right. I shouldn't be dragging up the past, especially in matters that can never be resolved. And for the record, I don't have all the answers and I don't have tangible proof of who's guilty, so I should probably keep my big old mouth shut.' The laughing continues. 'Enjoy the party, everyone. There's plenty of food and drink. Help yourselves.'

I hand the microphone back to Martyn.

So what about justice for Simon? the voice from earlier shouts again.

'I'm sorry, but who said that?' Martyn squints at the crowd, trying to shield his eyes, but the spotlights from above are blinding him. 'Why don't you come forward and say it to my face?'

Heads turn to see who it was, but no one replies.

'See what you've done?' Martyn hisses at me away from the microphone.

A shiver tracks down my spine. Isn't demanding *justice for Simon* another way of wanting revenge?

15

Can't prove anything, otherwise someone would have been banged up for it already, the second voice shouts out.

Murmurs and movement come from the right side of the room as a man wearing a beanie pushes his way to the front, head down. Martyn's face brightens and he steps forward to greet the man, patting him on the back. I frown. He's unshaven, coat collar standing up around his neck. Something about his face is familiar. Could this be *him*?

'Yeah, you're absolutely right.' There's a slight tremor in Martyn's voice that wasn't there before. 'It's so good to see you, mate, glad you could come.' He shakes the man's hand then speaks to everyone. 'And if the other heckler is brave enough to come forward as well, we could have an open conversation about this.'

He shields above his eyes again to search the crowd, but no one speaks or makes a move to join him. Martyn passes Tom the microphone and steers the man in the beanie towards me.

'Surprise!' Martyn says to me, beaming.

I break into a smile.

I knew I recognised that voice. Dan Jones. Moved away after we left school that summer when we were all sixteen. None of us has seen him since, as far as I know.

'You found him!'

Dan doffs his beanie, and as soon as he smiles, I see the boy I used to know. He opens his arms and I step into a warm hug.

'It's so great to see you.' I stand back, holding onto his arms while trying to take in the fact that he's really here.

'Thanks for inviting me, Heather. I'm so sad to hear your news. You of all people don't deserve this, after everything you went through.' His head sinks as he nods until he's looking down at his worn-out trainers.

He sounds like he's already had a skin full. Maybe

he'll tell us why he chose to disappear all those years ago. The troubled boy he was then has often visited my dreams. I wondered what had happened to him, if he was dead, because I could never quite project how he would look as an adult, and now here he is in front of me, virtually unrecognisable from how I re-member him as a sweet-faced boy with barely a hair on his chin. We were all so entangled in each other's lives that his going away without saying anything after what happened always felt like a betrayal.

'Can we get you a drink? Someone, bring Dan a drink please.' Martyn waves at a member of the bar staff.

'Yeah, a beer's good, thanks Marty. Good to see the old gang.' He spins round. I'm guessing he's looking for one person in particular, but he can't see her yet. He raises a hand at our mutual school friends and they wave back, accompanied by exclamations of surprise, their faces as stunned as mine must be.

Where've you been hiding DJ? a woman shouts.

'How have you been?' I ask and his gaze lands back on me.

'Not so bad. Working mainly. Lovely speech by the way, Heather, but I don't advise stirring up the past either. Excuse me for being blunt saying so, but it's us that will have to deal with the fallout, not you.

It's taken me a lifetime to forget that terrible time. Why do you think I kept away?'

'I didn't know why. I'm sorry it was so difficult for you,' I say quietly. 'I just wanted to put the record straight, do the right thing before I die.'

'You may have said too much already,' Martyn says through clenched teeth as he checks around the room. 'Why the fuck didn't you warn me you were thinking of saying that?'

His eyes flick to Dan, knowing he has his support.

'Because I knew you'd be like this,' I sigh.

'Someone who knows the Eyres could be listening and report back,' Martyn says. 'We know what they're capable of.'

'What happened to Alex was a terrible accident,' I remind him.

'Dangerous driving is not an accident.' Martyn folds his arms.

'He served his time. The police were satisfied.'

'And since when did they care?' he whispers. 'Do you know who was shouting about justice for Simon?'

'I couldn't see who said it.' Dan shakes his head.

'Wasn't a voice I recognise,' Martyn says.

'Nor me.' I rub my eyes. Stress makes me tire so

quickly now, and on top of the alcohol and medication, I could fall asleep right here.

One of the bar staff comes over with a pint of beer and hands it to Dan. Martyn stays standing beside him, still scanning the room, presumably hoping he'll see someone he can match to the voice, a face that will jog his memory. Tom had resumed the music with easy listening tunes but now 'Dancing Queen' has come on and I don't think I can resist even though my legs are begging me not to move.

'So where is she then?' Dan asks and drinks half his beer in one go.

'Come on mate, let's not spoil Heather's party.' Martyn pats his shoulder.

'Marty, I need to see her. You promised me. I came here for her too, remember?'

'You did what?' I say under my breath to Martyn.

'No offence, Heather,' Dan adds.

I shake my head at both of them. Part of me is not surprised he wants to see Cathy. 'Why didn't you get in touch with any of us before now? You knew where we were.'

'I've got to be honest with you, Heather. I was locked up for a good few years, prison then a secure psychiatric unit. It's all in the past. I do my best to stay out of trouble, but you know me, trouble always finds me wherever I go.'

'Seriously, mate?' Martyn and I laugh half-heartedly because that is how we remember him. In trouble at school for one thing then another. Outside of school there was shoplifting and running away from home.

Dan nods. Our faces drop. He's clearly not joking.

'So sorry to hear that happened to you,' I say.

'Yeah, sorry Dan, they must have been tough times,' Martyn says.

'Thanks. I live by the sea now fixing boats. It's a peaceful life.'

The dance floor starts to fill up and I'm grateful to have the spotlight taken off me. Lisa comes over and gently leads me to dance with her.

I'm not sure where Cathy's been half the time we were making our speeches, but she shimmies in front of us, glass of white wine in hand. She seems to be getting through the drinks a bit too quickly.

'Lovely speech.' She kisses me on both cheeks. 'How are you holding up? You look a bit peaky. Can I get you something to eat?'

I shake my head even though she doesn't wait for my answer but carries on talking. '*I* really need to eat something in a minute. I've been chatting to all the old gang. Did you know that Jane and Stewart got married?' Her eyes and mouth widen for several seconds, something she always does to exaggerate her surprise. Lisa and I can't help belly laughing, releasing the tension built up from the conversation with Dan. We link arms as we double over, holding onto each other. Maybe the alcohol has helped to loosen me up too. I'm determined to stay in the moment and not dwell on anything stressful.

'How does it go?' Lisa and I say in chorus, copying Cathy's facial expression.

All three of us crack up this time, in fits of giggles.

'Seriously though,' Cathy says, trying to get her breath back, 'it's so nice to see everyone. I recognised most people. They all seem to remember me.'

I smile to myself. She seems genuinely baffled by that. Out of everyone, Cathy's not changed a bit.

'There she is,' Dan exclaims, arms out in front of him.

'Who's this?' Cathy asks me. Martyn laughs, not sure if she's being serious, but I genuinely don't think she recognises him.

'You don't remember me?' Dan asks, his face the picture of disappointment.

'What? Are you... oh my God, is it you?' She frowns, then when he nods, she opens her arms and they fall into the biggest hug. Dan pulls back after several moments, and kisses either side of her face, then they gaze at one another like they're teenagers again meeting for the first time.

'How have you not changed at all? Still as beautiful as you ever were,' Dan says, his eyes glistening.

'That's so nice, isn't it?' She checks to see if Lisa and I are still watching. 'I'm sorry I didn't recognise you. You look so different, but in a good way.' They hug again, tighter this time, and for much, much longer. I spot Robbie striding across the hall, straight in their direction.

'Who's this?' Robbie bellows, coming up behind Cathy before I have time to warn her.

16

Cathy lets go of Dan instantly and Robbie holds out a glass of wine to her. She takes the drink, flicking her hair over her shoulder.

'Robbie, meet Dan, an old friend from school.'

'Oh yeah?' Robbie says, frowning.

'Calm down. He's been missing for about a hundred years.'

The surprise on Dan's face looks more like indignation. 'The last time we saw each other we were what sixteen, and she dumped me.'

'You dated *him*?' Robbie laughs, pointing at Dan.

Cathy sips her drink.

'Sorry. It was a long time ago. A lot happened.

Then I needed to be on my own.' Dan presses his hand to his brow.

'Who are you saying sorry to?' Robbie asks, folding his arms.

'Sorry for what?' Cathy wrinkles her nose.

'It's okay, I get it, mate.' Dan holds his palms up to Robbie and side-eyes me.

'Less of the "mate" eh? And if you think you're back here to rekindle what you think you had, you can think again.' Robbie jabs the heel of his hand at Dan's shoulder making him stagger backwards, leaving him looking bewildered.

My jaw drops at Robbie's behaviour. 'There's no call for that. Dan hasn't done anything wrong.' I snap, stop-signing my hand and nudging Martyn's arm. He dives in between them, arms wide.

'Dan's here to see Heather, so don't forget yourself.' Martyn is taller than Robbie and tips his head down to look him square in the eyes, his jaw tensing as he grinds his teeth. 'It's Heather's special evening, remember?'

'Yeah, yeah I know.' Robbie backs off, puts a protective arm around Cathy's waist and pulls her closer to him. Cathy doesn't say a word, just sips her drink instead. Some things never change. She always loved boys fighting over her at school and now it's grown men. Doesn't like to miss out on a scrap of attention, even if it's not the good kind.

'I'm actually here to see Cathy too, but I don't want to upset the chump,' Dan says to me behind his hand.

'I heard that.' Robbie spins round, and pumps his fist at Dan's face, catching him square on the cheek. Cathy screams.

'What the hell was that for?' I shout, reaching for Dan as he doubles over, blood dripping from his face.

'What'd you do that for?' Martyn yells. 'Get him out of here Cathy, before I lose it too.'

Cathy links arms with Robbie and they push through everyone who's crowded around and leave through the main door. The group of our old school friends come over and a couple of the boys Dan used to hang around with help him into a chair.

'Let me have a look at you,' says Sandy, who used to live down his street and is now a nurse. He is still doubled over, hand to his face. I encourage him to sit up straight so she can examine him. 'Come on, let me see.'

Sandy gently holds his wrist and pulls his hand away. There's a gash pumping blood from his cheek, where Robbie's signet ring must have ripped into the skin.

'It's not that bad.' Sandy holds a hanky to the wound and presses the skin around it. 'No broken bones. Just badly cut and bruised. You're lucky it wasn't nearer your eye.' She sends someone to get the first aid kit from the kitchen area then cleans up the cut and covers it in a big square plaster.

It's a while before Cathy comes back in, alone.

'Robbie's in the pub nearby calming down,' she says, hugging her arms around herself. 'I'm sorry he kicked off at you like that, Dan. I hope he's not spoilt your party, Heather. I don't know what gets into him sometimes.'

'It's okay, it's not your fault. Why don't you two get yourselves some food and take the opportunity to catch up with each other?'

'Yeah, good idea.' Cathy holds out a hand to Dan and leads him to the buffet tables. Martyn and I agree to circulate again, speak to as many friends and family as we can. While most people are sitting down eating, Scott and Ben accompany me as I stop at each table and chat to my guests. Martyn goes round in the opposite direction, making sure everyone is okay, although I suspect he's on the lookout for the other heckler who called out about justice for Simon.

I speak to old neighbours and people I used to work with before I started the kennels. I'm overwhelmed by all the love and hugs I receive. There are lots of tears and kind words.

I make my way back to the table where Cathy and Dan are chatting. There are empty paper plates with half-eaten sandwiches and vol-au-vents in front of them and they're eating huge helpings of trifle in paper dishes like we used to have at our childhood birthday parties.

'Dan says he's living by the sea, mending boats,' Cathy tells me. 'He's going to take me on a trip around the Island. I've always wanted to go there.'

I tilt my head at them, wondering what Robbie will have to say about that, and whether she's had a chance to finish with him yet.

'What?' Dan grins, mischievous as ever.

'Robbie doesn't own me. I'm allowed to have friends.' Cathy shifts closer to me and lowers her voice. 'Were you really going to say who killed Simon?'

'Yeah, I was.'

'Why?' She looks at me, then Dan.

'You don't think it's time it came out?'

'Not really, no.' She frowns and glances at Dan again. 'Bringing it up could cause all sorts of grief.'

'Why say something after all this time?' Dan whispers. 'What good will it do?'

'That's what Martyn said and maybe he's right. But what about Simon's family? It must be awful not knowing who's responsible.'

Dan shakes his head. 'Hang on, think about what his father did to your brother.'

'I know, and I don't stop thinking about it, but they lost a loved one too in such a terrible way. I just think they deserve to know what happened.'

'I don't think they deserve anything. They'll want everyone locked up.' Cathy crosses her arms and legs.

'Honestly, I'm glad Martyn stopped you. I'm sorry Heather, but I don't think you're thinking clearly, which is understandable in your situation, of course it is, but consider what could happen if you named who did it.' Dan steals a glance at Cathy, who nods in agreement.

'It's not that simple for me,' I say. 'I've not told anyone this, but I've been seeing a spiritualist over the last couple of months, to help me come to terms with my illness, and they've helped me see the burden this secret has had on me, bottling it up for so long. It might even have contributed to me becoming ill. They think speaking the truth would release me from its grip. It's not going to save me, but it would lift a weight.'

Cathy and Dan frown at each other, then at me

with pained expressions. Cathy lays her hand on top of mine. 'Haven't you always said that those kinds of people are charlatans who prey on the vulnerable?'

'My circumstances are a bit different now.' I snatch my hand away from hers. 'Aren't I allowed to change to mind?'

'Of course you are. I'm sorry.'

'You don't know what it's been like, losing Alex in such a horrific way when he was so young, then both my parents dying, and now this happening to me. Knowing who killed Simon on top of all of that has been like dragging Marley's chain around with me wherever I go.'

'I appreciate how much you've been through, but I'm begging you not to open this can of worms,' Cathy says.

'I think Cathy's got a fair point, Heather,' Dan says.

'It's fine. I've already told Martyn I won't say anything. So you two don't need to gang up on me.'

Cathy's face suddenly creases up and I think she's mocking me. I'm about to say something else, until I see the pain in her eyes.

'Are you okay?' I shoot a look of alarm at her then Dan. She stares at me with such fear as she grips her stomach with both hands and leans forward, groaning.

'What's wrong, Caz?' Dan jumps out of his seat and kneels in front of her as she cries out, kneading her palms into her stomach. He holds her by the shoulders and tries to make eye contact but her head lolls to one side.

'What's happening?' Martyn runs over, his face drained of colour.

'Call an ambulance!' I shout.

17

Lisa holds the door open while Martyn and Dan help Cathy into the foyer to wait for the ambulance. She can barely walk and is wincing and groaning in pain. I follow with her bag and jacket. There's nothing to point to it being something she's eaten, but the food has been removed by the catering staff for now, just in case.

'At least no one else seems to be feeling ill so hopefully it's not the food. Did you eat anything before you got here?' I ask Cathy. She thrashes her head from side to side and cries out, clearly in a lot of pain. Martyn and Dan look up at me with forlorn expressions. There's nothing any of us can do except make her comfortable.

'Didn't she have a bite of one of the cookies you made her?' Lisa says.

'Christ, it can't be that, surely?' I try ringing Robbie but there's no answer.

She shrugs and goes back into the hall to help Ben and Scott.

'I'll go with Cathy to the hospital; you stay with your guests,' Martyn says, dragging his free hand through his hair.

'Robbie should be here for that. I'll try ringing him again.' I leave him and Dan kneeling either side of her. She has a firm grip on their hands and is squeezing them every time she goes through a wave of pain. If I didn't know better, I'd guess she was in labour, but she never had kids after her abortion. We were still kids ourselves. They said she wouldn't be able to have any because of the infection.

I walk out of the main door for a better signal and press Robbie's number. He finally answers and it's clear from the noise that he's still in the pub.

'You need to come quickly,' I shout.

'Hang on, I can't hear you.'

'Hello? What pub are you in?'

'That's better. I'm in the Bright Star. You're not ringing to have another go at me, are you?'

'No. Cathy's ill. She's collapsed.'

There's no answer.

'Robbie?'

'Say that again?' The background noise has gone, and it sounds like he's near a road.

'You need to come back right now. Cathy's ill, severe pains in her stomach. I've called an ambulance.'

'What has she eaten?'

'I don't know, the same as everyone but no one else seems affected. Just get back here as soon as you can.'

'I will, I'm on my way.'

'You've been drinking, haven't you?'

'I'm leaving now. Tell her I'll be there.'

I cut the call and reach out to push the main door back into the foyer. But then I stop. Martyn is leaning over Cathy. I peer closer through the glass. His face is a hairsbreadth away from hers. Is he whispering something in her ear? I push the door open, and he sits up straight.

'Robbie's on his way so you won't need to go in the ambulance. He's been mooching in the Bright Star pub up the road.'

'Is he in a fit state?' Martyn looks at Cathy then back at me. There are fresh tears on her face. She groans again, cupping her stomach, and turns onto her side into a foetal position. Maybe she *is* pregnant.

Thankfully Dan seems to have made himself scarce and gone back to the party. I will not put up with another face-off between him and Robbie.

It's another ten minutes before Robbie crashes in through the main door.

'What's happened?' he demands. He skids down on his knees and tries to talk to Cathy, but her eyes are creased shut and she can't speak for groaning in pain.

'I think it could be her appendix,' I say, looking at the way she's clutching her side.

Martyn stands up and crosses his arms.

Robbie strokes Cathy's hair. 'I'm here Cathy, can you hear me?' He leans down and kisses her cheek.

'Where the hell is the ambulance?' Martyn looks out of the door then at his watch.

'Where is that little scroat?' Robbie says. 'Did he do this?'

'No, of course not. I imagine Dan is keeping well out of your way,' I say. 'Did Cathy eat or drink anything when she was at the pub?'

'Yeah, she had a small Bailey's.'

I frown. 'She's drunk a lot. Could it be alcohol poisoning?'

'More likely her appendix, being in that much stomach pain,' Martyn says.

A few minutes later an ambulance pulls up right outside the main door. Two paramedics bowl in carrying emergency equipment. Cathy is writhing on the floor again crying. I stand close to Martyn, turning my face into his chest. He puts his arm around me as we answer the paramedics' questions about what happened.

'Do you think it could be her appendix?' I ask one of them as she stands up after checking Cathy over.

'I'm sorry, we won't know that for sure until she's had a thorough check at the hospital.'

'Promise you'll keep us updated,' I say to Robbie as the paramedics carry Cathy out on a stretcher. He nods once, as he follows them with her handbag, shoes and jacket.

My breathing quickens as the ambulance whizzes off, sirens blaring. I hug Martyn tight and feel him swallow hard. I think he's trying not to cry.

'Let's hope she's going to be okay.' He sniffs and pulls away from me. We glance at each other's stressed faces and take a moment before we go back into the main hall. Dan rushes up to ask me how Cathy is, and I tell him as much as I know. Tom passes the microphone to Martyn.

'Cathy's been taken to hospital with a suspected burst appendix.'

His voice wavers as he struggles to keep his emotions at bay, so I take the microphone from him. 'We'll keep everyone updated with any development as soon as we hear it from Robbie who's gone with her.'

Tom continues playing the music, but the atmosphere has changed, as though the air has been punched out of the room.

18

'What happens now?' Lisa pats my arm. I hand the microphone back to Tom.

'Let's bring everything forward.'

Martyn and Lisa nod.

'I'll speak to the staff, if you could go and check that the fireworks are ready?'

Lisa squeezes my hand and heads for the side door into the garden.

'Are you okay?' I ask Martyn.

'Yeah, just a shock. One minute she was laughing and chatting and the next... Isn't the appendix on the right side? Cathy was holding her middle, the stomach area.'

'When Ben had it, it started in the middle. He felt nauseous and threw up.'

'I don't remember her saying she felt sick. Do you think she'll be all right?' Martyn rubs his forehead with his hand.

'She might have to have surgery, but you know Cathy, she always bounces back.'

'I hope so.'

'I think I'll have to call it a night soon.' I yawn. 'I'll see if one of the boys can drive me home so you can stay and finish chatting with people.'

'Yeah, whatever you want.'

The atmosphere perks up as soon as the chef brings out the celebration cake followed by a parade of waiting staff carrying bottles of champagne. The cake is placed on a pedestal in the middle of the room and Martyn, Ben and Scott stand beside me next to it. *Farewell, Heather* is written on it in fancy writing. My stomach clenches seeing those words. It never stops being a shock to me.

Tom hands me the microphone again.

'I'd like to thank you all again for taking the time to come here tonight. I can only apologise for the unexpected drama.' I smile at Martyn and Dan and they look suitably sheepish. 'Of course, we all wish Cathy a speedy recovery.' I pause for a short round of applause. 'It's been a truly memorable evening for me. Thank you for helping make tonight the special occasion I'd hoped for.' My voice cracks. I pause as everyone claps. 'Both my parents loved fireworks and took me to a display every bonfire night. They told me as a child that fireworks were magical, and if you shut your eyes and made a wish, it would send your hopes and dreams out into the universe. So make your own wishes tonight. Please help yourselves to a slice of cake and a glass of champagne, then join me in the garden to watch the fireworks and share a special last toast with me and my family.' Everyone stands, clapping wildly and whistling. Lots of people are wiping their eyes. Martyn shouts out, *Three cheers for Heather,* and a collective *Hip Hip Hooray* fills the room as I plunge the knife into the cake. Dan starts singing, 'For She's a Jolly Good Fellow', and the whole room seems to lift as everyone joins in.

The waiters and waitresses walk around handing out champagne flutes, and when all the guests have a glass and a piece of cake they follow me, Martyn and the boys out to the garden.

It's a warm August evening and has only got dark in the last half an hour. Sofas and benches are set out around coffee tables across the long terrace in front of a vast lawn.

'That was so lovely,' Lisa says and gives me a hug. 'Are you happy with how the evening's gone, apart from the obvious?'

'Yes, I am. Thank you for helping me organise it and keeping it running smoothly.' We clink glasses and sit at our reserved table. Martyn is on the lawn chatting to some old school friends. He checks his phone every few minutes. He has a similar look of worry on his face as the day he took Cathy to the clinic. I stayed with Dan, who was too distraught at her going for a termination. That day broke us all.

Lisa touches my arm. 'Are you okay?'

'Yeah, I am thanks. I'm sure Cathy will be fine. Martyn is waiting to hear from the hospital.'

'I didn't realise they were so close. He seems really upset.'

'He and Cathy were like brother and sister at school, although they dated before we did, but not for long. The four of us were inseparable back then.'

'Hopefully we'll hear some good news soon,' Lisa says.

'I hope so.' I nod.

Dan is standing in the middle of the lawn, gazing up at the inky blue sky. He's probably wondering how different his life would have been if he'd stayed with Cathy. He must be kicking himself, seeing her end up childless and with someone flashy like Robbie, when he could have been standing here with her as her devoted husband, perhaps with a couple of grown-up children of their own.

At the time, I tried to persuade Cathy to keep the baby. Sixteen *was* too young, but she had her adoptive family around her who I'm sure would have supported her. She loved Dan, and boy, did he love her. She'd never been particularly ambitious about going to college. A year or two out wouldn't have made that much difference to her future. But she'd looked me in the eye so intensely and said no, she couldn't go ahead with it. Dan couldn't understand why she wanted to get rid of their child. I stayed with him to try to console him while Martyn, who thought she was doing the right thing, took her to the clinic. The four of us had been a solid unit until then. But it was never the same after that day. Dan moved away without saying a word to any of us, and Martyn and I finished with each other. Crazy how our choices back then spun our lives in completely different directions.

A member of the firework team asks Dan and everyone else on the lawn to move back. Dan stands on his own to one side and my heart aches for him. I ask Lisa to invite him to come and sit with us, which she does. He looks over at me and follows her over.

He probably feels obliged to as I won't be here much longer. He sits next to me and I reach out to him and hold his hand. Lisa sits on the other side.

I capture all these moments like the click of a camera in my head as 'lasts' of everything I do.

'Please all raise your glasses again to Heather,' Martyn says, standing at the edge of the patio.

'To Heather,' everyone repeats.

'Thank you. And don't forget to make your wish.' I raise my glass too.

The firework display thrills everyone with collective oohs and aahs at the loud bangs as fountains of glitter light up the sky. Maybe I should have my ashes sent up in a firework, I think to myself.

As I gaze into the shimmering night, all the things I would do differently rush at me. If I had my time again, would I really change that much? Maybe not, apart from the one big thing I'm trying my best to put right before I go. I could have made more of a difference to the world, but perhaps it's not too late.

The final big rocket whistles up into the night, its tail aflame, and as it explodes into a glittering display, I close my eyes and make my last wish.

19

By the time the firework display has finished, the cake has been eaten and a chill has crept into the air. Scott wraps a pashmina around my shoulders and escorts me inside. Once everyone is in and the doors have been closed, Tom hands me the microphone again and everyone quietens down as I give my final speech, thanking everyone.

I stare at all the emotional faces in front of me and wish Cathy was here to crack a joke and lighten the mood. I wonder how she is and imagine her laughing with the doctors and nurses at all the fuss. Maybe it was nothing more than a stomach bug. She can be over the top when she's unwell, but it did seem serious. Ben gently takes the microphone from me.

'Thank you, Mum. Please will you all raise your glasses to our dearest mum, Heather.' Ben holds his glass up and everyone does the same, saying my name in unison. 'Finally, some of you already know that Scott and I have challenged ourselves to run in the London Marathon next year. So, if any of you feel like sponsoring us, all the money we raise will be going to Mum's favourite charity, Blue Cross, which does such a brilliant job of rehoming dogs after their owners have passed away. And before you ask, just to reassure you, Scott and I will be looking after Monty and Morris for Mum when the time comes. Lisa will be taking over the kennels, although Scott and I were looking forward to doing that ourselves.' He glances at me as he says it and indicates to Lisa with an outstretched hand and a tight smile. She nods, clearly unwilling to acknowledge any acrimony. I'm a little taken aback at Ben's remark. I think about Tom accusing me of giving away their inheritance.

'So dig deep in your pockets if you can. Thank you all again for making this the best going-away party Mum could have wished for.'

Debussy's sombre, melancholic piano version of 'Clair de Lune' accompanies a medley of photos of me from childhood to the present day, projected on the wall. Everyone is still and quiet watching my forty-three years flash before them. I wish it didn't have to be this way.

Thankfully, as soon as Debussy has finished, Tom cranks up the party music again and the atmosphere lifts. A few more people chat with me and we laugh and cry at their memories from work and school and days at the kennels.

Martyn comes over, mobile in his hand.

'Any news yet?' I ask.

'Nothing. How are you feeling?' He rubs my shoulder then squats in front of me so he can speak to me at my level.

'Exhausted but happy.'

'Say when you've had enough, and I'll take you home.'

'Thanks. I feel like I don't want to leave now. I want to hang on as long as I can. Some people have travelled miles and miles to be here. If I went home, I'd feel like I was letting them down.'

'You could never do that.'

'Did you work out who was shouting out about Simon?'

He shakes his head then scans the room. 'I don't know who would have the balls to call out something like that.'

'I half thought whoever it was might come up and say something to me.'

'As they haven't, hopefully it means they were just trying to stir things up and that will be the end of it.' As he finishes speaking, his phone rings. 'Hello? Hang on a sec, I can't hear you properly.' He points to the phone, his eyebrows raised and mouths Robbie's name. It must be news about Cathy.

He steams out of the room into the foyer. I need to know how she is, so I follow him but at a slower pace, helped by Ben.

By the time we get there Martyn has his back to us but he's no longer holding the phone to his ear.

'Was it the hospital?'

I know it's a stupid question, but he's standing there so quietly and I don't know what to say.

He turns slowly, clutching the mobile to his stomach. His face is pale and drawn. 'Yes, Robbie updated me about Cathy.'

I frown. 'Come on. How is she then?'

He shakes his head. 'He said the police are on their way. No one is to leave.' His voice sounds strange, monotone, robotic.

'But why?' Ben asks.

'What's wrong?' I squint at Martyn. 'What's that got to do with Cathy?'

'He said she's been poisoned, and whoever did it is probably still here.'

He said she'd been poisoned, and whoever did it
is probably still here.

20

'You have got to be joking?' I grab Martyn's arm, but
he shakes his head. 'How is she?'

'She's seriously ill in intensive care.'

'Christ,' Ben says, 'we'd better get back in there
and tell everyone.'

I daren't ask, but I have to know. 'Is she going to
make a full recovery?'

'They honestly don't know at this stage.' Martyn's
face creases up and he's on the verge of tears.

I open my arms and hug him. 'Who would do
this? And why Cathy?'

Martyn pulls back and stares at me, eyebrows
raised as if I'm stupid to ask.

'Do you want me to go and break the news to everyone?' Ben says.

'No, it's okay, I'll do it. But you go back in. Martyn and I need to talk first.'

'All right. Are you sure you're okay, Mum?' Ben frowns at Martyn then at me. He suddenly seems unsure of him. They've never been close.

'What shall I do if other people start feeling ill?'

'Come and tell me or if it's urgent, call an ambulance straight away.'

As soon as Ben has gone, Martyn throws his hands up. 'For Christ's sake, Heather, what have you done?'

'What do you mean?' I glare at him.

'You know what I mean. You know what this is all about.'

'No, I don't. What are you talking about?'

He clenches his teeth, but his voice quietens to a whisper. 'Simon, of course. Justice for Simon? Whoever was calling that out knows about Cathy.' He checks over his shoulder to make sure no one has slipped in and is listening.

'You can't know that for sure. It's more likely to be an ex-boyfriend of hers. There are a few here she dated from school.'

'What you mean, like Dan?'

'Dan wouldn't do this.' My voice rises. How can he even think Dan would hurt her?

Martyn glares at me. 'You don't know that.'

'What reason would he have?'

'Because of the abortion? We all know he wanted her to keep it.'

'But why do this now, after almost thirty years?'

'Why not? He's probably been festering about it. Look at the state of him. Maybe he looks at Ben and Scott and wonders about his child who'd be grown up now, maybe with kids of its own. This could be the first chance he's had to get his revenge.'

'I don't believe Dan is the sort of person who holds a grudge. He's vulnerable, fragile. He's not capable of hurting anyone.'

I can't believe he thinks that of Dan. They used to be best friends.

'Maybe that's what he wants you to believe. How well do we really know him?'

Martyn's had too much to drink; he's freaking out.

'Okay, so I'll go back to my original theory. What if Cathy being poisoned is just the beginning?'

'Of what?' I shake my head in disbelief.

'You know what. Who's going to be next? Do we have to wait and see before you believe me?'

'No way, you've got it completely wrong. It's nothing to do with that. This is a one-off.'

'Okay maybe not tonight, but someone thinks they know who killed Simon. And that person is here tonight, blatantly calling out for justice. They could easily come and find you, beat it out of you if you refuse to tell them what you know.'

'I'm dying, Martyn. There's not much they can do to hurt me.'

'What about the rest of us? Or what if they come for Scott or Ben?'

'If that's the case, perhaps you shouldn't have stopped me speaking out. People deserve to know what happened. That family deserves to know the truth.'

'Maybe Cathy's being poisoned was a warning. I'm probably next.'

'What's got into you, Martyn? I can't believe you're saying this. There's no way her being poisoned was deliberate.'

'The police seem to think so.'

'Maybe they're working on that assumption until they find some hard evidence.'

'Fine, but why would you go ahead and rip open a wound that's healed over? We've managed to keep it quiet for so long.'

'I'm sorry, but I'm struggling to live with this secret any longer. The guilt of knowing who did this to an innocent man is eating away at me from the inside out. The truth always comes out in the end, with or without me, so why not now so I can die peacefully, with a clear conscience?'

'Because you have to consider the damage it'll do.' He shakes his head woefully. 'The mess you'll leave behind for your loved ones.'

'Stop telling me what to do,' I shout. 'I've barely stopped thinking about Alex since my diagnosis, and how I'd feel if I didn't know who'd killed him. How much more tormented I would have felt not knowing. Like the Eyre family must have been feeling, every single day since it happened.'

'No, no, no!' Martyn shakes his head and paces in long strides around the foyer. He pauses and swallows hard. 'I totally get how you feel about Alex, of course I do. What happened to him was a terrible, terrible thing. And being terminally ill must have brought it all to the surface for you. But doing this, telling people who killed Simon – it will ruin our lives. Is that honestly what you want?'

I turn my back on him and stare blankly out of a side window. The sound of a police siren in the distance makes us both look towards the entrance.

'I'm sorry, I need to go and update everyone about Cathy's condition and make sure no one leaves. Can you wait here for the police?'

He nods and rubs his hands over his face then brings his palms together. 'Please, please promise me you won't tell them anything about who killed Simon.'

I sigh and push open the door back into the hall.

21

All eyes are on me when I walk into the hall. Tom hands me the microphone and Ben and Scott are instantly at my side, pulling up a chair for me. I sink into it.

'I'm afraid it's not good news,' I say, sitting in front of a series of black and white photos of me projected onto the wall. 'The doctors believe Cathy has been poisoned and that it more than likely happened here this evening, so I'm afraid no one is allowed to leave just yet.'

'Who says so?' a man calls out.

'I'm afraid it's the police who have requested no one leave until they say you can. They'll be here any minute. I think they'll want to talk to each person before they let you go home. I'm really sorry. It's not the ending to the evening I wanted.'

'How long's that going to take?' a woman asks.

'I'm sorry, I don't know.' My eyes are sore and scratchy and my body weak with exhaustion. I could easily shut my eyelids and fall straight to sleep. The sensible thing would have been to leave earlier, but then I'd have regretted not chatting with more of my guests, people who've made such an effort to come and see me.

'I need to get home to my elderly father,' says one of my old neighbours sitting near me. Her hand is half raised in the air the whole time she speaks.

'I'm so sorry, it's out of my hands but I will ask the police to prioritise people who are carers or have babysitters and other commitments.'

The door to the main hall opens and Martyn shows in two officers who stride up to me.

'Are you Heather Deal?'

'Yes.' I stand up and they promptly show me their badges.

'I'm DI Bradbury and this is DS Stone,' says the shorter of the two, a woman in her forties with mid-length brown curly hair and olive skin.

'How many people are here?' asks the DS, a tall, slim woman with cropped blonde hair.

'One hundred and ninety,' I say and she scribbles it in her notebook.

'We'd like to speak to everyone here, starting with you and your family. There will be a couple of special constables joining us to assist with the volume of enquiries,' says DI Bradbury.

'You really think someone did this to her on purpose?' I frown and look to Martyn who's pursing his lips, glaring at me.

'We'll need to take away samples of all the food and drink from the buffet.'

'But everyone else seems to be okay. I thought it must be something like appendicitis. Are you sure she's been poisoned?'

'According to the hospital, Cathy has ingested a poisonous substance.'

'Could it be from the pub or maybe she picked up a dirty glass or touched something contaminated?'

DS Stone shakes her head. 'Signs indicate it was deliberate. Which pub was this and who was she with?'

'The Bright Star. She went with her partner, Robbie. It's not far from here. About ten minutes' drive I think. Actually he... left here under a cloud, had a bit of a set-to with Dan. We had to ask him to leave.

Cathy went with him, had a drink there before she came back here, apparently.'

'And who is Dan? What's his full name?' DS Stone asks.

'Dan Jones. We know him from school, but he moved away and hasn't been back for over twenty years.'

DS Stone glances at the DI, who turns away from me and asks the DS to go and speak to the landlord.

'Does Cathy have any enemies that you know of?' DI Bradbury asks.

'I don't think so. She can rub people up the wrong way sometimes without meaning to, but I can't think of anyone who would want to harm her,' I say, looking round at Ben and Scott, who both nod in agreement.

Martyn rests a hand on my shoulder. His eyes are puffy. I think he's going to cry again.

DI Bradbury asks us questions about the buffet, who prepared it and what drinks and food Cathy ate as far as we're aware. Martyn mentions she took a bite of one of the cookies I made her.

'And how well do you know her, are you close?'

'Yes, we spend a lot of time together. Martyn and I both went to school with her. Been friends for thirty years, maybe more. Although she went to live in

France for five years. Came back about two years ago after her marriage broke down. That's when she met her current partner, Robbie.'

'And have you ever fallen out?'

'Oh loads of times, but never for more than a day or two. It would be boring if we agreed all the time. We're both headstrong people but I'd say we admire each other for that.'

'And is everything happy between her and Robbie?'

I pause a second before answering. 'They have a somewhat volatile relationship. He has a tendency to get jealous, you see.'

'And what was the disagreement about, between Robbie and Dan this evening?' she asks Martyn. He glances at me before speaking.

'He punched Dan because he's an ex-boyfriend of Cathy's. He thought they were getting a bit cosy. And I mean an ex-boyfriend from when we were at school, not a recent relationship. Robbie was completely out of order.'

DS Stone writes this all down. Martyn and I glance at each other.

After the police have finished questioning me and Martyn, they move on to those who need to leave quickly.

'I'm sure that man with blond hair has something to do with what's happened to Cathy,' Martyn whispers. 'I've asked around and no one seems to know who he is. Could someone have got in uninvited?'

'No one was checking at the door, so I suppose it would have been easy to stroll in.'

Martyn rubs his chin. 'Why don't we look through all the photos taken tonight, then at least if he's in one of them we have something to show to the police?'

We find Phoenix, the photographer, and ask him if he could show us everything he's taken of this evening. We sit at one of the empty tables while the police question the queue of guests. There are hundreds of images to flick through, but we know what we're looking for. It's not long before my eyes are aching from staring at the camera screen.

'I'll grab my laptop out of the car and download the ones you want to look at more closely,' Phoenix says.

We continue looking and when we come to the group photos, I suggest we get those enlarged first so we can spot the face we're looking for. Phoenix plugs the camera into his laptop and when the photos are downloaded, he selects the ones we've picked out.

A group photo in the garden comes up. It's one

taken from the first-floor window. We zoom in so the photo fills the laptop screen.

'Is that him there, on the right?' Martyn asks.

Phoenix selects the man's face and zooms again. It's too pixelated to see clearly, but the spiky blond hair says it's him.

'Now we have a slightly better idea of his face, let's see if we can spot him in any more of the photos.' We click through the slide show on the laptop and find one of him with Cathy. His face is turned to her so we can see his profile.

'That looks like them together,' Ben says.

Martyn leans forward in his chair. 'So how does she know this guy? She's never said anything about him to me.'

'Don't you think he's got a familiar bump in his nose,' Dan says behind Martyn and slaps a hand on his shoulder.

I tip my head closer to the screen, to see what they are looking at.

'You're right,' Martyn says to Dan and points at the blond man with his index finger. 'I'd put money on that bloke being something to do with the Eyre family.'

22

'Seriously?' I crease up my nose. 'I don't see the resemblance at all. Loads of people have noses like that and the Eyres all have dark ginger hair.'

'Actually, Heather's got a point,' Dan says, 'and why would one of them be here anyway?'

Martyn shakes his head. 'They could easily have heard about your party but can't have known that you planned to tell everyone who killed Simon, because even I didn't know about that. So I suppose you must be right. But it still leaves the question of who would want to harm Cathy?'

'The hospital could have made a mistake.' I take a sip of water. 'She probably just picked something up she shouldn't have. We all know what she's like nibbling on stray bits of food. Do you remember that time she pinched a half-eaten cake off the next table in that café in Brighton? So embarrassing.' I laugh in mock horror. 'The people had only just left. You'd never guess she was like that to look at her, with her expensive taste in clothes. Waste not want not she always says, and the five-second rule never applies to her.'

'You're not wrong there.' Martyn lets out a sorrowful laugh.

'Maybe she stopped by the kitchen and snuffled something that was meant for the bin.'

'I hope she's going to be okay.' Dan takes off his beanie and scratches his head. His hair is thinning at the crown and is white in places. We're all beginning to show our age.

'How are you all doing?' Lisa comes over with the guest book under her arm. We pull faces at each other which just about sums up our mood.

'There's not really an answer to that,' I say.

'I'm sorry. It's so awful, isn't it?'

We all nod.

'Thank you for being absolutely brilliant this evening, Lisa. You've been so busy keeping everything running, we've hardly seen you.'

She leans down for a hug.

'I promised to make sure everything was ticking over so you and your family could properly enjoy yourselves on your special night. I hope you've had a great time, obviously apart from poor Cathy falling ill.'

'I have, thank you.'

'You don't know who this is, do you?' Martyn taps the screen.

Lisa moves round so she can see.

'No, but I saw him talking to Cathy a couple of times. He kept ordering those fancy Blue Lagoon cocktails from one of the waitresses. He seemed to be asking Cathy a lot of questions.'

'Oh! I don't suppose you heard anything he said, did you?' Martyn asks.

'Something about his dad I think, I didn't quite catch what though.'

I laugh. 'He was probably the son of one of her old boyfriends.' Dan and Martyn glance at me but don't seem to think it's funny.

'Possibly.' Lisa taps her finger on her chin. 'Except the conversation became quite serious. At one point he grabbed her wrist and she tried to pull away from him.'

'Why didn't she say anything to me about this?' I turn to Martyn.

'Or me,' he says.

'Then later,' Lisa continues, 'I saw them outside, away from everyone. Cathy looked really upset.'

'When was this?' Martyn asks. This is news to me too.

We exchange a look of alarm. He's probably thinking exactly the same as me. Why did neither of us know this was going on?

'It's when you were making your speeches. I only saw them the second time because I went out to check on the team setting up the firework display.'

'And how did Cathy seem to you?'

'Her head was down. I think she was crying.'

'Did you see anything after that?'

'No. When I walked back across the terrace to come in, they'd gone.'

'Why didn't she come and tell us about this?' Martyn asks again, probably hoping one of us has a theory.

'I don't know, it's so odd. We really need to find out who that man was,' I say.

'He's not here now, at least I haven't spotted him for quite a while,' Dan says.

'No, he's long gone. I saw him leave while the fire-works were going off,' says Lisa.

'Oh, did you?' Martyn says. 'I hope you're going to tell all this to the police.'

'I will. That's where I'm going now. I thought you might like to flick through the guest book.' She hands it to me. 'I've had a quick peek. Everyone's written such lovely messages.'

'Thank you.' I take it from her. It's heavy and Martyn helps me lay it on the table.

'Anyway, I'm being called. Speak later.' Lisa heads off towards where the police are sitting behind a couple of make-shift enquiry tables.

Martyn glances down as I open the book and flick through the messages, smiling at who's written them. I pause at the only one without a name and have to blink a few times to stop the words jumping around.

It's written in the middle of the page across a few lines like a poem:

*I know who
was on the bridge
that day,
and I'm going to
make them pay.*

23

'Who the hell wrote this?' Martyn asks, scanning the room. 'Whoever it was could still be here. No doubt the same person who's poisoned Cathy.'

'How can anyone else possibly know who was on the bridge?' I say under my breath.

'Do you recognise the handwriting?' He looks at it again. It's almost childlike in the roundness of the letters, and hardly any are joined up.

'I don't think so. I can't even guess if it's written by a man or a woman.'

'Me neither. Shit. It's got to be the same person who was shouting out about Simon, doesn't it?'

'But who was that? Is it possible someone else saw what happened that day?'

'No. I don't buy it. It's got to be a hoax. Maybe someone from our school? Everyone knows from the news reports it happened on the bridge. Whoever it is, they're using that to scare us. I told you not to invite certain people. I did not get on with everyone. I'd go so far as to say I had enemies. Someone is out to rile me and you announcing that you know who killed Simon has given them the fuel they needed.' He stands up, scans up and down the queue of guests who are waiting to give their personal details to the police, but there's no one there I think he needs to be worried about.

'All right, I'm sorry, don't keep on about it. I can't help it if the guilt is eating me up. It's obvious it doesn't bother you.'

'Course it does, but what's done is done. I'm not losing sleep thinking about it.'

'Fine, so tell me who it could be?'

'I don't know. Could be one of a number of people. How are we going to find out which one?'

'I say we ignore it for now and test whether your theory is right, because I bet whoever wrote this doesn't actually know anything,' I say firmly.

'Yeah, maybe you're right. Because if we start making a fuss, they'll feed off knowing their little message is getting to us.' Martyn continues to watch the queue the whole time he's speaking to me.

Dan comes over from talking to the police and pours himself a glass of water from the jug on our table. He glugs it down and refills it.

'That was intense. They wanted to know all about my relationship with Cathy, even though it was almost thirty years ago. They were trying to work out if I'm holding a grudge about the baby.'

He slumps into a chair next to me.

'And are you?' Martyn sits down again.

'Course not.' Confusion is etched into Dan's face. He drinks a mouthful of water. 'Yeah, it was the worst day of my life because I loved Cathy, and I wanted her to have the baby. I had visions of our lives together bringing up our child. But she didn't see it like that at all. I'm not sure she even loved me. The truth is I've never got over it. Her having the abortion wasn't my choice, but she didn't care what I thought.'

'I'm so sorry,' I say.

'I want to thank you for being there for me that day,' he says to both of us. 'I couldn't have got through it without you. I'm sorry I took off without saying anything, but I wouldn't have been able to face her when she came back from the clinic knowing she was no longer carrying our baby. It felt like she'd had it killed.'

'It wasn't easy for her either,' Martyn says. 'She almost didn't go through with it.'

'Didn't she? That's news to me. Bet you encouraged her though, didn't you?' Dan says bitterly. 'Sorry Heather,' he adds quickly, glancing at me as though he'd forgotten for a second I was there.

I frown at Martyn, but he doesn't meet my eye.

Dan continues. 'I'm glad Cathy and I spoke about it earlier this evening, considering what's happened to her. She said in many ways she regrets having a termination. Not at first though – thought she was fine with it, but out of the blue she started longing to have a baby with her husband and of course couldn't. That's what split them up. She just couldn't let it go and he wasn't interested in having any.'

'She never said anything about it to us, did she?' I try to catch Martyn's eye again but he's staring into space. I gently nudge his arm.

'Um, no.'

'Apparently, they'd been happily childless since they met then suddenly she wanted to adopt, but he didn't.'

'Gosh, I had no idea. I can't imagine Cathy being

broody.' I blink at Dan in astonishment. 'You think you know someone, don't you?'

I nudge Martyn again. He looks like he's about to doze off with boredom. He'd never shown any interest in being a dad until he became a father figure to Ben and Scott. I wouldn't have wanted to have a baby in my forties. I'm so glad I had my two boys when I was younger.

'Yeah, can't imagine her with kids.' He nods.

Dan sips his drink. 'Anyway, she said they've been talking about the possibility of adopting.'

'You mean with Robbie?' I ask. 'I didn't know that.'

'She didn't say, but I presume so.' Dan drinks back the rest of the water.

'Did you know?' I ask Martyn but he grunts and shakes his head.

'Hopefully she'll make a full recovery,' I say. 'She'll be a wonderful mum one day, although I don't expect I'll be around to see it.'

Martyn's phone buzzes. He lazily reaches in his pocket for it and squints one eye to peek at the screen. When he sees who's calling, he sits up, wide-eyed, and pulls the mobile to his ear.

'Hi Robbie,' he says.

I take in a breath and touch Martyn's arm, but he

stands up and strides over to the bi-fold doors. He nods a couple of times then dips his head, spreading one hand across his brows and down over his eyes. When the call ends, he stumbles back over to us, crashing into tables and chairs. I reach out and take his hand.

'What is it? How's Cathy?' My voice comes out unnecessarily high-pitched. Dan moves to the edge of his chair, face tipped up.

Martyn's hand drags slowly down his face. He blinks as though he can't see. Tears are forming in his eyes.

'I can't believe I'm about to say this, but Cathy died ten minutes ago.'

24

'What? You can't be serious.' I press my hand to my forehead, not believing what Martyn just said. Cathy is *dead*?

'And it was Robbie you spoke to?' Dan is on his feet.

'Yeah, that was him calling. He was by Cathy's side when she passed away.'

'Oh my God.' Dan drops back down into the chair, his face ashen.

'This can't be happening,' I say, my eyes wide. 'I never thought I'd say *poor Robbie*, but he must be in a terrible state. Especially after everything that's happened tonight.'

'It sounded like he was holding it together, to be

fair. Must be the shock. Probably not had a chance to take it in yet.'

'One of us should go over there, although I'm afraid I'm far too tired.'

'Don't worry, I'll go first thing in the morning. He said they'll be taking her to the Chapel of Rest shortly.'

'And she was definitely poisoned?' Dan's face is creased up, as he tries to comprehend what's happened.

'Seems so. They've not said any more about it apparently. Robbie's been told it's a police matter now.'

'Do you mean a murder inquiry?' I ask. My heart thuds hard while my stomach seems to fall away from me.

'I don't know.'

We automatically look over at DI Bradbury who is speaking on her walkie talkie, probably getting the news too. They're still processing our guests' details. Ben and Scott have organised tea and coffee to be brought out for everyone, and along with Emma are busy talking to the guests, finding out who needs to get home for children or elderly parents and making sure they're at the front of the queue.

The guests who've already given in their details to the police come up and say their goodbyes to me before they leave. All I can do is apologise for the party ending like this, but it's hardly Cathy's fault, and everyone seems to be understanding about the situation. Should we tell them what's happened?

It's almost 11 p.m. I'm exhausted, but this news has given me a spike of adrenaline and now I'm in shock and wide awake.

'There must have been a murderer amongst us all evening,' Martyn says, his eyes darting around the room again from one face to another. I try to picture Cathy lying dead in a hospital bed, but I can't conjure the image, my mind has gone blank. It doesn't feel real. To think she was here less than an hour ago, living and breathing, laughing and dancing. And now she's gone. I'm in shock. Poor Cathy. It's a stark reminder, as if I need one, that the nothingness of death is what frightens me the most. Trying to imagine myself not here sends a painful spike of fear through my heart.

'I need to go outside and get some air,' I blurt out. 'Will you two come with me please?' I reach out to Martyn and Dan. My hands are shaking. They let me link arms with one on each side and assist me, walking out of a side door onto the terrace.

We sit around a small café-style table in the moonlight, overlooking the immaculate lawn. The cool evening air revives me as soon as I take a few deep breaths. I take off my shoes, step down onto the grass and gaze up at the clear sky. I'm grateful to be alive but am reminded what a tiny jot I am in the universe.

My thoughts wander back to Cathy chatting with me earlier and my stomach pulls and twists with anger and disbelief.

I walk back to the table and sit down. 'Do you really think it was that blond man she was speaking to who killed her?' I ask them.

'You don't think so?' Martyn sounds incredulous.

'Perhaps it is. I'm not sure.'

'What happened to Cathy has made me even more certain that he's something to do with the Eyre family and is out for revenge. Also, you said you didn't recognise him, so was he even invited?' he asks.

'He could have been someone's grown-up child I didn't have a chance to be introduced to. The invitations were open to people I know and their families. Anyway, don't you think we're overlooking someone more obvious?'

'Who?' Dan asks.

'Don't you think it could be Robbie who poisoned Cathy?'

They both squint at me to see if I'm joking.

'Because we don't know for certain that she was poisoned *here*, do we? What if he's the one who did this to her in the pub, away from everyone. Makes much more sense to me.'

'But *why* would he? Yes, he's a piece of work, but he loves Cathy. *Loved*.' Dan tuts and corrects himself.

'Because he'd found out she was seeing someone else,' I say.

'Was she?' Dan looks even more confused.

'How do you know about that?' Martyn's eye creases up with his frown.

'You knew about it then? Why didn't you tell me?' I fold my arms. He was closer to Cathy than I was in the last couple of years, but he never even hinted about her having an affair.

He nods and crosses his arms which means he's not saying any more.

'I guessed she might be following her usual pattern of one in one out when she was painting my nails.' I turn to Dan as Martyn clearly knows all of this. 'She'd decided to end it with Robbie. She was really worried about how he would react. Wanted to do it in a public place because she expected him to kick off. So I presume she told him in the pub.'

'Poor Cathy. It probably tells you everything you need to know about that scumbag,' says Dan.

'And why did he insist on staying by her bedside after she'd ended it with him? He could easily have slipped her another dose of whatever it was and finished her off.' I grimace.

'Do we know for sure she went ahead and dumped him?' Martyn asks.

'I think he knew she was going to end it and that was the real reason he thumped Dan.'

'Do you think he was the one shouting out about Simon?'

'It could have been him. I mean who even is he really? We barely know him. Robbie may not be his real name either, and I bet he's connected to the Eyres and dated Cathy just to get close to her and us?'

'Shit.' Martyn sighs. 'Are we going to tell the police what we know?' Martyn leans forward and whispers.

'We can't, surely?' Dan looks hard at us both. 'That only leaves three of us now.'

We all instinctively move one hand each to the middle of the table, so our fingers are touching. Dan has been away for so long, but the four of us were back together this evening for just a few brief hours. Now we are down to three. And the pact we all swore to keep our secret, and keep each other safe, is broken.

I pull my hand away and rub my eyes. 'There's something I should have told you.'

'What is it?' Dan leans back in his chair as if I might bite.

Martyn gently places his hand on mine.

I dip my head then look intently at them both. 'It could be my fault that Cathy's dead.'

25

'What are you talking about?' Dan sits up.

'You can't mean that.' Martyn takes his hand off mine.

'I've been getting these texts.' I take my mobile out of my pocket and swipe it open. 'Threatening me.' I find the thread from an unknown number and show them.

Martyn looks at me in alarm. He takes my phone and holds it in front of him and Dan. He scrolls down and reads the first one.

I know who killed Simon.

I point and he looks down at the next one and reads it aloud.

I saw all of you running away.

'Christ, Heather, you should have told me about this.' Martyn's face is pale.

'I didn't want to worry you, not with everything else going on.'

'I'd have done something about it. Prevented Cathy from being... killed.'

'We couldn't have known what they were going to do,' Dan says.

'Why didn't you block the number when you got the first message?'

'And pretend that whoever this is doesn't know I was there that day? They'd have got to me some other way and it wouldn't have stopped them doing what they've done to Cathy. I thought I could try to work out who it was. If someone knew this, I guessed it wasn't a prank.'

'Bloody hell, it means they saw all of us,' Dan says.

'So why aren't we all getting these messages?' Martyn asks.

'Cathy might have been, but she didn't say.'

'Do you think they only saw us running away? Nothing else?' Dan whispers. We eyeball each other as we consider the question in silence.

'You should have told one of us about this,' Martyn slaps his hand on the table.

'They were only sent today. What could you have done?'

Martyn taps his index finger on his lips. 'Someone has been biding their time.'

'Or was too scared to come forward before,' says Dan.

'No one else was there,' I say. 'I'm sure of it.'

Martyn flicks down to the next message. Dan reads it out in a whisper.

> If you don't want something bad to
> happen to one of your friends,
> you'd better tell everyone who
> killed Simon.

Dan and Martyn stare at me.

'You see how it's my fault Cathy is dead?' I bow my head and cover my face with my hands. I know they don't want to pass blame, but it's obvious it's all down to me.

'But you wanted to tell everyone. It was me who

stopped you saying it,' Martyn says, a hand to his face. 'Shit. It's *my* fault she's dead. It's all my fault.'

He chucks my phone on the table and dashes over to a row of low hedges and throws up behind it. Dan and I look away.

'If I'd said something sooner, Cathy might still be alive,' I say quietly.

26

'For Christ's sake, Heather. We need to tell the police about this,' Martyn says. 'That text is an admission and a threat to any one of us.'

Dan doesn't blink, like the proverbial rabbit in headlights.

'We can't tell the police because they'll find out what really happened the morning Simon died,' I say.

'But they can trace the number and find out who's doing this, who killed Cathy.'

'Everything all right?' Lisa steps forward, startling us. She's standing a short distance from us in the semi-darkness, on the edge of where the patio meets the lawn. How long has she been standing there? None of us heard her approaching, probably because of her soft footfall on the grass. She's carrying a pile of used firework rockets and other debris from earlier. I thought that was something the display team would have already cleared up. It was certainly supposed to be their responsibility, not ours.

'Er... no, of course it isn't.' Martyn glares at her. 'We've just heard from Robbie that Cathy's died and we're in the middle of a private conversation here. Have you been listening in?'

I cringe. Martyn's always blunt when he's agitated. He's never been keen on Lisa being close to me, and like Tom and the boys, he doesn't agree with me leaving the kennels to her.

Lisa jolts at his abruptness and looks to me to answer for her, but I honestly don't know what to say. I don't know why she's out here. It's not up to her to clear away used fireworks.

'Thanks Lisa, I appreciate all your help, but you really don't need to do that. The firework company said in the contract they would tidy up any mess they made. Why don't you dump them near the kitchen bins and get off home? We'll deal with it. I think most people have gone now anyway, and Ben and Scott have everything else in hand.'

'I'm sorry I interrupted you. I promise I didn't know you were all out here. The door on the left wing was open so I thought I'd make myself useful and tidy round.' She turns to go back the way she came then spins round. 'Did you really say Cathy's dead?'

'I'm afraid so. But we've not told anyone else yet, so please keep it to yourself.' I smile shakily, hoping she's not too hurt by Martyn's outburst.

'Of course. What a shock. I thought she was going to be okay.'

'So did we,' I say.

'By the way, I remembered something earlier after we spoke. I don't know if it's helpful, but when Robbie left after you told him to go, and Cathy went with him, I saw another man leaving a minute or so after them, the one with blond hair.'

'Did you?' Martyn side-eyes me, like he's not surprised to hear this.

'Yes, I'm sure it was the same man. He and Robbie said something to each other outside. The blond man started it by shouting something at Cathy, and Robbie responded. Cathy tried to hold him back. I don't know what they said but the two men squared up to each other.'

'Have you told this to the police?' I ask.

She nods.

'What happened after that?' Dan asks.

'Cathy managed to pull Robbie away and they

walked off in one direction and the man went the opposite way,' Lisa says.

'So he left the party? I wonder if this is on CCTV. We could see if he ever came back,' Martyn says.

'I think we need to leave that to the police.' I turn back to Lisa. 'I really appreciate you telling us that.'

'Glad I could help. I hope you get a good night's sleep. I'll see you bright and early, if you're up to it. Don't worry if not, I'll manage feeding the animals. Goodnight.'

'I hope to be up to help you. I'll text you. Goodnight.'

Martyn and Dan say goodnight to her too, and she takes the firework rubbish back the way she came.

'We really need to speak to Robbie, find out what the other man said,' I say when she's gone. 'I'm going to come with you to the hospital in the morning. We need to find out whether it was Robbie or the blond-haired guy who did this to Cathy.'

'How well do you know Lisa?' Dan asks me.

I frown at him before answering. 'Really well. We've been good friends for about five years, since she joined my team at the kennels. Business was slow and not really going anywhere until she came along with some brilliant new ideas, like playing classical music to the animals and using aromatherapy oils to calm them down. The customers love it and it really seems to work. We run the business together now, although she's been gradually taking the reins since this latest prognosis.'

'You mean she hasn't put a penny into your business, but you're leaving the whole lot to her anyway,' Martyn says, rolling his eyes at Dan.

'Who else is going to continue the good work that we do? We care about those animals. Most of them are regulars and we've built up good relationships with the owners as well as the dogs and cats.'

'But you've got to admit she's going to do all right out of you.'

'Martyn, don't say that! She deserves it. She's worked just as hard as me to make it a success.'

'I'm not so sure. Anyway, more to the point, she could have been standing there listening to every bloody word we said.' Martyn kicks the table leg.

'We weren't talking loudly. I don't think she could have heard much from where she was standing.'

'We didn't really say anything specific, but I did get the feeling she was trying to listen in.' Dan finishes his drink.

'I don't know, maybe she was curious,' I say. 'She

certainly wouldn't say anything to anyone if she had heard.'

'What if *she's* the one behind all this, who saw us on the bridge?' Dan says.

'Seriously? She's not even old enough. Just stop this now.' I swipe my hands between them and wrinkle my nose in disgust.

'But hear us out.' Martyn glances at Dan.

'It's "us" now, is it?'

I should have guessed they'd gang up on me. Funny how almost thirty years has fallen away and they're acting in the same way they used to when we were sixteen.

'What we mean is, haven't you noticed how Lisa's been snooping around all evening? She knew when the blond guy had been speaking to Cathy, and now she's seen him outside shouting at her and having words with Robbie. Don't you find that strangely convenient?'

'No, I don't, and anyway Lisa has absolutely no reason to hurt Cathy.' I pause. 'Let's wait and see what Robbie says when we see him in the morning, shall we? Does he know we're coming to the hospital? I thought *he* was our main suspect.'

'I think the police are going to question him tonight. Maybe they'll keep him in.'

Dan's mobile lights up and buzzes. He pulls it out of his pocket and fixes his eyes on the screen.

'What is it?' I ask. Dan doesn't answer. Martyn and I frown at each other.

'There's a text from an unknown number. What the hell? This is pure evil. Who would do this to me?' He shoots out of his seat, twists around and kicks his chair over.

'Show me, Dan.' Martyn stands and holds out a hand.

'Tell me it's not true.' Dan lets his phone drop into Martyn's hand.

'What does it say?' I yell at Martyn, but his face is frozen, staring at the screen. 'Show me,' I shout again and pull on his arm. He turns the phone round so I can read it.

Cathy's baby wasn't yours.

27

'What? That's impossible isn't it, Dan?' I pull at his sleeve but he's groaning, his face in his hands.

'Who the fuck is playing games with us?' Martyn presses a couple of buttons and tries to call the number, but the phone is switched off. 'This isn't true, you know that don't you? Someone is being vindictive, trying to upset you.'

'He's right, Dan. Cathy would have told you if she'd even suspected it might not be yours,' I say. But Dan is shaking his head.

'You're wrong. She'd never have told me if she'd slept with someone else.'

I frown at Martyn but he's staring at Dan.

'All these years I've spent mourning a baby who

might not have been mine. How could she do that to me?'

'You can't believe some random message. You don't know if it's true.' I put my hand on Dan's shoulder.

'What if it is though? If I wasn't the father, who was?'

'I have no idea, do you, Martyn?'

He shakes his head, staring into the distance as though his mind is elsewhere.

'I know this must hurt deeply, but there's nothing you can do to make this right, Dan. Please don't torment yourself.'

'She had the chance to tell me the truth this evening, but she didn't. She continued to lie to me. Why couldn't she tell me?'

'Because it wasn't true,' I say.

'But someone knows something we don't. If it's true, she betrayed me in the worst way and didn't even try to resolve it when she could have been honest with me, told me the truth. I should never have come.'

'We don't know that for sure. And if that's the case, we'll never know why she didn't tell you, mate. I'm sorry,' Martyn says.

'It was you who went to the clinic with her, didn't

she say anything to you? You should have tried to stop her. Unless she was attacked and raped and couldn't tell me. That would be different then,' Dan says, his voice softening again.

'She never said a word to me if she was. That's the God's honest truth.' Martyn holds a hand to his chest, his head to one side.

'I think whoever sent that message is just trying to upset you,' I say. 'How would they know more about something like that than you?'

'Heather's right. I wouldn't believe a word of it.'

'But why would they say that? How many people even know she was pregnant? That's got to narrow it down. Seems a lot of trouble to go to if they made it up. I can't believe someone plucked it out of the air.' Dan shakes his head.

'Look, whoever is sending these messages is probably closer to us than we want to admit, because they appear to know all sorts of secrets about us.' Martyn finishes his drink.

'Have you checked to see if it's the same phone number that sent texts to me?' I ask.

'It said *No Caller ID*, so I guess they've blocked it so we can't check.'

'It has to be the same person though, doesn't it?'

'I would have thought so.'

I stand up, swaying. 'I'm sorry but this is all too much for me on top of everything else that's happened tonight. I've overdone it as it is, and now I'm just so upset about Cathy. I really need to go home and rest.' The mixture of drink and tiredness has taken its toll on me. I dread to think what state I'll be in tomorrow. I send Martyn indoors to see if DI Bradbury is free for a quick chat before we leave.

'Where are you staying tonight?' I ask Dan.

'I've got a room here.'

'Will we see you tomorrow? I hope you're sticking around for a while.'

'Yeah, I'll be here for a day or two, visiting our old haunts.'

'Can we exchange contact details, so we don't lose touch again?'

'Of course.' He pulls up his mobile number and shows me. I tap it into my phone then send him a text, and he replies to confirm it's correct. 'Room 49 if you want to meet up?'

'I'd like that. I don't think I asked you where you've been living.'

'I took myself off to the Isle of Wight when I left. My dad moved there after he and Mum split up. I wasn't happy at home, so it made sense to go and join him. He'd been asking me to go for a while. I went to college there and after a short stint in prison, I started my own business as a carpenter, so I stayed on the Island. I like the quiet life. I hardly come to the mainland any more.'

'I'm pleased for you. You liked woodwork at school.'

He nods, seeming impressed that I remembered.

'Yeah, you made a box with different coloured layers of wood then made a big hole in the centre and flocked the inside with some sort of velvet. You gave it to Cathy as a birthday present.'

'I did, didn't I? I'd forgotten about that. I was kind of hoping tonight that Cathy might want to go out with me again, but I suppose it was wishful thinking that she'd be single or even want to be with me. Did she ever say anything to you about who the father of the baby was?'

'Nothing at all. I've believed it was yours all this time. And you know, it probably was. Someone is being vicious saying you weren't the dad. Do you know who that could be?'

'No, but I suspect it's something to do with me being there the day Simon Eyre died.' He shrugs. 'I gave up trying to work people out years ago. It took me so long to get over what happened. The guilt ate me up. And then losing the baby I was so certain was mine tipped me over the edge. I still see a therapist now and again since leaving prison and the psychiatric unit. Tried to end it a few times.' He hangs his head.

'Oh, Dan. I'd no idea. I'm sorry it took such a toll on you. It did for all of us I think in different ways.'

'Simon never deserved what happened to him. A young man killed in his prime.' He shakes his head. Every line on his face tells the story of his state of mind over the last twenty-seven years. 'That day still haunts you too, doesn't it?'

'Yeah, completely. It hides away in a little corner of my mind, then pops out at the most inopportune moments. That's why I wanted to clear my conscience, tell everyone the truth tonight, although I realise you wouldn't all agree with me because it would cause you trouble. But I think Simon deserves justice. He shouldn't have paid for what his dad did. It's time we faced that, don't you think?'

'Yeah, you're probably right, but I'm a coward locking myself away, not dealing with it. Don't you find the guilt makes you question everything you do? Asking yourself, do I deserve this nice thing happening to me, or will I need to tell everyone what I was involved in before I commit to this? Because if they find out I'm not a good person, will they kick me out?'

'All the time.'

'It's been so weird for me coming here tonight, seeing all the people from school and from the area we grew up in. I had that horrible feeling that they were all looking at me, as though they all knew I had something to do with it.'

'They can't know. No one can, which is why I don't believe those messages to you or me. Someone is making wild guesses.'

'I'm not so sure. Maybe my paranoia is going into overdrive, but I had a strong feeling someone here tonight knows everything that happened that day. And whoever it is, they are laughing at us. They want to get their revenge by picking us off one by one in plain sight. The question isn't just who is doing this, but who's next?'

28

We go back inside. Everyone has gone except the police. I take the opportunity to speak to Ben and Scott who are helping Tom pack up the sound system, projector, and microphone. I tell them the news about Cathy and we all stand together in shocked silence. Martyn calls me over to speak with DI Bradbury.

'I understand you've heard the news that sadly, Cathy has died,' the DI says.

I nod. 'Robbie called us.'

'My condolences to you both. As I said before, the hospital believes she was deliberately poisoned, but we need to wait for the outcome of the autopsy just to be sure. We've collected a comprehensive list of your guests' details and statements, so we'll be following up a few leads.'

'Thank you. It's so hard to take in that this has happened.' I draw my hand across my forehead. Tears fill my eyes. I can't seem to control my emotions.

'We'll do our best to find out who did this to your friend. Do you have any thoughts about who might want to hurt Cathy? Someone she fell out with perhaps, or who may hold a grudge against her for some reason?'

I shrug and shake my head.

'Because no one we've spoken to sprung out at us as disliking her strongly enough to want to do her harm. People who knew her seemed to... how do I word this... love her yet tolerate her. Does that sound like a familiar reaction?'

I nod and wipe the tears from my eyes.

The DI reads from her notes. 'Some said she was a show off, could be quite full of herself but she'd been a good friend to them and to you, so they tolerated her behaviour. Does that ring true?'

'It's harsh but they are fair comments. Not everyone knew Cathy as well as Martyn and I did. I'm not a shrink, but I think her behaviour stemmed from a deep insecurity. She was adopted at two years old and took the rejection from her birth mother badly. She played a part a lot of the time, scared of exposing her true vulnerable self. Her life never really panned out as she'd hoped it would. I think she found it difficult to accept her own failings. She tended to only tell people the good things that were happening in her life and exaggerate them to the max. That was how she expressed it to me. She couldn't bear failing at anything, and I think that stopped her moving forward. Especially in her career. She stuck at the same legal secretary job she had when she left school, apart from when she trained as a nail technician at college in the evenings. And more recently, her marriage broke down because she realised she didn't love her husband. She'd made a mistake marrying him because she was flattered that he loved her. She told us that.'

Martyn nods. I thought he'd have something to add but he's silent.

'I see. Quite a complex personality then, and someone who potentially upset a few people over her lifetime.'

Martyn frowns at me, probably as a warning not to tell the DI about the threatening texts I received or the confession I was going to make earlier.

'You could say that. We've been discussing it

amongst ourselves, and we think it could be Robbie.'
I mention again the reasons why he got upset with
Dan earlier and about Robbie punching him, and
that's why we had to ask him to leave.

The DI writes all this down in her notebook. 'So
you said before he's the jealous type?'

'Definitely. He freely admits that. His anger issues
are out of control. I mean, he hit Dan before we had
the chance to introduce him.'

'That's helpful, thank you. We're going to the hospital to speak to him now, but if either of you think of
anything else, please contact me.' She hands over a
business card each to us. 'My colleague went to the
pub Robbie and Cathy visited earlier this evening,
and we've taken samples from where they were sitting, but the glasses they were using had already been
washed so there's no evidence that Cathy was poisoned while she was there. We'll be checking the
CCTV at the front and back of the premises for any
suspicious behaviour. We're also going to be checking
the CCTV here from this evening, to see who has
been coming and going. We'll find out who the man
with blond hair is too as he's been mentioned a few
times by different people as someone Cathy was
spending quite a lot of time with, and we believe they
had cross words in the garden. We want to see what

he has to say about the nature of his conversation with Cathy, and how well they knew each other.'

'Thank you, we appreciate everything you're doing. Thanks for coming so quickly,' I say.

Martyn sees her out and I go back to Dan who is still staring at his phone.

'You okay?'

I don't wait for an answer and tell him the police are going to speak to Robbie. When he doesn't reply, I sit next to him and put my hand on his arm.

'What's wrong?'

'I can't tell you; you've got enough going on.'

'What do you mean? If it's important, I want to help.'

'Do you know, that's your problem.' He looks me in the eye. There are tears in his.

'What is?'

'Always thinking of others. You're too kind and there are people out there who take advantage of that.'

I don't know what to say.

'And you know what? The main culprit is right there, in the centre of your life, pretending to care about you and love you.'

'I don't know what you mean. I think we're all tired.'

He slowly shakes his head. I'm surprised by his frankness.

'Why are you being like this, has something else happened?' I ask, but he carries on talking, as though he hasn't heard me.

'You were going out with Marty, and I was going out with Cathy and we both thought we were loved and happy, but that's not true because they were seeing each other behind our backs.'

'No, they weren't.' I squint at him, trying to work out how drunk he is.

'They betrayed us and they're still lying to us today by not admitting to us what they did.'

'What did they do? Where's this coming from, Dan? It's the first I've heard of it.' I'm completely taken aback at what he's saying. How can he be so certain?

He slowly shakes his head. 'I've been sent another message and I'm telling you, whoever this is from knows a damn sight more about my life than I know myself.'

He sniffs, wiping his nose on the back of his hand and for the first time I see tears rolling down his face.

'Show me.' I frown.

He swipes open his mobile screen and the text

lights up. Received six minutes ago. He taps to open it.

I frown as I read the words, but I have to read them again and again because I'm so tired I can't believe what I'm seeing.

Martyn was the father of Cathy's baby.

29

'What? That can't be true!' I cup my hands around my mouth and stare as Dan nods sadly. As soon as the words are out of my mouth, I'm thinking how easily it *could* be true. At the time it was strange how Martyn became so invested in making sure Cathy went to the clinic to 'get rid' of this problem. And she didn't object either. I was happy to stay with Dan because I supported him in wanting to keep the baby, but normally for something so personal and sensitive, it would have been me going with Cathy, and Martyn would have stayed with his best friend.

Fresh tears spill from Dan's eyes. I snatch the mobile from him and try to find out who sent the message, but again the phone says *No Caller ID*. More than likely a burner phone used to send this one message, like throwing a grenade at someone's life, then running away.

'Whoever sent it knew how explosive this would be.'

'Cowards!' Dan screams.

Martyn comes rushing over. When he sees our faces, he stops abruptly. Tom and the boys look over, but I flick my hand at them to carry on with what they're doing.

'What is it, what's happened?' Martyn asks, his hands out in front of him.

'You and Cathy, that's what happened. You were never going to tell us, were you?' Dan screams and hits out with his fist but misses Martyn's face and staggers into a chair.

'What are you talking about?' Martyn asks, then his eyes flicker over to me. I'm stone still, arms crossed, waiting for a denial.

'Dan's had another text,' I say flatly. 'About you and Cathy. The baby was yours, wasn't it?'

He groans and looks down at the ground, rubbing his forehead with the heel of his hand. 'Of course it wasn't mine. Don't you see, whoever is sending these texts is trying to turn us against each other? And just look at us, they're succeeding.'

'How can we believe you?' Dan says. 'Was Cathy about to tell me about it? Is that why you killed her?'

'Don't be daft. I didn't kill her. I wouldn't do that. We were friends.'

'Was she carrying your baby and neither of you wanted it? That's why you insisted on taking her to the clinic, isn't it?'

'I offered to go and support her because you weren't man enough to go yourself,' Martyn yells, prodding a finger at Dan.

'I didn't go because I wanted her to keep it. I stupidly thought it was mine.'

'Why weren't you thinking about what *she* wanted?' Martyn sneers.

'Shut up! Shut up!' Dan runs from the room, his hands to his head and I have the feeling we won't see him until the morning. He never did like any kind of confrontation.

'You believe me, don't you?' Martyn asks.

'I don't know what to think. If you're saying it's not true, then I suppose I have to believe you've not been lying to me. But remember, one day you'll have to make peace with your ghosts too, like I'm having to.'

He sits in a chair and slumps forward, holding his chin up with his hands.

'Let's go home. I'll call a taxi.' I go over and say goodbye to Tom, Ben and Scott.

'We're nearly done here,' Tom says as he winds the last of the leads from the sound system.

'How are you holding up, Mum?' Ben asks and hugs me, then Scott hugs me too.

'I'm still in shock,' I say.

'Do you want to take your guest book with you?'

'Oh yes, thank you.' I'm so tired I could curl up on the floor under the table and fall asleep.

'We'll bring everything else, don't worry.' I kiss them both on the cheeks.

'Is everything all right?' Ben glances at Martyn who is pushing himself out of his chair.

'Yeah, we'll be fine.'

Martyn drags himself out to the foyer.

'Are you ready?' I ask him, phone in hand.

'Do you know which room Dan is in?'

'Number 49, I think, why?'

'I can't leave things like this.' He paces up and down. 'You go on home. I'll pop up and speak to him and catch you up.'

'Are you sure that's a good idea?'

'He's upset with me.'

'Why don't you both sleep on it, leave it until the morning?'

'What if he takes off again? I need to sort it out now.'

'Sort what? Wouldn't it be better to let him calm down?'

'There's something I need to tell him, and it can't wait.'

'What's so urgent?' I check my phone. 'The taxi is here.'

If Martyn heard my words, then he doesn't acknowledge them. 'Do you want me to get one of the boys to come with you?' he asks.

'No, I'll be fine, thank you.'

'You go and get in, I'll call Ben.'

'Honestly, I'm okay. Please tell me what's wrong.' I touch his arm and try to catch his eye, but he won't look at me.

'I'll see you at home,' he says as he starts to climb the stairs.

30

At home, I stand in the hallway and the silence closes in on me. I want to scream, make some noise. I've never liked a quiet house. I loved hearing the boys playing when they were younger. Chasing around the rooms playing hide-and-seek or tag. I wasn't one of those parents who was precious about the furniture or the flooring. I'd rather they felt at home and could play without worrying they would damage anything. Some of the parents would come round and turn their noses up at the dog hair or the sagging sofa cushions. But I prided myself on it being comfortable and lived in. When Tom moved out, I tried to keep it just the same. But now Ben and Scott have grown up and moved out, and I'm aware I'm not going to live long enough to know my grandchildren, the silence is particularly sharp and cruel.

I place my keys in the bamboo bowl by the coat stand and pour myself a glass of water from the kitchen tap. In the living room, I flick on the side light and sit on the sofa with the guest book on my knees. Despite being exhausted, my mind is too active and overwhelmed to sleep. All the familiar friendly faces and several I've not seen for years, but still recognisable. I wonder how many of them will remember me in five years, or ten, or twenty. I go over everything Tom said about the boys and what he thinks of me leaving the kennels to Lisa. And those text messages. I should have said my piece. Not allowed Martyn to stop me. And now Cathy is dead. It's so hard to take in.

I push the guest book aside and stand up. Reaching to the top of the bookcase nearest the TV, I feel around for a disc. Once my fingers have found it, I slide it down and press it into the slot on the Xbox. It's the only way we have now to watch DVDs. Doesn't seem so long ago that it was the latest technology. The menu pops up and I select the correct input on the screen. As soon as I press play, the image flickers and I appear, sitting at my desk, photos of the family either side of me. I didn't know where the best place was to film it. Ben helped me buy a ring light on a stand with a mobile phone attachment. He thought I'd bought it for a friend's child.

I watch myself for a couple of minutes. I seem a bit too stiff and sombre now, but I haven't got the time or the energy to change it.

If you're watching this, it must mean that I've died and you're looking for answers. All you really need to know, Ben and Scott, is that I love you with all my heart. Your support in my final months and weeks has meant everything to me. Anything I've done in my life has always been with the best intentions...

I hit pause. There's another half hour of this and I'm not about to relive it. The whole truth is in there, not a detail left out. So whatever happens between now and the day I die, I know that the two most important people in my life will find out everything from me.

I open my laptop and write an email to my solicitor, requesting some alterations to my will.

It's gone 3 a.m. by the time I hear Martyn get into bed. I'm aware of him tossing and turning for the rest of the night. My mind still won't switch off as I try to make sense of Cathy's death and everything that's happened. Eventually I sink into sleep.

By seven the next morning I'm wide awake although my body is aching all over. I text Lisa, apologising for not turning up to help her with the kennels. I hope she didn't mind doing it without me. She's going to have to, soon.

She replies telling me not to worry, she didn't expect to see me after such a late and emotional night. I thank her profusely. I'm lucky to have such a loyal friend.

At breakfast, I try to ask how it went last night with Dan, but Martyn shakes his head and leaves the room.

He's still quiet as he loads my foldable wheelchair into the back of the car. We take the short drive to the hospital in silence. When we arrive, Robbie is waiting for us outside the main doors, smoking a cigarette. He tells us he's let the mortuary staff know we're coming to see Cathy before she's moved to the undertakers. We're down as her next of kin.

'They did the autopsy first thing,' he says as he stumps out the cigarette on a small ashtray by the wall. He blows the last of the smoke out of the side of his mouth then glances at the ground before he speaks. 'They're still saying she was deliberately poisoned, but they're not giving me any other details.' His bottom lip trembles. 'I've already been questioned by the police in case you're thinking of accusing me too. They're looking for that blond bloke she was talking to. He threatened her at the party apparently.'

'Did he now? Lisa mentioned that he followed you both out as you were leaving for the pub, shouted something at Cathy?' Martyn says.

'That's right. Called her a lying old slapper. I'd have punched his head in if she hadn't stopped me. She was quite shaken up by it.' Robbie opens the main door and holds it, allowing us to walk in first. 'He'd been chatting her up to start with, and you know what she was like, enjoying it, flirting back, especially because he was much younger and good-looking.' He tuts. 'She liked to wind me up like that, make me jealous to drive me mad, like she did with that Dan fella. I'm sorry about hitting him. I hope he's all right?'

I nod, not wanting to interrupt his story.

'Anyway, the blond guy was plying her with Blue Lagoon cocktails, and she was eating a chunk of your chocolate cake that Martyn handed out. I tried to ignore the two of them otherwise I'd have been tempted to smash his face in there and then. Anyway, she said he suddenly leaned right up close to her face. She thought he was coming in for a peck on the cheek, but instead he whispered in her ear, accused her of killing Simon. Can you believe it? When she denied it, he said someone had seen her do it. She knocked back the last of her drink and stormed off without saying another word to him. I reckon whatever he put in those drinks killed her. In fact, I'd put money on it.'

'Shit.' Martyn turns to me, his eyes wide.

I look away not wanting them to see my reaction. Robbie's clearly trying to deflect suspicion away from himself and point the finger firmly at the man with blond hair.

'And you've told the police all this?' I ask.

'Yeah, that's right. Weren't you going to announce to everyone who killed this Simon bloke, but Martyn stopped you?' He points at me, puzzled. 'Did Cathy kill him?'

I exchange a look with Martyn. Robbie's looking us both over.

'Come on. What's it all about? If you two know something, you should say.'

I ignore his question and raise my hand at the mortuary technician who is walking in our direction. Hopefully it looks to Robbie like she called us over, because he's the last person I want to have a conversation with about who killed Simon Eyre. I'm glad Cathy didn't break her vow and tell him.

But still, the thought is there: if I'd told everyone the truth last night instead of letting Martyn stop me, would Cathy still be alive?

'If you're ready?' the woman says in a hushed voice and invites us to follow her. Bile rises in my throat as we walk along the bright white corridor and I hurriedly swallow it down. I can't face seeing Cathy dead.

31

We stand at a glass window overlooking a room where a metal trolley draped in a spotless white sheet hides Cathy's body. A male technician nods at the woman standing next to us. She asks if we're ready. Martyn says yes but I want to shout *no* and run away down the corridor, but the man pulls the sheet back.

Cathy's face is stone white with a waxy sheen. I imagine her head turning towards us and her eyes flicking open, as if all this is a joke she's playing on us and she's going to jump up any moment and roar with laughter at us being so dumb and needlessly upset.

How can a life as large and bold as hers be extinguished so easily? I whimper and turn away, covering my eyes, pressing my face into Martyn's arm, but the image is already burned into my brain.

A strange sound escapes Martyn's lips. He's crying too. Of course he is. I clench my teeth trying to get through this, but they start to chatter, my nerves in shreds. He sniffs as he drapes his arm around me and draws me in tight, his chin on my head. Cold tears drop onto my hair, down to my scalp.

'Who did this to her?' he whispers and leads me away. I steal a look at Robbie where he's standing near the exit and wonder if we can trust him.

Martyn and I link arms as we head back down the corridor, clinging to each other all the way. I can't help thinking of when Alex died. My dad put his arm around my shoulders to comfort me then. We'd just heard the terrible news that he'd been hit by a car and was being airlifted to hospital. For two hours we hoped he would pull through. When he died, I've never cried so hard. I couldn't stop. They wouldn't let us see him in the morgue. Mum and Dad were told it would be too upsetting for us, because of the state of him after the crash. We saw him when he was laid out at the funeral parlour, all tidied up. He looked like a waxwork in his small white coffin. My sweet little brother with the big kind eyes, always pulling funny faces and making animal noises, trying to make people laugh. I wanted to shake him and wake him up because he looked almost alive, as though he'd just closed his eyes and was about to open them again. But when I kissed his forehead, the cold solid skin startled me, reality hitting me hard all over again. I'd cried inconsolable tears at the thought of him never coming home.

We stand outside the hospital in each other's arms. A chilly breeze is blowing but it's not the only thing making me shiver.

'We'll have to arrange Cathy's funeral,' I say. 'She doesn't have any family left to do it for her.'

'What about Robbie?'

'She named us as her next of kin.'

'That's going to be grim.'

'I asked her a few weeks ago what she would choose when I was planning mine, and she said black horses with plumage and a glass carriage like Sleeping Beauty. Said she'd want to make a grand exit. But then she'd laughed nervously and said she was going to live forever so there was no point planning anything. Then she looked at me strangely and said what an odd question for me to ask because I wouldn't even be here to see it.' My voice catches in my throat. 'None of us really know how long we've got, do we?'

Martyn hugs me. 'Some people find it difficult talking about death, writing a will or planning a funeral, in case it's a bad omen.'

'That was definitely the case with Cathy. I think me being ill made her feel invincible. She really seemed to believe death would never come for her. Perhaps deep down she was hiding her own fear of dying. The day I told her I couldn't go running with her any more because the illness had progressed and I was struggling to catch my breath, she went out on her longest run yet and savoured telling me she was going to do a half marathon. She really could be insensitive verging on cruel sometimes.'

We walk to the car and get in. 'I'm sure she didn't mean to upset you,' Martyn says.

I blink hard at him. He always defends her. 'I thought it was uncalled for to say it so bluntly when I clearly wasn't capable. It was almost like she enjoyed me not being able to do things.'

'I doubt that. But I do think sometimes she didn't realise how hurtful she could be.' He starts up the engine.

'It felt like she knew exactly what she was doing. I mean look at how she treated Dan after not seeing him since school. She could have been more sensitive.'

Martyn switches off the engine. 'There's something I told him last night that I should have told you too.'

'What's that?' A trickle of ice runs through me.

He stares down at his hands, then out of the window. Focussing straight ahead, he lets out a sigh.

'The message he received was true. Cathy's baby was mine.'

32

I frown at him. 'What did you just say?'

'Cathy was pregnant with *my* baby. We both decided it was best to have the abortion.'

'How could you do that, behind my back?' I shout at him and thump his arm.

'I'm sorry. It was a mistake, for both of us, and we tried to undo it.'

'You lied to me all those years ago and you've kept on lying to me since. Both of you. You had so many chances to tell me the truth, why didn't you?'

'I'm so sorry.' He stares at the floor.

'Can you at least look at me?'

He turns slowly to face me. A face I've loved with all my heart from such a tender age. I used to think I could trust him with my life, but his mask has slipped. I'm not sure who he is if he's capable of doing this, of keeping this from me. He lied to my face. Made out he was like the big brother Cathy never had, looking out for her whenever he could, making sure she was okay. But they must have gone in that clinic as a couple. Boyfriend and girlfriend.

'I wanted to tell you everything when I came back into your life, but Cathy said it would be cruel to bring it up after all this time.'

'Did she? So while we were kick-starting our relationship based on lies, she sat right back and watched? And neither of you thought it would be better to be honest with me?'

'I guess we were too scared you'd push us away. We wanted to forget it ever happened.'

'So who else knew? I take it you're only telling me now because someone sent that text to Dan?'

'I don't know who else knows, but yes, I thought it was only fair, especially now Cathy isn't here. Nothing is worse than that. And I *was* going to tell you, I promise.'

'How can I possibly believe you?'

He sighs again as though it's me that's causing the problem.

'So how long was it going on, you and Cathy?'

'It was once, that's all. A mistake. I was an enthusiastic teenage boy, what can I say?'

'You're making excuses. You were *my* boyfriend.'

'That's why she had an abortion. And neither of us wanted to be lumbered with a kid.'

'What, did she come on to you or did you go after her?'

'I'd rather not go into it.'

'Well I'm sorry but I need to know,' I shout.

'A bit of both; call it curiosity.'

'Seriously? So why let Dan believe the kid was his? You knew how much it destroyed him at the time and it's ruined his life since. Wasn't that unnecessarily cruel? You were supposed to be his best friend.'

'We were protecting ourselves I suppose. Way too young to think of the consequences that far ahead. We were mostly worried about you both finding out, full stop. After what happened with the Eyres, and our pact to stay silent, we couldn't afford to let you know we'd cheated in case you decided to go to the police.'

'Unbelievable. I trusted you completely. Both of you. How could you betray me then act like nothing happened? Cathy was like a sister to me. How did you keep this secret for so long?'

'I don't know. Because I'm a complete shit? I'm so sorry.'

'I'm having trouble processing this.' I shake my head. 'Can we just go and see Dan? If you told him this, he's going to be as upset as me and need consoling.'

'I honestly tried to persuade Cathy to tell him the truth, but she said it would be like chopping off his arm, because losing the baby became part of who he was.'

'That's an awful thing to say.'

I sigh, trying hard to ignore the intrusive images in my head of Martyn making this baby with Cathy. He's pretended to me he was loyal when all the time he was a cheating bastard. I bite my tongue.

'I actually thought you'd be much more upset.' He goes to touch my arm, but I pull away.

I look at him face-on. 'I *am* upset, believe me, but I haven't got long left, have I? I really don't have the energy to deal with your selfishness. It's not like I can change things, can I?'

I burn my eyes into his and I'm sure I can see his teenage self cowering there.

As though sensing it, he looks away.

'You know I didn't mean to, right? We'd both had

too much to drink.' He glances at me sideways. It would almost be laughable if it wasn't so tragic.

'But you didn't say no. You always liked her.'

'I was drunk at a party, crashed out on a bed. She kind of sat on me. I don't remember much else.'

'And it was just the once, was it?'

'Yes, I swear.'

'Except you just told me you can't remember.' I have to turn away. Every fibre of my body tells me he's still lying. 'What happens now?' I try to keep my voice neutral, so the anger doesn't bubble over.

'Back to the hotel? I need to speak to Dan again. If he'll let me.' Martyn puts the key back in the ignition.

'I actually meant between us.'

'Oh. I don't know.' He looks straight ahead.

'So you didn't patch it up with Dan last night?'

'He was too mad at me to listen after I told him the truth.'

'And I suppose you want me to try to talk him round?'

'If you could, although I don't know if it will help.' He sighs. 'He was so upset I'd let him believe the baby was his. He told me he's held a mini memorial service for it every year on what would have been its birthday. Can you believe it?'

'I can actually. Maybe you would too if you'd felt the loss.'

Martyn starts the car and begins to drive in silence. I try to push away more images in my head of him being intimate with Cathy. I picture her feeling smug about sleeping with my boyfriend. She always wanted everything I had. I never let it bother me because she'd had such a hard start in life. I felt sorry for her, being put up for adoption at such a young age, then her adoptive parents not giving her the affection she craved. I thought her jealous streak was natural for someone who'd been rejected so early in life and given so little love. But she could be nasty with it sometimes. Now instead of mourning her I feel angry that she did this to me and kept it from me. We were good friends, weren't we? I thought so. But maybe she never really liked me as much as she pretended to.

I try to think how Dan must have reacted last night when Martyn told him the truth. I hope he managed to hold it together. He's tormented himself about the abortion his whole adult life and now he's been told the baby wasn't his. What's that going to do to him? Surely it will destroy him. He came back to see us, hoping to build bridges, but instead he's had to face his worst nightmare.

'Don't you ever think about the termination and have regrets?' I ask.

'Not really. It was a tiny group of cells, probably not even an embryo, certainly not a proper person yet.' He scrunches up his nose.

'Some people don't see it like that.' I cross my arms. 'It was still a growing human that was going to develop into your baby. A mother can have her baby's life mapped out in their heads from the moment they know they're pregnant.'

'Really?'

'Of course. Not necessarily years ahead, but the first few months, wondering if it'll be a boy or a girl, what name they might give it, if it will look like them or their partner, imagining holding it for the first time, its tiny hands and feet, proudly showing their baby to their mum and dad for the first time, wondering how it will feel taking their newborn out in its pram. Anticipating its first steps, and the magical moment when it says Mummy or Daddy. Your mind can do overtime, constructing your whole future with this precious baby. You already have a date for its arrival. The day your family will become three. It can be devastating when it doesn't happen for whatever reason. So please don't dismiss it as "just" a cluster of cells to Dan, me or anyone.' I stab my finger in his chest.

'I'm sorry.' His eyebrows rise and fall. 'I never wanted children. I'm not ashamed of that.' His remorse at being told off doesn't go unnoticed.

'I don't want you to be. But you're being ignorant and insensitive. I don't want you dismissing the beginning of a new life, because to most people, that's something precious. Cathy changed her mind only recently though didn't she? Apparently she wanted to adopt a child with her new man. Do you think Robbie is aware she was cheating on him?'

'Hasn't hinted at it if he is.'

'Except it would be a motive to get rid of her, wouldn't it?'

'You really think Robbie could kill Cathy?' His face screws up.

'I don't know. But someone did.'

The pulsing blue light is the first thing I see as we approach the hotel car park. Martyn and I look at each other in surprise. An ambulance and several police cars are parked outside.

Instinctively I try calling Dan's mobile, but when he doesn't answer, my blood runs cold.

33

'Why isn't Dan answering? What's going on?' I ask but Martyn's face is frozen in a grimace. Is he fearing the same thing as me?

'We need to go in and ask someone,' he says.

A policeman stops us in the foyer. 'Are you staying here?'

'No, but our friend is, and we've come to see if he's okay.'

'You can ask for him at reception, but no one is allowed beyond the tape.' He indicates to the police tape behind him.

'Why not? What's the tape for?' My heart is thumping.

He pulls a face like he shouldn't really say. 'There's been an incident.'

'Is someone hurt?' I ask him, then turn to Martyn. 'It's just that our friend is not answering his phone. Can you tell us what sort of incident?'

'I'm sorry I can't say. Reception may be able to help you about your friend.' He points to the desk beyond us in the foyer. There's a small group of people around the receptionist who is calling to a woman in a back office to come and assist him.

'Can you queue up here while I have a look around?' I whisper. Martyn looks alarmed but nods anyway. I try Dan's phone again in case he's slept in and only just checked it. But it's still going to voicemail. A woman wearing a raincoat is speaking to an officer at the bottom of the stairs. I casually dip under the tape and start walking up.

'Can I help you?' the officer calls after me.

'I just need to grab my purse. I left it in my room.'

The officer pauses. 'What number room?'

'Forty-nine,' I say straight away as if I know where I'm going. I remember Dan telling me last night.

'All right, be quick.' He turns back to the woman in the raincoat and she carries on talking.

I climb the stairs as fast as my aches and pains

will let me. On the first-floor landing is a limited view of the garden area out of a long window. All I can see are a few officers dotted around. I'm so cold, I'm shivering. I hurry along the corridor until I find Dan's door, and knock. No answer. There's a Do Not Disturb sign on the handle. I knock again, louder this time. I can't hear any movement inside. He was so drunk last night. Perhaps he passed out. I have visions of him splayed out on the floor having fallen and cracked his head. I call out his name, then text him but I can't get a response.

I'm about to walk away when I catch a glimpse of the chambermaid I passed along the adjacent corridor, so I hurry back and ask her to please come and unlock my door so I can grab my purse as I've shut it by mistake, leaving my card key inside. She doesn't question my story and walks back to number forty-nine and lets me in.

Dan is not in bed. In fact it doesn't look slept in at all, although there's a dent in the pillow so maybe he laid on top and had a nap. I scan around the room, and look in his rucksack in the corner. There are only folded clothes and a pair of trainers. The ensuite bathroom has barely been touched. There's no clue as to where he may have gone. I pick up his coat from the back of the easy chair by the coffee table and check the pockets. There's something odd, uneven, about the way the chair looks. I stand back and tip my head. There's a huge crack down the centre of it. Next to the kettle is half a mug of tea and in the bin is the other mug, broken into several pieces. Splashes of tea have dried up one wall and there are scuffs of dirt in the carpet. What has gone on here? Did he get mad and chuck a drink at the wall or has someone come in and they had a scuffle? Where is he now?

I call Dan's mobile again. Still going to answer-phone. Think. Where would he go? I open all the drawers in the wardrobe unit for a clue. Nothing. I find his wallet and phone on silent in the bedside drawer. Shit. I pick it up and it lights up, listing all my missed calls and messages. Where would he have gone without them? Not far is my guess.

I drop down on the bed.

My phone buzzes. I pull it out of my pocket and look at the screen. It's Martyn.

Have you found him?

He's not here. Any luck with reception?

> They say he didn't come down for breakfast.

> He's left his wallet and mobile up here. I think someone's been in his room.

I gravitate towards the window and draw back the georgette curtain which drapes along the ground. A small white tent is being erected by the side of the lake, but I can't see much beyond it. I expect Dan has gone down to see what's going on. He may even be speaking to an officer.

I leave the Do Not Disturb sign on the handle and let the door click shut behind me. Martyn texts asking where I am. I reply saying I'm on my way down.

As I hurry back along the corridor, I see the maid again.

'Do you know what's happened out there?' I ask her, pointing in the direction of the garden.

'I heard they can't work out who it is. No ID apparently,' she says.

'Thanks.' A shiver runs through me.

Martyn appears at the end of the corridor, running towards me.

'You need to come now, Heather.'

'Why, what's wrong?'

'They've found a body in the garden, and I think it could be Dan.'

34

'Don't say that!' I yell at him.

'I know, I know, but I explained to one of the officers about Dan not being in his room and not answering his phone and they want us to see if it's him.'

'It won't be. I told you, his mobile is in his room with his wallet. He's popped out somewhere, that's all.'

'Except it turns out he's the only person staying here who's not been accounted for. The only one who didn't come down for breakfast. They've spoken to everyone else.'

'Maybe he went out for a walk, and he's not come back yet.'

'You think he's still out since last night?'

'I meant this morning. Did he go out last night?'

'Possibly. He was in a state and needed to calm down, so he may have headed out into the garden.'

'Calm down from what?'

Martyn hesitates. 'We had another disagreement.'

'I thought you came to resolve your differences not make things worse.'

'I did but...' He looks away, pinches his lips together with his thumb and forefinger.

'But what? What did you say to him?'

Martyn runs his hand through his hair. 'I apologised and we spoke about what happened between me and Cathy, but he wouldn't stay calm, he was still too upset, maybe in shock. He called me all sorts and was flinging things around the room. You were right, I should have left it until today, which is why I wanted to come and speak to him again.'

'So you're saying you didn't resolve anything with him?'

'I think I might have made it worse. He couldn't even bear to look at me. Said he'd been mourning the loss of that baby his whole adult life, believing it was his. He was in shock that it wasn't. He blamed me for ruining his life, not telling him sooner. Said I should have been honest with him at the time and that he could understand a bit more why Cathy didn't speak up, but not me. He ran away not only because he split up with Cathy, but because he couldn't deal with the loss of his son or daughter.'

'Christ, Martyn. What have you done? I don't understand why you didn't say something sooner. You could have told me any number of times over the last few years since we got back together. Why didn't you?'

'You know I didn't want to go over the past. I've never wanted to talk about any of this.' He sweeps his hand out in front of him. 'Not about the abortion or what happened to Simon. As far as I was concerned, I'd put a lid on it. I was done with it. I made huge mistakes, I know that, but I can't bear it being brought up again. I suppose it's easier to block it out, pretend none of it happened.'

'We've all had to deal with what happened to Simon in our different ways, so I guess it's the same with the abortion. But they can never be forgotten. We can't pretend they didn't happen, just like you can't pretend you didn't cheat on me with Cathy and get her pregnant. But whoever sent those texts knows about all of it. I think they're trying to make us fight with each other.'

'But who could that be? We haven't told anyone

else any of this stuff, and I'm pretty sure no one else was there that day.'

'I don't know either, but I've been wondering, is it possible that Cathy or Dan confided in someone about it? I mean, as you've said, it's a big secret to lug around for our whole lives. What if Cathy told Robbie?'

Martyn gives a forlorn shake of his head. 'Cathy swore to me she'd kept to the pact. As for Dan, none of us have seen him for more than half our lives. He could have told anyone for all we know.'

'Where did you speak to Dan, was it in his room?'

'Yes.'

'And you argued?'

'He went for me. Started throwing things around. He smashed a mug against a wall and chucked a chair at me, so I told him I'd speak to him when he'd calmed down.'

'And when you left his room, he was still fit and well?'

'Yeah, apart from still raging at me and slamming the door. He'd been drinking more whisky by the time I got there.'

'So like I said, maybe he went down to the garden for a walk after that. It's possible he didn't see the edge of the lake and fell in.'

'Someone could have gone after him and pushed him in,' Martyn says.

'But who? If he's the person the police have found, they'll need to look at the possibility that who-ever killed Cathy has killed Dan and could be staying at the hotel.'

My phone buzzes. I glance at the screen. It's from the same unknown number as before.

Two down, two to go.

I show Martyn, and a chill runs through me.
One of us is next.

35

Two women in all-in-one white coveralls stride towards us.

'They're going to check Dan's room for clues,' Martyn says as they pause next to us.

I tell them I've been in there but tried not to touch anything.

'His wallet and mobile phone are in the bedside drawer. It looks like there was a disagreement in there. A mug and chair are broken. There's tea up the wall and he's not slept in his bed,' I say.

I steal a glance at Martyn, but he doesn't react. If he's got nothing to hide, why doesn't he tell them it was him?

'You shouldn't have gone in there,' the taller woman says to me.

'I'm sorry, I thought I'd find him still asleep.'

'DI Lyon is downstairs. She would like to speak to you both,' the second woman says.

'Come on,' Martyn says, touching my elbow, probably not wanting to say any more in case I drop him in it. I nod and let him guide me away.

Should I have told them that Martyn was in there with Dan last night, that he might be the last person to have seen him? But that's up to him to own up to, isn't it? He could be putting himself in the frame if something has happened to Dan. His prints will be in there, so they'll soon find out. I'm certain Martyn wouldn't hurt him intentionally. Although it's possible he could have reacted in anger when Dan started throwing things at him. Even the calmest people are capable of anything if pushed to the edge. I don't know for sure what he told me is true. I can't trust him.

His fingers dig in my arm as he leads me towards the stairs. I imagine him thrusting me to the edge then pushing me down them. I dig my heels in and twist away until he lets go of me.

'What's wrong? I'm trying to help you,' he says irritably. He must know the police are going to find out he was in the room and they had an argument. How sure am I that he doesn't know where Dan is?

Downstairs, a policeman escorts us into the garden. We follow him toward the incident tent. My head is woolly, numb but my heart feels like it's drumming loudly. Everything has gone into slow motion as we approach. This doesn't seem real. It's as though we've stepped into an episode of *Lewis*.

A plain-clothed detective strides forward to meet us on the lawn near the lake.

'DI Lyon.' She offers her hand and shakes mine first, then Martyn's. 'Sorry to bring you down here, but we'd like to get an ID before we move the body and so we can inform next of kin asap.' She doesn't stop for us to answer. 'My colleague said you were enquiring about your friend at reception, and they realised he hadn't been down to breakfast this morning, and I understand he's not picking up your calls, is that correct?'

'Yes, that's right and Heather went up to his room. We assumed he would still be in bed. We were all here last night for Heather's farewell party.'

Before Martyn can finish, the DI butts in.

'So you were also friends with the woman who was poisoned yesterday evening? Cathy Blake, is that correct?' The DI tilts her head ever so slightly, possibly to encourage a truthful reply. Her severely cut fringe swings to the side, her eyes fixed on Martyn.

'That's right,' I answer. She glances at me, as though not expecting me to speak. I suppose it looks like it's more than a coincidence that Martyn and I potentially know both these people.

The DI is called away and speaks on a mobile phone a short distance from us.

'I wish Dan would just bound up out of nowhere like he did last night,' I whisper.

'You didn't see the state he was in,' Martyn says under his breath as he kicks at the grass.

'What do you mean?'

But he doesn't have a chance to answer. One of the people in white coveralls comes out of the tent and nods at the DI. The DI beckons us over.

'Is there something else you wanted to tell me about last night?' she says, addressing Martyn face-on.

His head jerks, taken aback by her question. He doesn't answer, but he looks petrified.

'Let me help you. We've checked the CCTV and you didn't leave the hotel all evening until 1.05 a.m. We've also found Dan's mobile phone in his room. There are abusive messages from you at around 12.20 a.m.'

'What?' I glare at him. I can't help myself reacting. This doesn't sound like something Martyn would do.

'I don't remember sending those.' He sounds like a petulant sixteen-year-old again.

'One said you were "coming for him". Can you explain what you meant by that please?'

'I never sent that,' Martyn mumbles and frowns at me as if hoping I will back him up but I don't see how I can help him, so I don't say anything. I won't lie to give him an alibi.

'They're sent from your phone,' the DI says in case Martyn is in any doubt.

He's dropped himself right in it. I keep my face blank. If Martyn has hurt Dan, I won't have anything more to do with him.

36

'I went to his room to speak to him, that's all. We'd had a disagreement earlier in the evening about something, and I wanted to go and put things right in case he took off again.'

'Why would he take off?'

Martyn glances at me. 'We haven't seen him since we were sixteen. He disappeared and we lost touch.'

'Where did he go off to?'

'Isle of Wight, where his dad lives. I managed to track him down. Heather wanted him here for her party.'

'But not you?'

'I didn't really mind either way.' He sighs.

He's not coming across well. I wish I could nudge

him, wake him up. He could be a prime suspect here if something has happened to Dan.

'So you normally put things right by hurling abuse at people, do you?' the DI asks.

'No, no I don't, but I admit I was angry about his reaction to something he found out. I honestly re-gretted sending those messages straight away, so I went up to his room to try to fix things. I tried to calm him down, but he threw a mug of hot tea at me.'

'Someone in the next room heard you arguing. Loud and aggressive was how they worded it.'

Martyn raises his eyebrows at me. He knows he can't say too much about how the four of us are linked in case it leads onto questions about what hap-pened to Simon. I keep my face blank, but I'm trem-bling. I do not want to be a part of this. Whatever went on in there was between him and Dan. All about Cathy no doubt. I do not want to spend my final days in a prison cell.

'Like I said, he's not been back here for twenty-seven years so it was bound to come up and cause friction between us. Although I have to say he was the one who brought it up, not me. I'd have quite happily never spoken about it again.'

'So tell me what it was all about? Must have been important for two middle-aged men to fall out over.

Something to do with a woman, was it?' The DI turns to me, and I shrug.

'Partly.' Martyn pauses, but the DI is waiting for him to continue.

'Look, we were sixteen going on seventeen and I got his girlfriend pregnant, never told him. She had an abortion and he thought it was his. I'm not proud of it. I made a mistake. We were kids.'

'So you didn't tell him this until...?'

He nods slowly. 'Last night.' He draws his hand through his hair. 'At the time, I went with Cathy to the clinic. He wouldn't go, wanted her to keep it because at the time he assumed the baby was his.'

Martyn saying it aloud brings it back in a flash. Me standing with Dan defending him to Cathy and Martyn who were determined to get rid of the baby as soon as possible. I hadn't understood at the time why he was so adamant he should be the one to go with Cathy. He made out it was because she shouldn't be alone, that he needed to go if Dan or I weren't going to. I feel sorry for my younger self, how gullible I was. And look at me now, with him again. Why am I so stupid and trusting? Because I love him? How can this be love? If he's capable of keeping that from me, he's capable of anything.

'Ouch.' The DI's eyes flicker over Martyn's face,

perhaps searching for signs of remorse or signs that he's lying. 'You're a sly one, aren't you?'

He's not even sorry. He's not said as much to me, anyway. Yes, he confessed, but only because he's worried someone else knows about it. If I'd known then what they'd done behind my back, I'd have been heartbroken. I'd also never have got back with him.

The day Martyn took Cathy to the clinic, Dan was adamant he wouldn't go because he couldn't be a part of destroying his baby's life. I chose to stay with Dan, and we went over and over it. We hoped Cathy would see sense and change her mind, but I told him if he really wanted to stop her, he should go after her, try harder to persuade her to take more time to think about it, but he wouldn't, he was too weak. Martyn thought it was terrible that Cathy was going on her own as I wouldn't go either, so he went with her. Little did Dan and I know that it was Martyn's baby all along.

I didn't believe in abortions then unless it was in the case of rape or incest. I understood that Cathy thought she was too young to become a mother, but she loved Dan, and he loved her, so why not go ahead? I thought they could work through it. They broke up after the abortion and Martyn and I split up soon after too. I should probably go through my old diaries, try to pinpoint which day they probably slept together. If it really was only once. I don't remember being suspicious or noticing anything unusual.

'They're ready for us, if you both are?' DI Lyon says.

We look at each other and nod. She shows us into the white tent.

I jolt at the sight of the body lying on a ground sheet, fully clothed and soaked with water. The mop of hair is swept across the forehead, which has a greyish white pallor. I tell myself it's not him. It doesn't even look like him. I don't recognise the clothes he's wearing. Grey joggers, a pastel-yellow T-shirt and bare feet. Pyjamas maybe? There are dark patches on the skin around his neck.

I scramble to get out of the tent and once outside I double over, vomiting onto the grass and over the toes of my shoes. When I've finished, I daren't look up, unsure if there's any more to come. I'm shaking, dizzy. I can't look at the body again. Out of the corner of my eye, Martyn is staggering outside too, and doubles over to the left of me, covering his mouth. The DI is next to him. It's a few seconds before he speaks in a strange strung-out voice that doesn't sound quite real.

'Yes, that's Dan,' he says and retches into his hand.

37

'I'd like you to come with me to the station please,' the DI says to Martyn.

'What? Why? I haven't done anything.'

'You were possibly the last person to see Dan alive.'

'Except the bastard who killed him,' he says.

'I can always arrest you if you prefer.'

'Just go, Martyn,' I tell him. 'You might know something that will help them catch who did this.'

'It's more than likely suicide, isn't it?' Martyn says.

'He told me he tried a few times in the past,' I add.

'He was in a bad way after the baby news. He wasn't expecting it and took it harder than I thought he would,' Martyn adds.

'It may well be,' the DI says. 'We'll have to wait for the autopsy results. But for now, all we know is you had an altercation with him in his room not long before the estimated time of his death. We need to ask you some more questions about last night.'

'Okay, okay.' He holds up his hands, looks away.

'Do you want me to come with you?' I ask, not really wanting to because I can't see how I can help and I'm not certain if he's innocent.

'No, you go home, you should rest.' He runs his hand down my arm then turns to the DI. 'Do you realise Heather's condition is... terminal? You're giving her all this added stress which isn't good for her.'

'I'm sorry, you can go now,' she says to me.

'Thank you,' I say before turning back to Martyn.

'Can you get yourself home okay?' he says.

'I'll get one of the boys to come for me and pick you up when they've finished with you.'

As I watch Martyn walk away with the DI, I take my phone out of my bag and call Ben. He arrives a few minutes later.

'Isn't Martyn coming?' he asks as he links his arm through mine.

'Haven't you seen, Martyn's got his own transport,' I say under my breath, indicating to Martyn waiting in the back of a police car. We stop and watch him being driven away, then walk to Ben's car and get in.

'What's all that about? What's he done?' Ben starts the ignition.

I explain about Martyn going back to the hotel last night to smooth things over with Dan, but them continuing their argument about Cathy's abortion and Martyn admitting he was the dad, not Dan.

'It was a bad idea him telling Dan the truth. He didn't know they had betrayed him, and me. It sounds like he lost it with Martyn and threw things at him in a rage,' I tell him.

'Do you think Martyn hit back?'

'I don't think he would have hurt anyone on purpose, but now Dan's body has been found dead in the lake, I don't know what to think.'

'Jeez Mum, that's heavy shit. Did *you* know about Martyn being the real dad?'

I shake my head. 'He lied to me too. He and Cathy kept this to themselves all these years. I'm still in shock.'

'You don't seem that upset with him. What if he's lying to you about other stuff?'

'Of course I'm upset, but what's the point in getting angry? In the grand scheme of things, it doesn't really matter any more. It's in the past. We were teenagers who made mistakes. We're all different people now. I don't want to spend my last weeks hating and resenting him. It's exhausting, a waste of energy and ultimately doesn't change anything, does it? I know you've never really taken to him, but I won't be around for much longer, and I really want to try to enjoy the time I have left, so please don't say anything to him. It's difficult enough with everything that's been going on. I really don't want to be involved in a relationship break-up when I'm at death's door. That reminds me, we'll need to start planning Cathy's funeral. If I concentrate on that it'll keep my mind off everything else.'

'But that's two people dead in less than a day, Mum. What the actual fuck is going on? Is it possible Martyn could be responsible for both?'

I don't answer straight away.

'Mum?'

'I suppose he had the opportunity, but I can't think why he would poison Cathy.'

'Is this something to do with the confession you were going to make last night?'

'Look, I've decided it's better if you don't know anything about that. It's far too complicated.' I turn away and open my window an inch to breathe in some fresh air.

'But why was it Martyn who stopped you saying it? It's something to do with him isn't it, something he's done? Don't tell me you're covering up for him. Has he hurt someone before?'

'I really can't say, I'm sorry.'

'Are you sure about that?' he says sarcastically.

It's understandable he's annoyed. I don't usually keep much from my sons, but I'm trying to protect them from my past mistakes, as well as attempting to put things straight. I wish I could tell them everything about Simon's death.

'I just don't want you getting involved,' I tell him and he meets my glance, then concentrates on the road ahead.

'If you're in any danger Mum, you need to tell the police.'

'I'll be fine, I promise.'

Maybe I will have to tell them... in the end. But for now, the less they know, the safer they will be from the person hell-bent on revenge.

My silenced mobile flashes in my handbag. I catch a glimpse of a new message from the same unknown number. I need to get home so I can deal with this in my own way.

38

Ben drops me off at home, telling me to call him if I need anything. We kiss on the cheeks, and I let myself in.

The dogs trot up to greet me and lick and nuzzle their noses into my hands. Lisa is tidying up in the kitchen annexe. I check the time. It's after lunch. She'll have been checking on the animals, walking the dogs. We sit together in the kitchen, and I tell her everything that's happened this morning. She reaches for my hand and gently squeezes it, then – without me having to ask – she gets up and makes me a sandwich and a cup of tea.

'How long do you think they'll hold Martyn for?' She places the plate and cup on the table in front of me. The sandwiches are cut into triangles and there's a substantial serving of fresh salad on the side. Next to it she leaves my packet of tablets and a glass of water. She's so kind the way she looks after me.

'I've no idea, they didn't say. I'm not exactly sure what went on between him and Dan. Only what I've told you he said, but of course there's always two sides and now we'll never know.' Tears spill over my eyes.

'You don't think he could have hurt Dan?' She sits opposite me with a cup of coffee and a sandwich, and takes a large bite.

I shake my head. 'For all Martyn's faults, I don't think he's got it in him to be a killer, even an accidental one.'

'Could it be Robbie who killed Dan and Cathy?'

'That would make more sense since he was upset with both of them. But I think the police are exploring the possibility it might be suicide. The autopsy will tell them more. Finding out Cathy's baby wasn't his was too much for Dan to take in; he was fragile, despite so much time passing. He came here to see me of course, after we invited him to the party, but he was also hoping he might be able to rekindle his relationship with Cathy. But it feels to me like there's more to his death. There's something not right about it. I mean why go in the hotel garden to do it?'

I sip my sweet tea and immediately feel fortified by it.

'It must have been an awful shock seeing him like that.'

'Honestly it was utterly horrifying. I don't think I'll ever erase that image from my head. It looked like he'd drowned, but there were marks around his neck. Maybe someone did kill him. I can't even bear thinking about it. He was wearing what looked like pyjamas and nothing on his feet. Isn't that a bit odd? I mean, what would he have been doing out there dressed like that in the middle of the night?'

'Maybe someone messaged to meet him, and he was ready for bed?'

'Could be. But he'd had so much to drink, I doubt he was in a fit state to leave his room. Perhaps he took the lift down, staggered outside but couldn't see very well, then tripped and fell into the lake?' I pick at the salad, but I've lost my appetite.

'Possibly, in which case it was an accident. If someone did message him, it would have been Martyn, wouldn't it?'

'I think so. And to go back to your question, I think Robbie was still in custody answering questions about Cathy's death when Dan was killed. But maybe they'd let him go by then.'

Lisa finishes her tea. 'Right, I'm going to get off home, but I'll be back again later to feed and check on the animals. Are you going to be okay on your own?'

'I'll be fine. I'll take my tablets and go have a lie down.'

'All right. If you need anything, just give me a bell. I've got my key, so I'll let myself in, just in case you're still asleep, okay?'

'That's great, thank you.' We hug and she lets herself out.

I close my eyes for a second and breathe in the stillness. The dogs are lying at my feet. As soon as I move, both of them get up and traipse after me into the kitchen. I cover the sandwich with foil and put it in the fridge for later. I check my emails on my laptop in the living room. There's one from my solicitor confirming the changes I asked for. I take my phone out of my pocket and frown at the message that arrived earlier.

Now it's your turn.

I switch my phone to silent and make sure all the

doors are locked. I haven't got the energy for these games right now; I'm dead on my feet and I need to rest. I trudge upstairs to my bedroom and change into comfortable clothes. Loose jeans, a T-shirt and a thin fleece. I check my face in the mirror then lie down on the bed. The dogs gather around me. I pull a light blanket up and over my shoulders and shut my eyes.

My mind plays tricks on me as I drift between consciousness and sleep, drawing me back to that day twenty-seven years ago. An almighty crash rings out in the misty morning air, shattering the peace and quiet. Echoes of footsteps pounding on metal, white clouds of breath and ribbons of laughter trailing behind us. Alex is standing in the middle of road, arms by his sides; everything about him is grey including his skin, and the crash is the car hitting him.

I wake up with a jerk to someone banging on the front door. I catch my breath. I'm sweating. Alex's forlorn grey face is still in my mind. None of them considered the trauma to me of what they made me do to Simon.

I sit up and scratch my head, pick up my phone and look at the time: 4.03 p.m. I slowly stand up. I'm aching all over. Out of the window is a sleek silver car half parked on the pavement, engine exhaust billowing out. A car door slams. I glimpse someone in a black hoodie standing near my front door shifting from one foot to the other. I really don't want to answer right now, I'm not in the mood to talk to anyone, but they must sense I'm in because they bang on the door again. I frown at the message on my phone.

I take my time coming down the stairs, making sure I hold on, because my ankle is still hurting where I twisted it falling off the stage. There is one person who could be at the door, but I don't particularly want to talk to them right now. Although I have a feeling it's urgent and they're not going to go away.

'Won't be a minute,' I call out. I shove my phone in my fleece pocket as I herd the dogs into the kitchen and shut them in. People who don't like dogs tend to get nervous, especially with two showing up at once.

I open the front door, and something flashes in my face. I scream as I catch a glimpse of a man's mouth moving, speaking. It's not a voice I recognise and it's not who I thought it was. Something rough and scratchy is pulled over my head. I shout *help* but my voice is already muffled. I'm bundled backwards into the house and against a wall.

The rough material is lifted momentarily while a strip of cotton is forced across my mouth making me cough and squeal in pain, and then the material is tied tightly behind my head. Two hands grab my elbows and bring my hands together behind my back. I breathe heavily as someone else ties my wrists with something, making me cry out in pain.

I'm hoping one of my neighbours sees something or hears the dogs barking madly and calls the police. I try to make as much noise as I can but the grip on my arms pinches tighter. I picture Mrs Walker next door sitting in her front room, watching daytime TV with her knitting in her lap. If she could just look up for a moment. Stand up, walk to the window to find out what's going on. *Call the police. Please,* I scream but my words are just noise.

A car door-lock bleeps open and I'm pushed into the boot and rolled onto my back. The door is slammed shut, sending in a rush of air. My heart thuds against my ribs. I can hardly move. I'm glad I can't see as I hate enclosed spaces, although I can sense the coffin-small area I'm in. I've thought a lot about that lately. Being buried in the ground. In a box. Sometimes I have nightmares where I'm in my coffin but I'm not completely dead and I've gone into such a deep sleep my pulse is undetectable. It happens sometimes to people who've been found in extremely cold temperatures. In my dream I have to scratch my way out, but the earth I'm buried in starts to fall in and that's usually when I wake up.

The engine purrs into life and the car silently speeds away.

What happened to Simon was wrong. I didn't ask for it. I've tried so hard to put things right.

But someone thinks it's not enough.

39

It's hard to breathe with a sack or whatever it is over my head. I'm sweating from the heat of being encased by such thick material. Whatever cloth is wedged across my mouth touches my tongue and the wet from my saliva makes me gag. I swallow and swallow, but the bitter taste of it won't go away and I'm trying hard not to be sick because I'd probably choke on my own vomit. My heart is pounding out of my chest. I'm scared I'm going to have a heart attack. In here. All on my own.

The smell of rubber and synthetic carpet is overpowering. I wish I could shut my nostrils because it triggers another wave of sickness over me. If only I could move but it's impossible. The more I think about where I am and what this is, the more fear creeps like a giant spider up my spine, onto my neck and over my scalp. My face is rigid, muscles aching with fear. What if they leave me here? No one would know where I am, where I've gone. I'd die a slow, lonely death. Not how I envisaged my last moments, which I've thought about a lot. I've written in my end-of-life care plan that I want to die at home in my bed, surrounded by my closest family. It's important to be able to see their faces, feel their warm hands holding mine before I close my eyes for the final time and sink into nothingness. Do I deserve to be treated like this? Maybe I do. I didn't mean for anyone to get hurt. I remember exactly how it feels to lose someone. Is this really how it ends for me?

I imagine the dogs howling in the kitchen, wondering where I am, scratching the door trying to get out to find me. I sob loudly, gulping down air. What's the use, no one can hear me. Taking slower, deeper breaths, I try to control my rapid breathing. If I can just focus on a list of things I need to do, it'll help distract me. Although it seems utterly pointless, it's my default for anxious situations, especially since my diagnosis. If I don't occupy my mind, it goes into overdrive. In my head I go around all the windows and doors at home and visualise locking them. Then I go through the evening chores at the kennels. Lisa will be coming back to do the final animal feeds for the day and then won't need to return until the morning. She'll assume I'm upstairs asleep and will probably not notice I'm missing, although hopefully she'll hear the dogs and wonder why they're locked up. Martyn is my only hope, but I gave him instructions to text me as soon as they let him go at the police station. My mobile is in the zip-up pocket of my fleece. If only I could reach it and alert someone. I won't be able to answer when he calls. How will he know where I am? Will he be able to find me?

Then a little worm of doubt crosses my thoughts. Could this be his doing? Does he know I've found out what he's done?

40

It's hard to say how long I'm in the boot of the car while it's moving. It feels like hours but maybe in reality it's only about twenty minutes. It's impossible to tell. The car turns a sharp corner then slows down as the tyres crunch over gravel and then stop.

Once the engine is switched off, I hear three doors open and slam in succession. Does that mean there are three people? A mix of light and heavy footsteps walk away over the gravel. A door opens with a metal-sounding creak and shuts with a heavy slam. Then silence. I scream and kick out, forgetting I'm only wearing slippers, and cry at the agony of stubbing my toes. I try to move my hands round to my fleece pocket but no matter how much I twist and turn and stretch, I cannot reach my phone.

The boot suddenly opens and a rough-skinned hand hauls me out. Whoever it is keeps a tight grip, pinching my upper arm and marching me across uneven ground. I stagger forwards, feet dragging, fearing what's going to happen to me and with a feeling I'm going to trip over at any second. There's a clang of the metal-sounding door grating open, and a gruff voice tells me to step up three stairs and into a room smelling of stale alcohol and cigarette smoke. Dance music is thudding at a low level somewhere in the building. I'm guessing it's a bar or pub or possibly a restaurant, although I can't detect any food aromas. There's a draught coming from somewhere – maybe a window or a door is open to air the room. It could be my way out of here.

The person holding my arm lets go. My skin feels sore and bruised. I start shaking, not being able to see my surroundings, not knowing where these people are, who is there, what's coming next.

Heavy-booted footsteps come towards me, echoing on what I guess is a wooden floor, then they stop in front of me. The person clears their throat but doesn't speak.

My mobile vibrates in my pocket. I can make out

flashes of light as it pulses from a gap in the material where it's not quite zipped shut. Someone pats their large hands down my clothes, finds the phone, and pulls it out. I groan inwardly. If there was a chance of letting Martyn know where I am, it's just vanished. Although I'm not sure if he'd be in a position to help me anyway. Or worse, if he's in on whatever is going on here.

There's probably enough of the message on the locked screen for them to see what it says and who it's from. Scott's always telling me to disable that function for safety reasons, so messages can only be read if you know the log in, but I never believed it was necessary.

'It's Martyn,' says a gruff man whose voice I don't recognise. 'Been released, wants a pick-up from Luton police station.'

'All right, but first, let's have a look at her.'

I start at the familiar voice.

The rough hood is whipped off my head, scratching my skin as it rubs past my nose and ears. Someone unties my gag. I'm in what looks like a back storage room with scuffed matt black walls and boxes of alcohol piled high. A door in front of me swings open and the corner of a pink and orange neon sign pulses from a darkened room with twinkling lights on the ceiling.

The blond man from my party strides up to me, grinning. The stubble on his upper lip and around his chin is light ginger – strawberry blonde you'd call it if he was a woman. He's not a natural blond after all, his hair is bleached. He's got model looks teenage girls probably swoon over.

'Hello, Heather.'

'Is this some kind of joke?'

He shakes his head and holds my phone up to my face, unlocking the screen.

'Shall I reply to Martyn for you, or do you want to do it?'

Next to him are what I can only describe as heavies or bouncers. Four skinhead muscle men in ridiculously skin-tight black jeans and shiny black bomber jackets with a gold crown and ball logo on the left. There's one older bouncer standing to one side of them who has a white stubbly goatee, dark tanned skin and bags under his eyes.

'What's all this about? Untie me now.' I raise my voice and wriggle my arms helplessly behind me. Whatever they've used to tie me is cutting into my wrists and my joints ache. I'm going to need my medication in a couple of hours, and I don't have it with me.

'Nah, I think you're all right like that for a bit longer. I'll text Martyn back for you. Get a couple of the boys to go and pick him up from the police station. Can't wait to hear what he says when he gets here. Any idea why they've not charged him?'

'Why are you doing this to *me*?' I continue.

'You know, things can change very quickly.'

'What are you talking about?' There's a tell-tale waver in my voice.

'Dan and I had a little chat only last night.'

I shudder and swallow the lump in my throat. I daren't ask what they talked about, what happened.

'I don't think you've been entirely honest with me, have you?' He shuts one eye and points at me as though he's holding a gun. One side of his lips rise in a crooked smile as he pretends to aim at my head and shoot, then he laughs to himself.

'What do you mean?' I cry. This isn't how it was meant to be.

He looks down at my phone and starts typing with one finger, reading it out as he goes.

> Hope all okay. Sending a mini cab for you.

He points to two of his men and chucks a set of keys at them. They go outside and moments later we hear an old-sounding car being driven away.

'Not good about the police letting Martyn go. They should be charging him, banging him up.'

'Maybe they don't have enough evidence,' I snap.

'But they know he was the last person to see Dan alive. He argued with him. There are abusive texts from Martyn's phone. Should be case closed.'

'How do you know all that?' I narrow my eyes.

'Walls have ears, Grandad used to say.'

I prickle at the mention of him.

My phone flashes in his hand.

'Martyn will be on his way shortly, so let's get the gag back on you.'

Two of the bouncers come towards me.

'Tell me what's going on. What are you going to do?' I shout. The older man and a rotund-looking man with a thick silver ring through the centre of his nostrils bring over the piece of cloth. One holds me still while the other wedges it between my lips and pulls it tight around the back of my head, despite my noises of complaint. Somehow the man with the nose ring secures the two ends into a knot with his chubby fingers.

Part of me wants to warn Martyn not to get in that

car, but he isn't the person I thought he was and I'm still not sure if he's part of this plan to kidnap me. I should have left the Martyn I loved firmly in the past. Now I know he betrayed me with Cathy in the worst possible way, I can't trust him. He's shown me his true self and deserves everything that's coming to him.

41

As soon as the car pulls up outside, my back stiffens. I try to speak but the cloth in my mouth makes it impossible. My first instinct is still to protect Martyn, but I check myself, remember that he lied to me back then, and he's still lying to me now. He doesn't deserve my loyalty.

The door opens and the heavies drag him in by the elbows. His hands are tied behind his back and a potato sack covers his head. Panic shoots through my veins. No one else knows we're here.

They push Martyn into a chair opposite me and when the sack is pulled off his head, it takes him a few seconds to realise it's me sitting in front of him tied up too.

'What are you doing here, are you okay?' he says in a strange, muffled voice through his gag, as if no one can hear him but me. He looks around at the bouncers standing to attention, their hands over-lapped in front of them.

'Nice of you to join us.' The blond man strolls to-wards us from what must be his office at the back of the room. He indicates for the gag to be removed from Martyn's mouth.

'Who are you and what do you want with us?' Martyn yells, narrowing his eyes at him.

'Aren't you going to tell us how you got on at the police station?'

'Hey, aren't you that bloke who was heckling us at the party? You're the one who was flirting with Cathy, getting her all those weird-looking cocktails.'

The man holds out his hands and slow-claps Martyn for finally beginning to understand. 'Yes, I'm that bloke.' He laughs, nodding his agreement. 'Cathy was a very attractive woman.'

'Piss off. She was too good for you. She thought you were a joke.'

'Did she now? Is that why she gave me her details?' He slips his hand in his jacket pocket and pulls out a piece of paper folded in two. He takes his time opening it and then shows Martyn what presumably is Cathy's name and mobile number.

'She wouldn't have given you that.' Martyn raises his chin.

'Why not? Are you jealous?'

'Because...' He glances sideways at me. If he was about to blurt something out, he thinks better of it and manages to hold himself back. 'Who are you?' he asks, frowning.

'Tell him, Heather. It's you who invited me to your party. I don't want to steal your thunder.' He grins at me, rubbing his chin, clearly enjoying this.

One of the bouncers who has a slight limp unties my gag.

'What? You said you didn't know who he was. Why did you lie to me? *Did* you invite him?' Martyn throws a look of incredulity at me. I turn away and focus on the ground. He has the gall to call me a liar.

'His name is George,' I say in a low voice, then look up and stare Martyn in the face, daring him to carry on with his lies.

'Is that supposed to mean something to me because I still don't have a clue. Where do you know him from?' He shuffles to the edge of his chair.

'We met a couple of weeks ago and we've got to know a bit about each other.'

'What? You haven't told me about him.'

'Do you tell me about everyone you meet, everything you get up to?' I glare at him.

'No, but Christ Almighty, Heather, look at us now. I think I've got a right to know who's dragged us here and tied us up.'

'Tell him.' George thumps the side of Martyn's chair.

I take a deep breath. 'This is George... Eyre.'

I pause for Martyn to take it in.

He frowns and his eyebrows rise as the penny drops, then he can't stop himself staring at this younger man standing in front of him.

'That's right,' George says, puffing his chest out. 'Simon Eyre was my dad, and I was just a baby when you killed him.'

42

'What? I didn't kill him.' Martyn frowns at George then at me. 'If you knew who he was, why the hell did you invite him to your party?'

'Bob Eyre died three weeks ago,' I say, not answering him directly. 'I spotted his obituary in the local paper and felt a sense of relief – at last the man who ran down Alex was dead. But the mention of Bob having a grandson shook me up. I'd only ever thought of Bob as this monster who'd killed my brother. But nothing is that clear-cut; he'd been a family man too. I had no idea Bob's son Simon had a baby son when he died. George had to grow up without his dad. Bob helped to bring him up. It changed the way I thought about him. It got me thinking that it was time to put things right before I die. And I decided George had a right to know what happened that day, so I contacted him.'

Martyn stares at me, crestfallen at what he sees as my betrayal.

George nods. 'Not long before he died, Grandad told me for the first time how my dad died sitting right next to him in his car. He said he still woke up in the night reliving it in his nightmares. He kept it from me to protect me. Wanted me to grow up without hate and resentment. Said he'd always thought it had to be something to do with his car accident that killed Alex, but the police were so stupid they didn't investigate it properly. They couldn't believe school kids had done it.' George swings round, making me flinch and grabs Martyn's head in an arm lock. 'So instead, they questioned a couple of college boys who'd been seen messing about on the bridge around that time. But there wasn't enough proof to charge them. There were no fingerprints because you lot were wearing gloves.'

Martyn whimpers and grunts as he tries to release himself. His eyes shut tight as he twists and turns, spit flying from his lips. In moments his face quickly turns bright red with the strain and lack of oxygen.

'My dad didn't deserve to die. He was only twenty-two. He'd just become a father. Did you even know that about him?'

Martyn's reddened face grows darker as he coughs and tries to protest. George lets go of his throat and Martyn splutters and coughs. 'I did not kill your dad.'

George sighs. 'That's not what I've been told from a very reliable source.'

'You told him?' Martyn pulls a face of disgust at me. 'I didn't know Simon had a baby, did you?' he says to me then looks back at George. 'Anyway, you can't throw accusations around when you have no evidence.'

'I spoke to an eyewitness – Dan. I went to see him in his hotel room. He told me what you did,' George says. 'In fact, he told me everything that happened that morning. Who was there, who did what.'

'You're lying,' Martyn shouts at him, his voice gravelly and strained. He starts coughing again.

'And you knew he was the one who would eventually spill, didn't you? That's why you wanted to get him to leave. You offered him money to go away and not come back.'

'Is that true?' I yell at Martyn. He's never told me this. Whenever we discussed why Dan had left so suddenly after Simon's death and Cathy's abortion, he pretended he was as clueless as I was.

'Come on, Heather,' Martyn says. 'You know Dan was weaker than everyone else, struggling with what had happened. If anyone was going to blurt to the police, it was him. I thought if I encouraged him to start a new life, go and live with his dad in the Isle of Wight, he'd be able to put it all behind him. And he seemed to have done just that, until you insisted I find him and ask him to come to your party. Just so you could say a final goodbye to him. I knew it would be a mistake.'

'I cannot believe *you* made Dan go away.' I squint at Martyn, trying to digest that he's told me yet another enormous lie. 'Why didn't you tell me you did that?'

'Because I knew you'd go mad, try to make him stay. You wouldn't have listened to me. But I'm telling you now, he would have given us all away.' He stamps his foot.

'That's not true. He was a good friend to us. He would never have betrayed us. He was kind and caring and I happened to agree with him that he should have had a say about the baby. But then I didn't know it was yours.'

'You don't know how close to the edge he was. He

couldn't live with the abortion or what happened to Simon. He was talking about ending it all and I spent all that night sitting with him, persuading him not to. It was a no-brainer suggesting he reconnect with his dad. He'd hardly seen him since his parents' divorce. He'd not been getting on with his mum and her new partner, which didn't help his state of mind. He felt pushed out.'

'I knew he was taking Simon's death and the abortion badly, but not so much that he'd consider ending his life.'

'I was honestly trying to help him. I had some birthday money saved up, so I gave it to him for the train and the ferry ticket. His dad had been asking him to go and live with him since the split, so his new life was there ready and waiting for him. All I tried to do was help him to see that.'

George steps closer again, grabs Martyn's chin and tips it up. 'He looked up to you and you betrayed him. Marty, he called you. Affectionate, isn't it? He told me how you helped him move away and start again, but he didn't know he wasn't the baby's dad. He couldn't believe you'd betrayed him, shagged his girlfriend, getting her pregnant behind his back. As if that wasn't bad enough, you passed the baby off as his, left him with a life sentence of guilt, shame and regret.'

'I said sorry to him. I was just a stupid kid, full of ego and hormones.'

'Did you kill him when you argued?' George continues. 'Because he was alive and well when I left him. They'll try to pin that on you eventually, Martyn, so maybe I'll get some kind of justice for my dad.'

'I didn't touch him, and I didn't kill your dad,' Martyn protests as he tries to work his hands out of the ties.

'You had a fight with him though. The police think you're guilty, so why haven't they charged you yet?'

'Because of one simple fact: I didn't do it. That is why they don't have any evidence. There is none.'

George spins round. 'Except for the glass in Dan's sink.'

'What glass?' Sweat shimmers on Martyn's top lip, shown up by the spotlight above.

'The one I planted there. Took it from your table at the party. The one you'd been drinking from.'

'What?'

'You've been clever at wriggling out of things haven't you, Martyn? Got away with my dad's murder.

So one more is nothing to you, is it? Or is it two more? Did you kill Cathy as well?'

'I'm not even going to answer that. Tell me what Dan said to you.'

'He told me about how you planned everything in advance.' George's face darkens as he speaks.

'We've only got your word for it that he said that.' Martyn looks to me, obviously hoping I'll back him up in his false triumph, but I'm past helping him now.

'How you went up there after school to practise, even used a timer. And when you were ready, you got Heather up there to show her how it could be done. How you could drop a rock from a bridge onto my granddad's car and get away with it. Give her the justice she needed for her brother's death. Except you got the wrong man, didn't you?'

'That wasn't meant to happen, you have to believe me.' Martyn thrashes his head from side to side.

'And then Heather announced she was going to tell everyone. I bet you didn't see that coming. You must have been shitting yourself,' George bellows, then bursts into laughter. 'But what you didn't know, is she'd already confessed everything to me.'

43

'Why?' Martyn looks desperately at me, but I keep my face blank.

'Don't worry, I know it was Cathy who came up with the idea, not you. But she roped you and Dan in, didn't she? She told me herself when we were drinking those disgusting blue cocktails at the party. Once I told her who I was and everything I knew, she let it all spill out. Seemed rather proud of having two boys hanging on her every word, doing exactly what she wanted. Unfortunately for her, she didn't know who she was speaking to when she first started flirting with me.'

'So you killed her and now you're trying to pin it

on me?' Martyn dips his head, swallows and looks up again. 'You did, didn't you? You bastard.'

'Wasn't me.' George exaggerates a nasty grin on his face. He's playing with us. With me. I thought we had an understanding but now he's targeting me too. If he didn't kill Cathy and Dan, who did? I'm not so sure it was Robbie because he didn't seem to know Cathy was going to finish with him. He genuinely loved her.

George continues, 'But it seems only fair that she should pay for it considering how callous she was, planning to kill my grandad. And you're no better. You helped her work out how to execute it. So now it's your turn.'

'What do you mean?' Martyn frowns, his face strained with anxiety. He's still looking at me to intervene.

'You seemed overly upset at Cathy's death, wouldn't you agree, Heather?'

I nod but panic is rising in my chest. I'm no longer sure where I stand with George. He's double-crossed me, and I don't know how the hell I'm going to get out of this.

'Because she was a good friend. She didn't deserve to die.' Martyn's voice becomes higher-pitched.

'You may as well tell him,' George says to me and

nods at one of the heavies to untie my hands. I stand up slowly, keeping my eyes on him. I'm not sure what he's going to do to me. I rub the sore skin around my wrists.

'Why are you letting *her* go?' Martyn spits blood and saliva on the ground.

I could ask the same question. I can't trust George. Kidnapping me, treating me like this. How dare he! This was never part of the plan.

'I don't think you quite understand, Martyn.' George nods at one of the heavies who jabs a punch at Martyn's face, making his head shoot backwards with the force.

'What the fuck was that for?' he growls, blood dripping from his nose as his head lolls forward. His face is a mess of snot, saliva and blood. His nose could be broken.

George opens his palm out to me as if he's introducing me to Martyn for the first time. I fold my arms high on my chest and step forward, legs astride, enjoying watching Martyn squirm. 'That's payback for carrying on with Cathy behind my back.'

'Seriously? I told you about that. Anyway, I thought you were okay with it? You said it hardly mattered in the grand scheme of things, especially as it was decades ago.'

'Except you're still lying to me.' I throw my hands up in despair. 'And why would I be okay with it? Because if I'd known, I'd never have let you back into my life. You're a liar and a cheat and now for all I know, you killed Dan too.'

'I did not. And what happened between me and Cathy is ancient history, surely you forgive me so we can put it behind us?'

'But it's not though, is it? You were together last weekend when you told me you were golfing with your mates. You started seeing her again eleven months ago to be precise. A matter of weeks after I received my initial diagnosis. What kind of monster does that?'

I smack him around the head as hard as I can. Blood and saliva spin off in all directions.

'No, no, no.' He roars out his anger, grinds his teeth, leaning forward then back, rocking the chair, trying to make it tip over.

'Stop lying to me!' I scream, 'I thought you loved me, wanted to care for me when I needed you most, but all you wanted to do was be with her, strip me of my dignity when I'm at my most vulnerable.' I cry into my hands, shaking all over. George guides me away as two of the heavies start laying into Martyn with their fists.

44

'Enough!' I scream, covering my ears so I don't have to listen to fists pounding Martyn's flesh any longer. George raises a hand, and the heavies stop and move away to the back of the room and sit on a pile of up-turned pallets. Martyn groans, still tied to the chair, which has fallen sideways onto the ground. He opens one eye but it's just a slit of skin swelling up. I wanted this. I wanted to stand up for myself for once while I still have the chance. I wanted Martyn dead for what he's done to me, the heartbreak and humiliation. I wanted all of them dead for making me part of their sick plan that went so horribly wrong and left a young father dead, but I can't bear the violence and the burden revenge brings. I thought the answer was to clear my conscience, but now I may be partly responsible for two more deaths. This is so much worse than I imagined. Wanting something and following it through are two very different things.

'How did you find out?' Martyn gasps out the words. He coughs up a globule of phlegm and blood and spits it onto the floor. The heavies side-eye each other, nodding and smirking, evidently amused at the damage they've caused.

'It was at the dinner party when we broke the news of my terminal diagnosis. I saw the look you and Cathy gave each other when you thought no one was looking. Then later when you were in the kitchen on your own, I saw you touch the side of her face in a way you used to do to me. It hurt so much yet I daren't let myself believe it was anything. I made every excuse I could think of for you both. You'd known each other since school, dated once, it was natural that you cared for each other, but my suspicions got the better of me and the more I saw you together, the clearer it became. I'd been so blind to it all those months, assuming it was because you knew each other well.'

A loud click interrupts me. I shoot a look at the

heavies sitting together at the back of the room. The older guy grins as he holds up a spliff and tucks a shiny silver cigarette case back into his pocket. He brings out a lighter and strikes it with his thumb, inhaling deeply on the roll-up before passing it to the man next to him and blowing white smoke in our direction.

'I checked your phone,' I continue saying to Martyn. 'Your history had been cleared, something you never used to bother to do, except for a meeting with each other you'd planned but not told me about. So I followed you to a restaurant you'd arranged to meet at. Still I came up with reasons why you'd be meeting alone. Something to do with work or a special surprise for me. But you stood at the bar face to face and I watched from the shadows as you kissed on the lips.'

'I'm so sorry. It honestly meant nothing compared to you.'

'How can you say that? I don't believe you. I know what I saw.'

'I couldn't bear to be alone. I thought she would look after me, after you'd gone.'

'Is that what you told yourself? So you're saying neither of us meant much to you, we were just there to prop you up, make you feel better? I think you

were both waiting for me to die, so you could be together properly. In fact, I know so.'

'That's not true! You know how much I love you.
You have to believe me.' He pauses to catch his
breath. 'But I admit, at times it became too hard to
cope with your illness. Cathy was there for me, as a
comfort. That's all.'

'I bet she was. She was always jealous of us being
together, back in the day. Hated me when you broke
up with her and asked me out. She made damn sure
you cheated on me with her and then surprise surprise, you've cheated on me with her again. What a
fool I was not realising you were both disloyal to me.'

'We weren't. Nothing happened. Honestly. We
would just talk and maybe kiss and cuddle.'

'You can't lie to me any more. I know what you've
done.' I kick his ankle and he moans in pain.

'What are you talking about?'

'You got her to forge my signature to transfer my
half of the house to you, so when I die, my children
don't inherit anything.'

'No, I would never do that to you.'

'You're lying! When I was sorting through my papers and reviewing my will with my solicitor, she
showed me an up-to-date copy of the title deeds from
the Land Registry. I couldn't believe that my half of the

house was in your name instead of mine. Tom's name is still there as owning the other half. We changed it to tenants in common as part of the divorce, which means he won't automatically inherit from me.'

'Your solicitor has made a mistake, you've got to believe me.'

I shake my head in disbelief. 'The transfer document shows my signature, and I know I didn't sign it which means it's been forged. When I found out you and Cathy were seeing each other, it all started to make sense. She's the only person who could sign my name so convincingly, because we used to copy each other's signatures as teenagers. Unless it was you?'

'I swear, you've got it all wrong,' Martyn pleads with me.

'Are you going to believe this shit?' George laughs.

'And that's not all, is it?' I pace around Martyn still lying on the floor. He raises his head an inch momentarily to see where I am, what I'm doing. 'Explain to me why you were going with Cathy to see an adoption agency?'

'You know why.' He sighs. 'Because she wanted to have a family with me.'

'So that's why she broke it off with Robbie?'

'I think so. She said her biological clock was

ticking and she suddenly had a yearning to be a mother and that should be with me, as recompense for getting rid of our first baby. I went with her to explore the options, but I didn't plan on going ahead with it.'

'She told me she was going to leave Robbie but failed to mention you were the secret lover she was planning on adopting a baby with.' A peel of laughter escapes my lips at the irony of the two people in my life who always least wanted to be parents making such a decision together.

'She knew you'd laugh at her wanting to be a mother. Felt you'd always looked down on her for not being interested in having children as though there was something a bit wrong with her.'

'That's not true. I tried to understand, but I respected her choice. I merely said I thought she was missing out on one of the most fulfilling aspects of being a woman. It's only my opinion.'

'Anyway, it's too late now, she's gone. Someone has stolen her life. I'm sorry, I didn't mean to hurt either of you.' He groans as he tries to move.

'You're not sorry you lied to us. You're only sorry I found out. Did Robbie find out about you two?'

'It's possible he thought it was Dan and that's why

he killed them both.' He turns his head to George as if he might be able to confirm it.

George raises his palms. 'Don't ask me. I have no clue. But at least I still have you two.'

I unfold my arms and take a step back. I've been so naïve. My plan for him to kidnap and question Martyn, get him to admit to his part in Simon's death and own up to seeing Cathy, has completely backfired.

One of the bouncers hands him a gun. I freeze. George intended to come for me all along.

'Dan and I had quite the chat in his hotel room. He told me you were on the bridge that day with the rest of them. That's not quite what you told me though, is it?' He waves the gun around then slowly points it at Martyn while looking at me.

'I admitted to you I was there and saw what happened.'

'But not involved, that's what you said. You're a fucking liar,' George yells, making me jump.

'You told him what?' Martyn's voice is hoarse, and his words tail off into a coughing fit.

George points the gun at Martyn's forehead.

'Tell him the truth, Heather!' Martyn shouts, his chest heaving up and down as his breath quickens. The barrel of the gun is almost touching his skin.

'Dan said *she* was the one who dropped the rock. But she told me the three of you did it.' George swings back in my direction, arms extended, pointing the gun at my head. I cup my hands around my mouth, shaking my head.

'*You* killed my dad.'

45

'Don't shoot.' I flinch and hold my arms up over my face and head. 'You can't listen to him, it's not true. I admit I was there, but Martyn and Cathy were the ones holding the rock.' I'm shaking, waiting for the bang and a shot of pain through my body.

'Tell me what happened again, starting from the very beginning,' George says, nodding to one of the heavies to give me a chair and put the gag back on Martyn. I sit down and glance at Martyn. He's cheated on me, betrayed me, he'll do nothing to help me out now, even if he could.

I tentatively sit in the chair, convinced he's going to pull the trigger because he's still pointing the gun at my head. I'm shaking so hard I think I'm going to wet myself. My legs won't stay still.

'Your grandfather, Bob Eyre, killed my little brother. My parents never got over his death. Dad started drinking heavily. Eleven months later Mum took her own life. Dad developed heart failure from the stress of it all and died of a heart attack seven years later. Your grandad ruined our family.'

Aiming at my temple, George squints with one eye and steadies the gun with his other hand. I hold my breath and clench my teeth as he speaks, expecting him to pull the trigger at any moment. 'He paid for it heavily too. He never forgave himself for what he did to your brother, even though it was deemed to be an accident. Every day he questioned his actions and how unfair life was that he was still breathing when that little lad had died so young. Then when Simon was killed right before his eyes, he knew deep down that rock was meant for him. He said it felt like he'd killed his own son.' He brings the gun down by his side and slumps into a chair opposite me. I let out a slow breath and feel the tension release in my face and neck. 'He sunk into a deep depression and had to give up work. He'd lie in bed all day not being able to get up.' He pauses and rubs his free hand over his face and into his hair. 'He started looking after me when Mum went back to work. He said it saved him. Gave him a reason to get out of bed every day. We were so close but neither of them told me exactly how Dad died until a couple of months ago. Grandad was dying and he said it was time I knew the truth.'

I nod. 'That's how I felt, but it seems to have backfired.'

'Before he died, I promised Grandad I'd find out who killed Dad and get our revenge. He didn't want me to because he didn't want anyone else getting hurt. But now he's dead, I don't have to honour my promise to him.' He stands up again, holds the gun in his outstretched hands, pointing it at my face. 'So I want you to tell me every single thing that happened that morning, do you understand?'

46

I swallow but my mouth is dry. 'I need a drink.'

George nods at one of the heavies and he goes through a door into what I imagine is the bar area because of the neon glow in the otherwise dark space. He brings back out a small bottle of water and hands it to me. George stands over me as I crack open the seal of the bottle and glug a mouthful of water. My hands are trembling as I drink. I catch Martyn's eye but quickly look away. I don't want any more contact with him. I cannot trust him and I'm glad they've gagged him.

I clear my throat and explain to George how the four of us went up on the bridge before school that day, when it was just beginning to get light. Martyn and Cathy were the ones carrying a massive rock. It was Cathy who made sure we all wore gloves and scarves over our faces up to our eyes, and insisted we pull our coat hoods up too, so we wouldn't be recognised. I tell him that when they asked me to go with them, I wasn't sure at first, but then I knew I needed to watch, see for myself what they were going to do. They kept saying they were doing it for me. I never intended to take part. I didn't know that Martyn and Cathy had been going up there to practise every day for about a week. They'd made a note of the precise time Bob drove under the bridge every morning on his way to work. It was a quiet back lane, barely any traffic. There was only a minute or two difference at the most in the time they noted each day. Martyn and Cathy marked a point a little way down the road where the car would pass. This was for one person to keep an eye out for Bob's car approaching, then the idea was they'd give the signal to drop the rock at that moment and hopefully hit the target. I tell him they explained to me they'd figured out he drove at about the same speed every day because of a speed restriction down there.

I take a sip of water. Martyn makes strange noises, trying to speak. George stares at me intently, taking in every word. I hope he believes me – throwing a rock onto Bob's car was not my idea. I had nothing to do with the planning and was only meant to witness it. I swallow hard and describe how Cathy and Martyn stood back from the edge of the railing so as not to be spotted. They were holding the rock ready in position above where the driver's side of the car would be, near the centre of the road. They were chewing pink bubble gum non-stop, which I remember smelling so sweet and sickly. They were joking about who could blow the biggest bubble while we waited, as though this was some kind of game we were playing. Even now I can't smell it without feeling sick. I struggle to swallow at the memory of it.

'Carry on,' George snaps.

'Martyn told me to put my hand on the rock too, and say a prayer for Alex, feel the grit and sharp edges that were going to land on this man, because this had to come from me, it was justice for my brother. I felt I had to do it. And then I remember Dan shouting *now* and Cathy and Martyn looking at each other, then glancing down as they let go of the rock. My hand had only been touching the top of it but maybe Dan thought it was all from me. Maybe that's why he told you I did it.' Martyn thrashes his head from side to side making grunting noises from the back of his throat. I do my best to ignore him and when he doesn't shut up, George kicks him in the shin. I have an image of us standing there, the rock leaving our hands in slow motion as it fell, gaining speed like a meteor. 'We all stood back and heard the almighty crash, smashing glass and a deafening thud on metal. They ran down the steps and as far away as possible. I ran behind them, but my legs felt like they were moving through treacle. I couldn't seem to pick up any speed no matter how hard I tried to be quicker. All I could think of was Alex and a car hitting him. There was a second bang but we carried on running. None of us knew, even then, that we'd hit the target. The two of them were laughing ahead of me as they ran.'

I pause again and take in a slow breath to calm my racing pulse. Hot tears fill my eyes.

'It wasn't until later we heard the shocking news on TV, that there had been a second man in the car, and the person who had died wasn't Bob. It was his son Simon.'

George bows his head.

'I've tried so hard to block out the sounds and smells of that morning repeating over and over in my head, because the terrible moment we killed an innocent man haunts me. We never intended to hurt anyone let alone kill them. It was just meant to be a stupid prank to scare Bob, make him swerve, get him back for running over Alex.'

George kicks the legs of my chair. 'So you *were* part of it all along. You told me you only saw them do it from a hiding place in the bushes.'

I nod solemnly. 'It's been so hard to admit it to myself, but the truth is Martyn and Cathy made me do it. They were the ones in control, holding the rock. They planned it all and all while I was still grieving for my little brother, and my mum. I've been angry about what they made me do for so long. I should have spoken up and said no, walked away. Would they have done it anyway? I think so. Because Cathy and Martyn had taken so much trouble to plan it. They said they involved me because they believed they were helping me get revenge for your grandad killing Alex, but I don't know, they took great pleasure in what they did.'

Martyn starts making animal-like noises again, thrashing his whole body until the chair moves. George waves the gun at two of the heavies who go over and slap Martyn's face until he's still and then they stand either side of him.

'The sentence Bob got did make a mockery of how severe the crime was, taking a little boy's life, but that doesn't excuse what we did. What we all took part in was wrong. Nothing we could have done would have made me feel better or bring Alex back. Of course it wouldn't. Alex's death was a terrible, terrible accident that we all had to come to terms with.'

George slumps in the chair again, the gun hanging down from his hand. 'My grandad cried when he told me a boy had died because of him. He didn't want me to know. Contemplated taking it to the grave because he was so ashamed. He said he was angry when he got in the van that day. Something stupid someone had said to him, he couldn't even remember what. He said he started the car and just put his foot down, not even considering he should check his mirrors because he was so worked up. Said it took all his courage to admit to me what he'd done. He never had a good night's sleep after the accident. Alex haunted him constantly in his dreams. It took him ages to pluck up the courage to drive again. When Simon was killed, he considered taking his own life. It was only my birth that gave him something to live for.'

Martyn groans and shuts his eyes. But I don't care what he thinks, George has a right to know what happened to his dad, what we did.

There's a noise outside the main door. It bursts open and two armed police officers storm in.

'Everyone stay where you are. Hands above your heads,' one of them shouts.

In seconds, the room is swarmed with half a dozen police, each of them pointing guns at us.

47

George is hand-cuffed and arrested for kidnapping and possessing a lethal weapon. I stand back and keep my mouth shut, rubbing my forehead with a mixture of anxiety and relief. I seem to have got away with my involvement in Martyn's kidnap. I suggested it but George planned it all, promised to bring me along so I could confront Martyn, but I did not expect him to kidnap me too. If he tells the police I was involved, I'll just deny it. They'll never believe him. There are CCTV cameras down our road, so there'll be evidence of them bundling me into the car.

Two paramedics rush in and see to Martyn still tied to the chair on the ground. Another comes over to me to check I'm okay and to see if I need anything. Once George and the bouncers have been taken away, Ben, Scott and Lisa run in. The boys come straight over and wrap me in a warm hug.

'Mum, you gave us a right scare,' Scott says, frowning.

'We didn't know where you'd gone,' Ben adds, worry giving him temporary lines around his eyes.

'Thank God it's over and you're here,' I say. 'George was going crazy waving a gun around. I honestly didn't know if he was going to let us out alive.' I'm shaken from George kidnapping me and pointing a gun at my head, believing I'm as guilty as the other three when I'm not. I thought he understood that I had nothing to do with planning what happened to his dad. What made Dan drop me in it? I was only on the bridge because Cathy and Martyn made me go. I'm the one who told George who was up there that day, otherwise he wouldn't have a clue. I can't believe he's double-crossed me.

I hug both of my boys again. Lisa steps towards me, arms out, but as we go to embrace, we both stop and watch Martyn being lifted onto a stretcher. She hesitates then looks back at me and smiles, bringing me in for a hug.

'Are you okay?' she asks, slightly breathless.

I nod and swallow down the relief that George didn't use the gun.

'What happened to Martyn? He looks in a bad way.'

I move slightly away from her, but still close enough to feel her breath on my face, and explain that George is Simon's son, and he was a baby when his dad was killed. 'Martyn got the rough end of George's wrath about his dad,' I say in a low voice. 'He's convinced Martyn killed Dan, maybe even Cathy.' I hope no one else can hear.

'He wouldn't do that, would he?' Her face creases up but she quickly pulls it straight again. 'At least you're okay. You gave me the fright of my life.'

'Tell me how you knew we were here.' I look from Ben to Scott, then to Lisa again.

'I let myself in. I brought the messages from the tree and other stuff left over from the party, but you weren't at home,' Ben says. 'Lisa had just arrived but didn't know where you were either.'

'I'd gone over early to give one of the dogs in the kennels its medicine,' Lisa explains, 'and thought it was odd for you to have gone out considering you were supposed to be resting. And it wasn't like you to lock the dogs in the kitchen, you normally keep them with you, even if they do disturb your sleep.'

'So we checked your doorbell camera and lo and behold it showed you being bundled into the boot of a car,' Ben says. 'We couldn't believe it! Anyway, we managed to catch a glimpse of the car's registration plate, so we called the police and they were able to get a clearer image and trace who owned it. They soon found out it was George Eyre's car, so they guessed you might be here at his nightclub, and sure enough his car is parked right outside.'

'He was upset with us about what happened to his dad, which is understandable but this was not the best way of dealing with it, especially with a gun.'

'But kidnapping you? What was he going to do?' Scott says.

'I don't know, but when he pointed it at me, I honestly thought he was going to kill me.'

'What did he do to you both?'

'The bouncers beat Martyn up and George pointed a gun at him and me. He knows Martyn killed his dad, with Cathy, but he thought I was behind it too. Which, I guess, is sort of true. But it was Martyn and Cathy who planned it all. They coerced me and Dan into helping. They were the ones in control.'

'So George killed Dan and Cathy?' Lisa asks.

'He doesn't seem to be behind it from what was said.'

It's not long before the police and the medical team give me the all-clear to go home. Ben and Scott support me either side as I walk out to the car. Martyn is being lifted on the stretcher into the back of an ambulance.

'Good riddance,' I say.

'Why do you say that?' Ben asks as Scott and Lisa stand waving. Martyn raises his hand just before the ambulance doors close. We all watch as it drives away.

'He was seeing Cathy behind my back. Can you believe it?'

'Shit, Mum. I'm so sorry.'

A policewoman who I remember from the hotel comes over and wants a quiet word with me. I walk with her a few paces away from the car while everyone else gets in.

'An autopsy has been carried out on Dan and his toxicology results have come back.'

'Is it bad news?' I ask stupidly, knowing full well that it's not going to be good, whatever the answer.

'I'm afraid so. He was poisoned with the same substance that killed Cathy.'

'He didn't drown?'

'No, there was no water in his lungs which indicates he was dead before he went into the water.'

'Christ. Who is doing this?'

'Unfortunately, at the moment we don't know.'

48

Ben drives me, Scott and Lisa back to my house. Lisa offers to stay with me for the night which I take her up on as I'm still shaky from the experience of the last few hours.

'Come in for a cup of tea,' I say to Ben and Scott as we pull up on the drive, 'there's something I need to tell you all.'

The tears come easily as soon as the dogs come running to greet me. I sit at the bottom of the stairs and let them lick my hands and face.

Lisa speaks as she bends down to fuss one of the dogs. 'When I popped in to give the new pug Chi-chi his medicine earlier, Morris and Monty were so miserable from being locked up in the kitchen. I let them in the garden, but instead of following me down to the kennels, they moped about looking for you.'

My heart breaks and I can't speak because all I can think of is one day not long from now, I'll never come back, and they won't understand that I've not willingly abandoned them. A knot of grief pulls across my chest. I must add to my will that the dogs are to be allowed to see my body. Let them sniff it, then they'll understand I've died.

Once the dogs have calmed down, Lisa insists on making everyone a cup of tea so I can sit back and relax after my ordeal. Scott rings for takeaway pizza while Ben lights the wood burner. By the time the food arrives, the living room is toasty warm and I'm grateful to be back with my family.

'What was it you wanted to tell us, Mum?' Scott asks, taking the last slice of pizza that no one else can manage. He's still young enough to have the appetite of a small village. I smile at him chomping away. His world is changing fast now he's moved out of the family home. Renting a flat with some of his college friends was a big step but the four of them managed to land full-time jobs so it seemed a natural next move. It's hard to believe he's not going to be a teenager for much longer. I'm so proud of him. He's developed into such a good-natured, thoughtful and caring young man. I hope he'll manage okay when I'm gone. It'll take time to grow accustomed to the loss, but with Tom and Ben's love and guidance, I'm confident he'll get through it reasonably unscathed. None of this stops me feeling anxious though, that I won't be here whenever he needs advice or a shoulder to cry on. I still miss my parents and wish they were around for me to ask advice or lean on for moral support.

I sense everyone has stopped talking, waiting for my answer with expectant faces.

'Sorry, I was miles away.'

I explain about my brother Alex being hit by Bob's car, the shock of his death, and Bob being convicted of death by dangerous driving as he deserved to be, except the sentence back then was so short, he would have got longer if he'd burgled a house.

'The pain and anguish it caused my parents was hard to bear. I was still a child, only thirteen when Alex died, and I didn't know how to handle it. Mum couldn't live knowing that "that man" was going to be walking around free in less than three years, breathing air, living his life while her little boy would never grow up. And Dad tried to obliterate everything with drink. He lost his job because he couldn't get up in the mornings. He'd be in bed with a hangover and neither of them were capable of looking after me. Our next-door neighbours Ros and Reg fed me most days. I'd get myself up for school and go to their house after school. At night Ros would drop me back home, but some days when Mum and Dad were at their worst, I'd stay over in their spare room.'

'Oh Mum, I'm so sorry. Why have you never told us this?' Ben asks.

'I was ashamed, I suppose. And my parents had been good to me up until Alex died. When I met your dad, I tried to build a new life. And when we had you two, I wanted to be there for you as much as I could.'

'And you have been, and we're grateful,' Scott says.

I take a deep breath and tell them what happened on the bridge that day. How Cathy, with Martyn's help, concocted a plan to scare Bob Eyre, maybe even cause him to have an accident, but none of us intended to kill him.

'Fucking hell, Mum,' says Scott.

'Does Dad know about this?' Ben's face is as white as a sheet.

I shake my head. 'I couldn't ever tell him. The four of us made a pact not to speak of it again. I thought if I told Tom, if I trusted just one person, I'd have broken my promise, and our secret could get out. We'd go to prison for murder or manslaughter. And I had you two by then and you needed me, and I couldn't bear the thought of not being there for you.'

The irony of what I'm saying makes me shake my head. Here I am leaving them too soon anyway. Not for the first time, I think my illness is a punishment for what I did.

'I know what you're thinking, I should have tried to stop them. Told them I didn't need them to fight my battles for me. But I was so fragile. I'd lost my brother and my mum almost a year after. I couldn't talk to Dad because he was always drunk. The way I saw it then was that my best friends had risked going to jail for me, the least I could do was keep my mouth shut. And I suppose I worried if I said anything, they'd call me ungrateful, get mad at me and reject me. I needed my friends. I didn't feel I had anyone else.'

'What about your marriage vows? Surely you promised not to keep secrets from each other?' Ben asks. He's probably thinking of himself and Emma and can't imagine keeping such a huge secret from her.

'I know,' I sigh. 'Maybe not being able to confide in Tom was the end of us before we'd even begun. It was so hard keeping it from him every single day.

Sometimes I worried I'd open my mouth and the words would fall out by themselves, so I had to stay vigilant at all times. Never get too drunk, never get too close in case I opened up about my past and gave something away.'

Lisa blinks at me. There's a strange look on her face I can't work out. She's been silent up until now. I'd almost forgotten she was here.

'I read somewhere that keeping a secret becomes like a poison coursing through your veins,' she says. 'Eventually it makes you ill and destroys you.'

She's looking at me so intensely, I have to look away. I don't know what she expects me to say to that.

'I think you're right. It's all such a mess. This is why I wanted to confess at my party about what we did. Speak up about what really happened that day. Tell everyone it was the four of us who killed Simon Eyre. We didn't mean to. It was a stupid, irresponsible thing to do. The police came to see if we knew anything about it, because of our family's connection to Bob being the driver who caused Alex's death. There had been a spate of kids dropping stones and rubbish from bridges onto moving vehicles, but the police had already made up their minds it was some older college boys. They arrested and questioned two of them although they were later released due to insufficient evidence. Their families were raging over it ruining their children's futures and made a complaint to the police authorities about wrongful arrest. But ultimately none of this was fair on Simon's family, not knowing the truth. I thought it was time for us to face our punishment, but Martyn didn't agree and stopped me saying it. And now Cathy and Dan are dead.'

'Do you think you and Martyn are still in danger, Mum?' Ben asks.

'I don't know. George swears he didn't kill Cathy and Dan, and he had the chance to kill us and didn't, so I guess he could be telling the truth.'

'It's not your fault, Mum.' Scott takes my hand and laces his fingers through mine.

I nod, acknowledging his kindness, trying to make me feel better, but the guilt and shame is embedded in me, it's become part of who I am. And I'm a bad, bad person for doing what I did.

'But if George didn't do it, who did?' Ben asks.

'I don't know. Someone is out for revenge. Whoever it is, they're still out there.'

49

'Could it be Martyn, given how he's betrayed you?' Scott asks.

'It's possible, although I'm not sure why he'd kill Cathy if they were planning on being together and adopting a baby.'

'Were they?' Ben frowns.

'I also found out he got Cathy to forge my signature and transfer my half of the house to him,' I say.

'What? Sneaky bastard,' Scott says.

'They were already cheating on me, so I suppose this was just another step in their grand plan. It wouldn't have been that difficult for her to copy my signature. As teenagers then later when we first started working, we'd practise signing our names on a big piece of paper and sometimes we'd attempt each other's.'

'Maybe it's someone else in the Eyre family?' Lisa asks.

'That's more likely, I think. There's something else I need to tell you all, but it's to go no further, okay?'

They all nod, looking around at each other.

'The police have told me that Dan's toxicology results came back from the autopsy. I wanted to tell you all the outcome.'

Everyone nods again solemnly.

I take another breath in. 'It's hard to believe this, but Dan was poisoned with the same substance that killed Cathy.'

'What?' says Scott.

'I know. It's been a massive shock to me too.'

'So do they think the same person killed both of them?'

'They didn't say but I'm guessing that's the police's assumption. I thought he'd drowned in the lake. But they said the autopsy showed he was dead before he hit the water.'

'Oh my God,' says Lisa. Scott and Ben look just as shocked. For a moment no one speaks.

'So does that mean he died then fell in the water

or did he die somewhere else and was moved there to make it look like he drowned?'

'I have no idea. They didn't give me any other details.'

Someone bangs on the front door, making me jump. I press a hand to my chest and freeze. My heart is racing. My mind instantly re-runs the banging on the door just minutes before I was kidnapped.

Ben frowns with concern at my reaction. 'It's okay Mum, I'll get it.'

I'm having a flashback to the banging sound waking me up. I'd checked my emails on my laptop in the living room after Lisa had left, then gone up for a nap. But my laptop isn't here. Where's it gone? The table is clear. How odd. I'd been sitting right there. I'm certain I left it open because I felt sleepy and went upstairs to lie down. Then I was woken up and came down to answer the door and that's when I was bundled into the boot of the car. I have a quick look around the room, but I can't see it. Someone has moved it. They could have seen the private email I was responding to on the screen. A message with information I wasn't planning on anyone knowing until after my death. I never got the chance to come back and put it away.

Ben stands in the doorway. He rubs his chin, something he does when he's not sure how I'll react.

'Who was it?' I ask. He comes into the room and Robbie is standing behind him.

'Can we help you?' I say, not standing up.

'I take it you've heard about Dan's toxicology results?' Robbie says.

'Yes, the police told me, and I was just this minute passing it on.'

'So you know they've ruled out George and Martyn as the perpetrators?'

'Really? I didn't know that.'

'I think they're on to something, but they're not giving out any more information.'

'You mean you think they know who did it?'

'Possibly.'

'But if it wasn't either of them, who was it?' Out of the corner of my eye I see Ben and then Lisa's eyebrows rise.

'Maybe they'll announce something soon. If they know.'

I don't know what to say. We all stare at Robbie, but no one answers, because we all suspect he did it.

'Actually, I've just been to the hospital to see Martyn.'

My eyes widen. I didn't know they were that friendly.

'The doctors say he may be home tonight. He's got two broken ribs and severe bruising around his face, but they've strapped him up.'

'How did you know he was in there?' Ben asks, then glances at me.

'He texted. Told me what had happened with your mum and George.'

'I didn't know you were that pally with him to be honest,' I say, standing up and showing him into the living room. I indicate an empty chair and he sits down, sinking into the softest seat in the room – it'll take an effort for him to get out again. I sit back on the sofa.

'Yeah, I know how it looked when we argued at the party, and he asked me to leave, but we actually get on okay.'

I can't say I've noticed. All I do is nod.

'Cathy was holding back telling you something,' Robbie says.

'Holding back? What hadn't she told me? I thought we were good friends.'

'She... she was worried about letting you down. Was always seeking your approval. Said she couldn't live up to your high standards.'

'What? Why didn't I know this? I had no idea she felt like that.'

Robbie nods slowly.

'So can you tell me what she was holding back?'

'Our big news. She decided it would be better to save it for another day, but sadly for her that never came.'

I glance round at everyone to gauge their reactions. They're listening to every word Robbie has to say. 'Why did she wait?'

'She didn't want to overshadow your special party.'

I wince as though the pain is physical and brace myself for the answer. 'So what was the big news?'

Robbie stares down at the ground then stretches out his legs. He sucks the air out of his cheeks, struggling to control his emotions. Then he looks up at me, tears shining in his eyes. My stomach drops.

'We were going to get married at Christmas. It was all planned. She was hoping you'd still... be able to come. We were going to ask you to be her maid of honour.'

'Oh Robbie, I'm so sorry.'

All I can think is that he has no idea about Cathy seeing Martyn and their adoption plans. She told me she was going to finish with him. Perhaps she didn't get the chance.

He nods and bites his lip. 'Ironic, isn't it?' He leans his arms on his legs and laces his fingers together, head down.

'Just a bit. I'm so sorry.' I wonder if Martyn knew about this?

'She was good for me, you know? It probably didn't seem that way from what you saw, but I've calmed down a lot, got my jealousy under control.' He half smiles and shakes his head. 'I know, I'm still a work in progress. She loved to wind me up, especially with Martyn, and then Dan came along, and I couldn't handle it and snapped. I'm so sorry about that. I wish I hadn't lashed out at him. Poor sod.'

'Wasn't you then?' Lisa pipes up, straight-faced.

What is up with her today? She's not normally so confrontational.

'Me?' Robbie frowns.

'Who killed Dan?'

'Seriously?' He grimaces at me as though Lisa's told him the worst joke and I'm the one who'll explain it.

'Are you okay, Lisa?' I tip my head at her to see if I've missed something, but she looks away.

'Yes, of course. Anyone want another drink?' She stands up.

I help her collect everyone's mugs and follow her out to the kitchen.

'Has someone upset you?' I ask and she spins round, back to the sink, not expecting me to be standing behind her. I spot Chi-chi's medication on the side.

'I said I'm fine,' she snaps, then more softly, 'thank you. Sorry.'

'That's good. I forgot to ask you, how was Chi-chi?'

'Seemed well, he ate all his food.' She nods.

'Good, good. Because his tablets are still there.' I point to two green capsules in a saucer by the back door.

'Oh God, what am I like? I must have gone up looking for you and completely forgotten to put them in his food.'

'You did feed him then?'

'Yeah, yeah. I'll go and give them to him in a sec.'

'Okay. Thanks.' I didn't mean to embarrass her, but she seems completely unnerved by something. I suppose the kidnapping has been an awful experience for her too.

'Was there something else?' Lisa flicks the kettle

on and faces me again.

'There was actually. When you let yourself in, was my laptop on the coffee table by any chance?'

She turns away and busies herself with filling the mugs with teabags.

'It's just I was in the middle of something important before I went up for a nap, then when the door went, I was bundled out to the car so didn't get a chance to close it.'

'Um, yes, come to think of it, it was. I thought it was odd, you leaving it there like that. I thought you must have been distracted, gone upstairs or something. That was why I went up to check on you. You're usually so careful.'

She's right, I am careful. I always shut it down without fail but this time I was too tired and distracted. Would she have been able to see what was on the screen or would it have locked itself? I can hardly ask her.

'I closed the lid and put it in the sideboard drawer. Why, is there a problem?'

'No, no problem. Thanks for doing that. It's fine, I just didn't know where it had gone.'

Except it's not fine at all. Because now I'm concerned she read the email from my solicitor, and that's the reason why she's so rattled.

50

As soon as I sit back down to drink my tea, my mobile rings. It's the DI. I glance round at everyone and take the call in the hall.

'We have some news,' she says carefully. 'I'm nearby and would like to come and speak to you if you're in and feeling well enough?'

'Okay. I'm not planning on going anywhere. I'm still recovering from my ordeal.'

'Yes of course. About that, George Eyre has been charged with kidnap and ABH and granted conditional bail.'

'Oh, I wasn't expecting that. That means they're releasing him?'

'I'm afraid so. He'll be up for his hearing at the end of the month.'

'Thanks for letting me know. See you soon.' I end the call and walk back into the living room, wondering what the DI is going to tell me. Robbie is still here, chatting with Lisa, Ben and Scott.

Robbie seems genuine to me despite his jealous streak. I had no clue that he and Cathy were going to tie the knot. Was she really going to leave him for Martyn and adopt a baby? I suppose I assumed she didn't like kids and wasn't the sort of person to change her mind. I feel bad now. Although to be fair to myself, that's how she's always joked about it. Perhaps she wasn't joking any more. People can change if they want to. She clearly had and I hadn't noticed. I treated her like she was the same person she was at sixteen.

'We were just talking about planning Cathy's funeral,' Robbie says to me, 'and I wondered if you wouldn't mind giving me some advice, maybe come with me to the pick out a casket for her?'

I raise my eyebrows.

'I hope I'm not speaking out of turn,' he continues. 'I know you're going through a difficult time yourself.'

'Not at all. In fact, I need to go and pick my own,

so we could do it at the same time. Maybe they'll do a two for one deal?' I laugh but no one else does. Scott looks horrified. 'Seriously, I'm happy to help you. I was expecting to arrange it as I think she had me and Martyn down as next of kin. Have they released her body?'

'Not yet, but they told me they're expecting to, in the next few days.'

'Does that mean they know who killed her?' Lisa asks.

'They must know something because the DI is on her way over here right now.'

Lisa gathers up all the empty mugs again and slopes off to the kitchen. I can't seem to work out what's going on with her. I open the sideboard drawer. My laptop is inside, just as she said. I open it and thankfully it has locked itself which means the battery life has been preserved. I then follow her into the kitchen and sit at the table. While Lisa makes the next round of teas and coffees, I type in my password.

As soon as I have access, I see that the email from my solicitor is still open on the screen. I glance over at Lisa who has her back to me, stirring sugar into a mug of instant coffee. I don't think it's possible for her to have seen it. The screen would have locked down by the time she arrived.

I tuck my laptop under my arm and climb the stairs to my office. I thought the door would be shut but it's not, it's ajar. I never leave it open because of the dogs jumping over everything. I look around the room but can't see anything out of place. Maybe I'm imagining it and I had left it open, or one of the dogs pushed the door with their nose. I close my laptop down properly.

As I'm about to leave, I notice the red light on the printer is flashing with the message, *out of paper*. From the top of my desk I grab an unopened ream, open it and take out a wad. I fan the ends back and forth so none of it sticks and slide it into the empty printer tray. As soon as I push it shut, the printer kicks into life, making all its quirky start up and con-figuration noises. A minute later it churns out a single page. I can't remember what I last printed, but it was several days ago. Maybe there was a page missing and I didn't realise. It's happened to me before.

I pick up the sheet and my heart thuds hard. It's the last page of the updated document sent by the solicitor. I definitely did not set this to print. I only viewed it on screen, yet the date printed at the bottom is today's date.

Someone has printed off a copy of my will.

51

As I'm making my way back downstairs, the doorbell rings.

'I'll get it,' Lisa says, coming out of the kitchen. She rests the tray of fresh teas she's holding on the hallway console table and lets the DI in. I grip the newel post to catch my breath.

'Is there somewhere we can speak in private for a moment?' the DI asks me.

Lisa takes the drinks into the living room, while I show the DI into the kitchen and shut the door.

'We've made a significant development in our investigation into Cathy and Dan's deaths. Is Cathy's partner here?'

'He's in the living room, why?'

'I've been trying to get hold of him. I feel I should tell you both first, away from everyone else.'

As I reach for the door handle, my mobile rings. I take it out of my back pocket and check the number.

'It's Martyn, can you give me a sec?'

She nods and I answer the call.

There are no pleasantries between us. He tells me he's being discharged and needs a lift home. The line goes dead confirming to me there is no future for us together, as if I needed any. Not even a goodbye. I suppose after what happened with George, it's not entirely surprising.

I lead the DI to the living room.

'The hospital has discharged Martyn,' I say. 'They need the bed or something, and he wants me to pick him up.'

'I'll go,' Lisa offers straight away.

'I don't mind,' Robbie says, sitting up.

'It's okay, I've already said I'd go,' Lisa says firmly, already reaching for her coat.

'Actually Robbie, the DI needs to speak to us privately. She's got some news.'

Robbie shrugs.

'Thank you,' I say, touching Lisa's arm.

'The DI can say it to me in here, in front of everyone. I'm not hiding anything,' Robbie says.

'Are you sure? It's about Cathy and Dan. She thought you might want to be told alone first.'

'No, no. Here's fine. I've got nothing to hide.'

The DI is standing right behind me. I move aside and she steps into the room. Everyone stops and looks up. Any smiles and chatter fall away.

'Afternoon, everyone. As friends of Dan, I thought you'd like to know that we've made contact with his parents and they're coming up tomorrow. I'm not sure if they're collecting his body or will be planning on holding his funeral near here, but I'll give them your number, Heather, and perhaps you can speak to them and let everyone else know so you have the opportunity to pay your last respects.'

Everyone nods, and although Robbie didn't know him, he nods too.

'I'll see you shortly,' Lisa says.

The DI waits for the noise of Lisa shutting the front door and driving away before she begins. 'I thought you'd like to know that we found a poisonous substance amongst Dan's possessions.'

'What, you think he killed Cathy?' Robbie sits up.

'Did he take his own life?' I ask.

'We believe so. We suspect he poisoned Cathy's drink at the party.'

'Oh no.' I drop onto the sofa between Ben and Scott. They both reach for my hands.

'What did he do that for, the stupid little shit.' Robbie rubs his hand over his face.

'There was a suicide note with an empty vial of poison. According to his dad he had attempted suicide before. Unfortunately, this time he decided to take Cathy with him.'

'Oh no. I knew he was fragile, but I had no idea how bad he felt.' I cup my mouth with my hand. The blow of seeing his lifeless body hits me all over again.

'But why kill Cathy too?' asks Ben.

'What did the note say?' Robbie asks.

The DI takes out her notebook and reads.

'I still love Cathy and this way I can be with her for all eternity. May God forgive me.'

'Was it handwritten?' Robbie asks.

'Yes, all in capital letters.'

I press my hand on my forehead. 'If only I'd spent more time talking to him. I should have seen what a terrible state he was in. Martyn and George going to see him after the party can't have helped his state of mind. I shouldn't have insisted on Martyn tracking him down. What a mess.'

'George went to see him?' the DI asks.

'Yes,' I say.

'I don't think we've got him on CCTV. Did he have a room there that night?'

'I'm not sure.'

'You can't blame yourself, Mum,' Scott says.

Part of me selfishly wonders if Dan mentioned to anyone apart from George, what happened to Simon Eyre. Maybe he didn't get the chance, but there's no guarantee that George won't.

52

Soon after the DI has left, Ben, Scott and Robbie leave too. My boys both hug and kiss me goodbye.

I bring down my laptop and open it. I switch it on and log in. There's a new email from my solicitor, asking me a question. I stare at it for a long while before answering it, stabbing at the keys as I reply. I check the printer history and note the time my document was printed.

When I hear Lisa's car pull onto the drive, my stomach lurches even though I was expecting her and Martyn to be back soon. I close my laptop and put it away. I'm not ready to face him. After everything that happened with George, I don't want to see him again.

He deserved everything he got. I know the lengths he will go to, to get what he wants.

I stand at the window and watch Lisa open the passenger door and offer Martyn her arm. He holds on to her as he pulls himself up. His face turns towards the house, and I move away from the window so he doesn't see me watching him. I should make myself scarce, go up to my office or into the kitchen but I'm curious to see what state he's in and what he has to say for himself.

He hobbles towards the front door, Lisa's arm linked with his. She's talking to him, but I can't hear what she's saying. The sound of her key in the door sends a stab of panic through me. I don't want them to think I've been waiting for their arrival, but on the other hand I need to know what's going on. I grab a book and sit in my favourite armchair and only look up when they're standing in the doorway.

'You can put him on the sofa,' I say to Lisa, as though she has a stray dog with her. 'I brought some cushions and a duvet down for him to use,' I say.

I can't even bear to say his name. If he thinks he's going to sleep in our bed, he's mistaken. I need to keep a close eye on him. When he's better he can move out, find his own place.

'Thank you,' Lisa says for him. 'They've given him

these tablets. Two every four hours for the pain, muscle relaxants and these to prevent infection.'

I shrug because quite honestly, I couldn't care less. It has nothing to do with me any more.

Martyn mumbles his thanks. He's stooped over and glances up at me then down again, defeated. I don't move. I'm not clearing out of the way; why should I? And I'm not offering to make him a drink either. He's only here because he has nowhere else to go. All this time I've trusted him, believed he loved me and that he was sad I was dying and was going to be lost without me, when all the time he was cheating on me. To think I've wasted my last few months and years with him. It sickens me.

Lisa helps him sit on the sofa then she takes off his shoes with great care, one at a time. She plumps up the pillow and lays it on the arm rest. Then she slides her arm beneath his ankles and lifts them onto the sofa as he swivels at the same time so he's lying down. She opens the single duvet, and fluffs it out before covering him in it right up to his chin.

I can't stay in the same room as him any longer. I stand up and go into the kitchen to make myself some soup and take my medication.

While I'm cutting onions and carrots, Lisa comes in and takes two mugs out of the cupboard to make tea. I don't speak to her, waiting for her to say something.

'Do you want a cup?' she asks.

'No, thanks.'

I can't look at her. I'm biding my time. I need to pick my moment to ask her if she printed a copy of my will.

While the soup is bubbling, I quietly look through the gap in the door. Lisa is fussing away trying to straighten Martyn's pillow while he's sitting up. His hand rests on her waist. She looks down at him and he up at her. Their faces are so close. I quietly move away, grinding my teeth.

Back in the kitchen, my phone beeps. I pick it up but it doesn't say who it's from. There's a two-word message on the screen.

Unfinished business.

53

An hour later, I'm getting ready for bed when I hear Lisa come up. I could ask her about the printer now, but I'll wait. The dogs sit at the end of the bed as I get in. I listen to every creak of the floorboards and the spare room door opening and closing, even the sound of Lisa brushing her teeth and getting into bed across the landing. I should have told her to go home. I don't want her here any more. I thought she was my friend, but she's shown her true colours, snooping around my private emails, printing my will. I keep my side light on. I'm so tired I can't help shutting my eyes.

At midnight, the front door sensor alert on my phone goes off, stirring me from my light sleep. I open the app and check the camera, replaying the last few seconds. There's a figure in a hoodie approaching the front door.

I swing my legs off the side of the bed. The dogs jump down with a thud, the sound enough to wake the dead. I wait a few seconds but there's no reaction from next door or the living room. I doubt if Martyn could get up even if he wanted to with all the drugs he's had to take.

In what feels like a matter of moments I am in my dressing gown, creeping down the stairs. My fingers grip the banister. I mustn't rush and miss my footing or slip on the edge of a stair. My ankle is still sore.

The silence in the house is palpable but every step I take seems too loud. The stairs creak. My joints click and crack. The dogs sniff under the door. I should have closed it completely.

'What's wrong, Heather, where are you going?' Lisa calls out from the top of the stairs, making me jump. Her tone is accusatory, menacing. I didn't hear her leave her room. Did I wake her? Is that why she's stalking around in the dark?

I glance up at her looming over me, larger than life in the shadows and darkness. Her skinny arms and legs remind me of a large insect from a children's book. I'm suddenly disorientated and shaky and I instinctively reach for the banister with my other hand to steady myself. This is my house; she has no right questioning what I'm doing.

'I'm fine, go back to bed.' I silently berate myself for the uneasiness in my voice. Now she knows I'm nervous, scared even, because I don't know what she'll do. She saw that email and printed off the document. She knows what I have planned. But I had to do it for the sake of my boys; surely she understands that?

'Let me come and help you.' Without waiting for a reply, she takes a step towards me, the stairs creaking. I wish she'd go away and stop pretending to care about me. I grip the banister tighter, worried she's going to rush forward and unbalance me, sending me tumbling down the stairs.

'I can manage on my own.' My voice is strained and high-pitched like an old lady. What's happened to me? I used to be so strong and confident. I inch down to the next step, holding the banister so tightly my hands are sweating.

'Leave me alone,' I say as I twist round.

One more stair and I'll be on the ground. The security light flashes on in the porch and a face peers in through the small pane of glass.

'Who is that?' Lisa asks and suddenly she's

stomping past me, clipping my arm and unbalancing me, and I have to grip harder to stay upright.

'What's going on?' Martyn's feeble voice calls from the living room.

Lisa unbolts the front door and thrusts it open in one sweeping move.

A tall, slim figure is standing there with their back to us in a dark raincoat, jeans and white trainers.

'What do you want?' Lisa asks.

'I've come to sort out some unfinished business,' he says turning to face her, a menacing grin on his face.

54

Lisa tries to shut the door on him, but he thrusts out his hand and it bounces back, narrowly avoiding hitting her face.

'Where is he?' George pushes the door wide and steps inside.

'Who?' Lisa says, frowning in my direction, fingers touching her lips, shock in her wide eyes.

'Martyn.' His voice is flat. He shuts the door behind him and suddenly Lisa is by his side, holding his arm, smiling up at him. What is she doing?

'He's in here.' She flicks a smug glance at me as she slides her fingers between George's and leads him into the living room. I stumble down from the last stair, reeling. Dots of light swim across my vision. I shut my eyes for a second.

What is going on? How do they know each other? Why doesn't he push her off? I shuffle along to the living room where George is standing over Martyn with a cushion in his hands.

'Wait, what are you doing?' I pull on the crook of his arm, but he elbows me away.

'I told you, I've got unfinished business.'

'What do you mean? You can't do this in my house, then disappear and make me look guilty.'

There is fear in Martyn's eyes. He's not moving an inch. What is wrong with him? I thought he'd be sitting up defending himself, even if he is in pain.

'That's what he wants you to think.' Lisa grins at me then gazes at George, stroking his arm.

'What are you talking about? How do you know his business?'

How have I not noticed these two together before? Were they like this at my party?

'I know everything,' Lisa says, her sickly grin going up to her eyes so they're almost closed. She's like a cat taking great pleasure in licking a dish full of cream, tipping her chin up at him, but he seems indifferent to her cloying attention. 'Your kidnap was supposed to be the end of both of you until Ben turned up and called the police.'

'I thought we had an understanding?' I say directly to George, bypassing Lisa. 'I told you the truth, gave you the names of everyone involved so I could atone for my part in what we did to your dad, and you were to deal with the three of them in your own way. I wasn't expecting you to add me to that list. Bundling me into the boot of a car and threatening me with a gun.'

George's face changes to a grimace as he grips the cushion tighter. 'I figured you were still involved in my dad's death. You were the *reason* Cathy came up with the plan, whether you knew about it or not. But you failed to tell me you were involved in dropping the rock from the bridge. You were complicit in your silence, letting my family suffer all these years, not knowing who killed my dad, not having the justice he deserved.'

He comes towards me, clenching his teeth and I slowly back away holding my hands up. Lisa sits on Martyn's chest so he can't move. Why doesn't he even speak?

'Don't forget I lost someone too. My brother was only a child when he died because of your grandad.'

'And I told you, he suffered for it for the rest of his

life,' he bellows. 'People shunned him in the street, knowing what he'd done. He lost friends, his job, his health.'

'We've been over this. My family suffered too. Don't you think I've been through enough? I've carried the guilt of what I did for so long. I'm dying anyway, so why make me suffer more?'

'Because I need it to end. Right here, right now.' He pounds his fist into the cushion. 'If I let you go, what does that say about my loyalty to my dad, and to my grandad?' He drops the cushion and takes a box of matches out of his pocket.

'Please, don't do this.' I back away. 'You said yourself that your granddad didn't want you to take revenge, that's why he didn't tell you what happened to your dad sooner.'

'But you all came after my grandad, so now I'm coming for all of you.' He shakes the matchbox next to his ear and listens to the sound.

'How long have you known Lisa?' I'm finding it difficult to keep the alarm out of my voice but I need to delay him. I'm in shock that Lisa has hoodwinked me. I glance behind me. Maybe if I distract him for a second or two, I can get to the utility room and lock myself in then get out of the back door.

'Georgy and I go way back to when we were both

little kids.' She stands up and strokes his face, one finger at a time. It's disturbing the way she says his pet name in such a baby voice.

'Lisa?' Martyn's voice is croaky. He's finally clocked the way she is with him. He's clearly put out by seeing her like this with George.

'What do you want, old man? Did you really think I was interested in you?' She uses the same weird breathless baby voice to show how sorry she is for him. She leans down and pushes out her bottom lip, tilting her head mockingly to one side then the other. When Martyn doesn't respond, she laughs cruelly in his face.

I've never seen her like this before. Has she been putting on an act with me all this time? It's as though she's become a different person. Martyn isn't saying anything. I don't understand why he's so subdued, not sticking up for himself in his usual bolshy way.

'What do you mean? Why are you saying that to him?' I ask, as if I haven't noticed the attention she's been giving him, like going overboard showing concern for him when the police came into George's nightclub to free us. She couldn't stop checking to see if he was okay, even when she was speaking to me. Then making sure it was her who went to pick him up from hospital and fussing over him when he got here. What was it all for? Now she's being cruel to him because she's clearly with George.

'Don't you know yet? Are you so blind?' she says, as she caresses George's arm.

'Know what?'

'That Martyn's in love with me. He told me he's wanted me for weeks.'

'But he was having an affair with Cathy, I saw them together in a restaurant, kissing.'

'Yeah he was, and it helped me put you off the scent while I was reeling him in.'

'Why are you doing this to me? I thought we were friends.'

The kind, quiet, caring woman I've come to rely on as my business partner and best friend is not a friend at all, she's been undermining me at every turn, and now she's being rude and disrespectful to me in my own home.

'Why can't I move?' Martyn shouts but the words are slurred and his mouth makes strange shapes as though he has no control over it. The panic in his voice gut punches me. His body twitches as he attempts to move.

'Do you need the toilet?' Lisa asks him in her babyish voice again. 'Aww, are you going to piss yourself, old man?' Her voice becomes deeper, guttural and sarcastic.

'Why can't he move, what have you done to him?'

'What, are you telling me you care about him now? You've practically kicked him out of your house. He's only sleeping here because he's just come out of hospital, so don't make out you give two hoots about him,' Lisa shouts at me in a much deeper voice.

'You can talk, you clearly don't care about him either. Tell me why he can't move.'

'I might have added a few extra muscle relaxant tablets to his drink. Just to make sure he doesn't cause us any trouble.' A smile creeps up one side of Lisa's face.

A shiver runs through my body. I steal a look at Martyn then away again. Whatever happens, I'll never be able to lift him up and carry him out of here.

I need to save myself now.

55

'It's you who's been looking at my laptop, reading my emails, isn't it?' I ask her.

'Not much gets past you does it, Miss Marple?' Lisa laughs and even that sounds different to what I'm used to.

I draw in a short breath at her cutting sarcasm. We've barely had a cross word in all the time we've known each other, and she's certainly never been rude or cheeky to me.

'No, it does not. And I was right to change my will, wasn't I? Is that what this is all about, trying to get money out of me?'

'Don't worry about that, we still can,' George buts in. 'Lisa's messaged your solicitor using your email, instructing her to change it back, saying you made a mistake. So when you die, Lisa will still get the kennel business and buildings you promised her.'

'I saw that, but my solicitor won't accept your request because it's been flagged as fraudulent. I've given her your name as the culprit.'

Lisa's eyes widen then she spits at me with full force. I recoil in disgust.

'You would never have got this past my ex-husband anyway,' I yell at her.

'He'll be our next target. He must have known your dirty little secret all the time you were married to him. Thought it was okay being married to a murderer, did he?' George snarls.

'He didn't know anything about what happened on the bridge,' I shout. The thought of them harming Tom, cuts deep.

'Aw look, she still cares about him,' Lisa says in her baby voice again. 'Maybe it's time to put this one out of his misery, because, let's be honest, no one gives a shit about him.' She slaps Martyn across the face.

'It seems there's only one solution remaining.' George's voice is low and menacing as he slides the matchbox open.

'You can't do that!' My voice is uncontrollably

high as I yank on his arm. He swats me away, sending me across the floor, then he swings round to face me. 'This was *our* plan all along. Did you think I was going to let you off for killing my dad?'

'I told you they made me do it.' I grip the coffee table and pull myself up.

'Hey, don't forget about my mum, she was injured as well,' Lisa says.

'What the hell are you talking about?' I scream at her. She's making all this so much worse.

'My mum was driving a Mini behind Bob Eyre's car that day. She had to brake so hard when Bob came to a sudden halt that her legs got trapped and she had to have physio for weeks. I was in the back in a child's seat aged three. Yes, I survived uninjured, but my mum has struggled from that day and it's all your fault our lives have been so difficult. She's never been the same since. I lost the happy, carefree mum I'd known and loved and it's all your fault.'

I stare at her, dumbfounded. I remember hearing a second bang as we ran away. But we'd kept on running.

'I'm so sorry Lisa, I didn't know what had happened to your mum. What we did was a terrible, cruel thing. I've regretted it every single day since. But we were kids, angry and impulsive. It's not an excuse but we didn't understand the full consequences of what we were doing. Honestly, we thought the worst that would happen would be to make Bob swerve. It was such a quiet road, it seemed unlikely another car would be involved. Martyn and the others convinced me that Bob should pay for what he did. His prison sentence was laughably short, and they said I should get justice for Alex, but I didn't know that meant killing him. Bob Eyre was happily back with his family, walking around a free man. How could that be right? I don't remember hearing about another car being involved or that someone else had got hurt. We were all so in shock at Simon's death that we promised each other to keep away from the local news and we never spoke about what happened.'

'Save the lecture.' Lisa's voice is cold and curt. 'I've had enough of your pathetic excuses, your whining and privileged moaning, to last me a lifetime.'

'I'm so sorry, Lisa. I know I can never make it up to you, or George.'

'We'll see about that,' George says, tapping the box of matches.

'I've come to rely on you so much, as a colleague and a friend.'

'Yeah, yeah, all while taking the credit for the growth of the business. Remember when the local paper came to do a story on you? You put your glad rags on and had a lovely photo shoot while I was with the dog walkers and helpers in the background, shovelling up shit. Admit it, you've used me as your personal slave since I've been here, and I've had enough.'

'That's not true. The journalist spoke to you as well. You didn't want to dress up and be in the photos with me. You said I should be the one in the limelight. I told them how hard you worked and that you saved the business with your innovative ideas. I don't know why they left it out of the article. I thought we worked well together, as a partnership as well as friends.'

Lisa shakes her head. 'Never friends. I let you think that, but every day I was plotting against you, gaining your trust.'

'But that's why I was leaving the business to you, because I valued your friendship so highly.'

'It was all in your head. Anyway, you changed your will, took all that away and didn't think to tell me.' She gives me an ugly snarl.

'Only because Tom persuaded me to leave it to the boys. Said I should be keeping it in the family and

helping them out more. He thought you'd understand.'

Lisa grinds her teeth together. The dogs have
started whining, shut in my bedroom.

'Did he now? Charming. I only took this poxy job
to find out if all the rumours were true.'

'What rumours?'

'Mum talked about the rumours – who everyone
thought was up on the bridge that morning. All sorts
of names were flying around for years. Martyn's name
was one of them. Your dad's name was always in there
too. Everyone said it had to be connected to what
happened to Alex. And at the time, Mum said a lot of
people thought it was justified. In that position they'd
probably have taken matters into their own hands
too. They were raging over his behaviour, not looking
before pulling out. But that didn't help us. After the
accident, Mum had to go on sick leave for weeks.
Went down to half pay at one point but she couldn't
do anything about it until she got better. She has mobility problems with her legs now and it restricts
what sort of work she can do. Our lives were never
the same after that. We scraped by. Not to mention
the pain Mum is often still in and the medication she
has to take.'

George smacks a fist into the top of the sofa.

I step back. His expression has darkened.

'And so you see, that's why Cathy and Dan had to pay for their part in killing my dad, and now it's Martyn and you.'

56

'But I thought the police cleared you of that because of the suicide note. They said he killed Cathy, then himself.' I was so convinced Dan had taken his own life, but the culprit has been staring me in the face, along with the person pretending to be my loyal friend.

'We were careful to make it look like that, weren't we?' Lisa says and George nods. 'I fixed Cathy's drink at the party and George handed it to her. Then I gave Dan a small dose in his glass of whisky before he went up to his hotel room. George was in our room next door. I texted him to say Dan was on his way up to bed, and Martyn was following him. George listened to their argument through the wall, and he was the one who complained about it to the police the next day. So after Martyn left Dan's room, George went there with a bottle of whisky, and they had a little chat. Once he'd got all the information he needed, he laced Dan's drink. I knew someone who used to work there so it was easy to get a spare key card and let myself in earlier in the evening while you were all downstairs, hide the vial of poison with the suicide note, to be discovered later by the police.'

'No!' I shout. Martyn lets out a mournful groan.

'It was his own stupid fault for wandering down to the lake in his pyjamas when he was probably not feeling well and of course he was very drunk, which helped. He must have collapsed and fallen headfirst into the water.'

'But he was already dead when he hit the water. You killed him,' I say, slowly shaking my head.

'Shame there wasn't enough evidence for the police to charge you, Martyn, even with that glass of yours I left in his room. Wore my heavy overcoat so he'd think I'd come from outside not the room next to him, and when he wasn't looking I switched my glass for yours in my pocket. He was so drunk, he probably wouldn't have noticed anyway. You could be safe in police custody right now,' George adds.

'How is it they haven't caught you on CCTV going into his room?'

'Disguised myself as staff.' Lisa grins at my seemingly stupid question. 'The whole thing was laughably easy.'

'So was it you sending those threatening text messages to me and Dan?'

'Of course it was,' Lisa laughs.

'But how could you have known about Cathy's abortion?'

'My nan worked at the clinic for ten years, said she recognised a girl from my year. Told me she turned up with a boy and they sat in the waiting room holding hands, heads together, whispering. Didn't take much to work out it was Cathy with her ginger hair and the heartthrob of the school.'

I don't know what to say. She's completely fooled me.

'Heather?' Martyn whimpers.

I try not to look at his pitiful face. We've let each other down and now we're on our own.

'And I told you what you wanted to hear,' George says, cutting in. 'Lisa and I have been following you and Martyn for months, years in fact. My grandad and Lisa's mum long suspected your family must be behind Dad's death, but we couldn't prove it. Bloody police were useless, not finding any evidence or questioning you kids about where you were that morning.'

'George and I met at a memorial for his dad three years ago,' Lisa says, taking over. 'We had an interesting chat shall we say. I was already working for you by then of course, gaining your trust, waiting for my moment to prove you were involved. It made sense for George to jump on board and join me in my quest.'

George nods his agreement. 'When you came to me to confess what you knew about that day, it only confirmed what we'd already suspected – that all of you were involved in killing my dad.'

'It wasn't like that for me, I didn't plan anything, I already told you.'

'I only have your word for that.'

'Not her fault.' Martyn's words are slurred. He tries to shake his head, but it doesn't move more than an inch in either direction.

'Sweet, loyal Martyn.' Lisa laughs. 'Like I said, my nan clearly remembers seeing you being all lovey-dovey with Cathy in the abortion clinic waiting room when you were supposed to be dating Heather. She knew your nan from the WI. Mum was in hospital from the crash, and no one knew who was responsible for her injuries or Simon's death, but your family's name was on everyone's lips.' She stabs her finger at me.

'Whatever. I'm sick of all of this.' George strikes a match and lights a candle in a glass jar on the coffee table. Lisa takes her outdoor gloves from her pocket and runs upstairs. My pulse quickens at the thunder of the dogs jumping off my bed and running downstairs. They run straight to me and I reach out so they can lick my hands, but as soon as Lisa calls their names, they follow her into the kitchen. She's been as much a part of their lives as I have. I can see now she's made sure they are trained to her command. We hear the back door open in the utility room and Lisa sends them outside. Then she locks the door and comes back in.

'They don't deserve to be harmed,' she says without looking at me, then picks up the candle with a gloved hand.

'What are you going to do?' I cry and follow them as they parade one after the other into the adjacent dining room as if they are performing some kind of ceremony. George rests the candle on a side table near the thick velvet curtains, then gives the glass container a sharp nudge. It tips onto its side and the flames lick the curtain fabric, instantly setting them alight.

57

'What the hell are you doing?' I scream and grab a vase from the table and fruitlessly chuck the tiny volume of water along with the roses at the growing flames.

'We'll keep these.' George picks up my keys, laptop, our mobile phones and the Ring doorbell batteries, and drops them in a black rucksack he's left by the front door. 'All the windows and doors are locked and we have the keys, so don't bother trying to get out.'

'Good thing you upgraded to double glazing.' Lisa grins. She was the one who persuaded me to have it installed this time last year.

'Enjoy watching each other die,' George says. They high-five each other then both put their hoods up and quietly leave by the front door, locking it after them. I watch out of the window to see where they go, but there's no car, no engine starting up. Instead they walk off round the corner. Maybe they parked in the next street or they could be on foot so as not to draw any attention to themselves.

I quickly grab a blanket from the arm of the sofa, close the living room door and shove the material in a roll along the gap to stop the smoke getting in. That should keep Martyn safe for a while. Then I grab a bucket from under the sink in the utility room and half fill it with water; it's all I can carry. Going back-wards and forwards half a dozen times, I chuck water again and again at the curtains, but the flames keep climbing and spreading.

It's not long before almost the whole wall is alight, and the air is thicker now with smoke. Pulling open a drawer next to the sink in the kitchen, I hunt through it for a clean dishcloth. There's one left in a packet under some leaflets. I dampen it with water and hold it to my nose and mouth so I can breathe.

There must be other ways of contacting Ben and Scott or alerting a neighbour. I'm sure there's a spare mobile phone in the junk drawer or an old laptop of Martyn's in my study. But where are the chargers? Why did I let Lisa persuade me to get rid of the land-line? I always kept an old-fashioned dial phone plugged in at the wall, which we could use if there was a power cut. She insisted people don't need or use house phones any more and that it's just an added expense. I shouldn't have listened to her, but she made me feel old and out of touch. I thought she was being frank with me, helping me because she was my friend. Her betrayal and my realisation she didn't want the best for me hurts like a kick in the chest. Her spiteful words spin around in my head.

I can't worry about what Lisa's done to me now. I take a deep breath, I need to focus, hurry, or we're not going to get out of here alive. I'm not sure Ben or Scott will find out what's gone on here. The smell of smoke is acrid with chemicals from the curtains and paint. There must be a way out that I haven't thought of.

I climb the stairs and try to be quicker than my usual snail's pace, but my legs feel so heavy and sore, I need to sit down, but I can't waste time. My eyes are already watering from the smoke. I don't find any-thing useful so go back downstairs and through to the utility room, shutting the door behind me. At least the smoke hasn't reached here yet. For the moment the fire is on the other side of the house and there are only fields beyond, so it's unlikely anyone will see anything for a while.

I perch on the pullout steps. I'm so tired but I need to wrack my brains. What should I do? *Think.* What would Ben tell me to do?

Then it comes to me. He and Emma gave it to me in case of an emergency. I'm supposed to carry it around the house at all times. Something that could save us. If only I knew where it was. I get up, groaning inwardly and stand on the first step. The wall cupboard isn't as tidy as I'd like it to be. There are baskets on the top shelves of all sorts of odds and ends. On the bottom shelves are packets of cleaning sponges and free sachets of washing liquid, plastic bottles of paint from when the kids were still at home, and a half bottle of bubble mixture that's probably been there ten years. On the middle shelf is a box of Halloween decorations, half used candles and an oil burner. I move up to the next step, hanging onto the cupboard door for support.

I rummage through the boxes. Maybe I gave it away. I can't remember because I never used it even though Ben set it up for me. A little fizz of hope rushes through my veins, pushing me on. But as soon as I pull out one tub, I have to stop and double over coughing. The smell of burning is much stronger now. I glance round at the door. Smoke is drifting under and around the edges, silently curling upwards. My eyes dart about the room. I need a cloth to cover the gaps or I'm going to be unconscious in a matter of minutes.

Carefully I step back down the steps. The washing machine is full of wet towels. For once I'm grateful I forgot about them. I tug them out and chuck them at the bottom of the door with a slap. The sloppy heap should be enough to hold back most of the fumes for now.

Back up the steps I pull at basket after basket. I used to keep spare keys in one of them, but they're not there now. Maybe I gave them to Tom or one of the children. I need to find the personal emergency alarm Ben and Emma bought for me a few months ago. He sat at the kitchen table setting it up. I wanted to tell him not to bother. My face was flushed hot with embarrassment. It was thoughtful of them, but it made me feel so useless. I didn't think I should need something like that at my age. I couldn't bring myself to use it. But I remember now, he said it stored emergency telephone numbers so when I pressed the SOS button, it would automatically call his mobile. If he didn't answer, it would try Scott, the next number on the list, and so on. Said it was better than a basic one that went through to a central contact centre. I put it somewhere out of the way. I think back to when I opened the package, Emma saw how much it upset me. I was so stubborn and in denial when I first got my diagnosis. Daft really because I only made it worse for myself turning away help, pretending this wasn't really happening to me.

But now I'm glad. Lisa doesn't know I have this. And now this emergency button is my only hope of getting out of here alive.

Finally, I spot it on the top shelf tucked away at the back behind a DIY manual, hidden away so no one would find it. I pick it up in its ugly little carry case and bring it down the steps.

It's fiddly undoing the press buttons on the carry case, they're so tight, my nails bend and almost tear off, but I manage to open it and switch the unit on. It still has 10 per cent of its battery life remaining. I press the emergency button hard. As soon as I hear Ben's voice, I start tearing up.

'Mum, what's wrong? Have you fallen?'

'I'm okay, but please call the fire brigade quickly,

send them to my house as soon as possible. The house is on fire and Martyn and I are trapped inside.'

I slump down on the steps, coughing. The almost invisible smoke is seeping in around the door.

All I can do now is hope they arrive before it's too late.

58

I don't know how long it is before I hear the fire engine's siren, because I've lost all sense of time. I feel so sleepy, slumped on the floor. The fire must have reached through the kitchen by now because the wisps of smoke are growing into thicker ribbons coursing through the cracks around the door. I daren't open it for fear of being overwhelmed by flames and fumes.

At last, someone is pounding on the front door, making the whole house shake. I presume it's a fire-fighter attempting to break it down with one of those metal battering rams. A man's voice shouts from the garden, asking where we are. It takes all the energy I have left to bang on the door with the wooden end of a scrubbing brush. I shout back that Martyn is lying on the sofa in the living room. They tell me to stand clear, they're going to break down the door. A couple of minutes later the outline of a firefighter's yellow helmet appears through the glass. In two thuds it opens and I'm being covered in a blanket and led into the garden to safety. The dogs run up and greet me as they always do with licks and barks of joy.

'Mum, are you okay?' Ben cries as he and Scott rush forward and wrap their arms around me.

'We were so worried,' says Scott.

'What happened? Is anyone else inside?'

'Martyn, but hopefully they've found him.'

At that moment they carry him out on a stretcher, oxygen mask to his face. A paramedic comes up to me and says they want me to go to hospital for a check-up. DS Stone comes over and takes down some details. I tell her they need to catch up with George and Lisa quickly. I give her as much information as I can before my throat is too sore to carry on.

Ben comes with me in the ambulance while Scott stays to check on the animals and promises he'll be along shortly. The kennels are far enough away down the garden not to be in any danger, thank goodness.

As we drive away, it's clear that at least half of the house has been destroyed. The firefighters are still wrestling to put out the flames. The firefighter who helped me get out told me that another ten minutes and I'd have been overwhelmed with smoke and may not have survived.

On the way to A&E, I explain to Ben as best as I can what happened, although I have to keep stopping to cough and the paramedic insists on me using the oxygen mask.

'I always thought Lisa was such a kind person. I can't believe she was plotting against you,' he says.

'Neither can I. Cathy and Martyn too. The people who I thought I could trust the most were only pretending to be my friends, and were the ones out to hurt me, and I didn't see it.'

'I'm so sorry they let you down, Mum. You have us though,' Scott says.

'And you two are more important to me than anyone.'

EPILOGUE
SEVEN MONTHS LATER

Emma strolls out of the patio doors carrying baby Alfie.

'Would you like to hold him?' she asks me, beaming.

'I'd love to, thank you.' I move the book from my lap and she places the sleeping bundle in my arms. He's already five months old and has brought me so much joy in the short time he's been alive than I ever thought possible. Ben and Scott come out of the kitchen and lay the trays of burger rolls, sauces and salads on the table in front of me.

'Sausages are ready,' Tom calls from behind the BBQ.

I stare at Alfie's perfect face and gently kiss his

soft creamy skin. Although I won't be here to see him grow up, I feel I can die happy now that I've spent plenty of precious time holding my beautiful grandson in my arms. In the end, life is about the small joys each day brings us and the love of those we care about most in the world.

It took a couple of weeks for my throat to feel near normal again after all the smoke I inhaled from the fire. Ben and Scott took it in turns looking after me at Ben and Emma's house, while the police and the insurance company carried out their investigations. The house is slowly being renovated and I won't be able to move back in for at least another six months.

Martyn passed away in hospital that day from the effects of smoke inhalation. He didn't deserve to die like that, but I can't help thinking how much he betrayed me. I tried my best to save him, but my heart wasn't in it like it once was. He always had that lying streak in him and I just wish I'd been aware sooner.

George and Lisa were caught trying to board a boat to France after a nationwide manhunt. DI Bradbury told me that in his defence statement, George accused me, Martyn, Dan and Cathy of causing the death of his father, but as there is no new evidence, he was told there was no case to answer, plus she said

it had no bearing on his own charges of kidnap and
ABH. Lisa's been charged with the murders of Cathy,
Dan and Martyn and of attempting to defraud me.
George was further charged with being an accessory
to murder and fraud.

'What can I get you, Mum?' Scott asks, holding a
plate ready for me at the table.

'Hang on.' Ben puts his plate down, opens his
phone and takes a photo of me holding Alfie. There
are so many photos and short videos of me now, it
really feels like I'll never be forgotten.

'I'm okay at the moment thanks, you get yours
first.' I gaze down at my sweet grandson and wish for
this afternoon to stretch on for as long as possible
because I'm enjoying every second I have left.

ACKNOWLEDGEMENTS

Tomorrow is not guaranteed for any of us, so my mindfulness app reminds me. This was a tough book to write for many reasons, especially being the subject of someone who is dying before their time.

I couldn't have written this story without the help of a small, dedicated army of people. Thank you firstly to my supportive agent, Jo Bell, for always being so encouraging and positive. Enormous thanks to my incredible editor, Emily Yau, for trusting me to write this story and for her thoughtful and incisive notes, which helped to make this a better book. Thanks to the whole dedicated team at Boldwood Books, led by the inimitable Amanda Ridout.

Thanks once again to Candida Bradford for catching all my errors in the copy edit. Any mistakes remaining are completely down to me. Thank you to Aaron Munday for creating the most stunning cover of *Guilty*. I loved it at first sight! Thank you to Rachel Sargeant for your proof-reading skills.

Special thanks as always to my husband Richard, my children, daughter-in-law and my parents, for their unwavering belief in me. To all my writing friends for their support, especially Rose McGinty, for her advice and lovely chats.

This book is dedicated to Lucy Fassett, a thoughtful, brave and brilliant old schoolfriend of mine, who inspired the seed of this story with her own farewell party, held just weeks before her death in 2017 aged just forty-eight. I was unable to attend because of my own health reasons, but in hindsight that distance allowed me to create this story guilt-free, mainly from my own imagination but also inspired by photos from her party. All the characters and plot in my story are pure fiction, but I have named a minor character after Lucy. I think she would have liked that.

I'd also like to pay tribute to Lindsey Mooney, the fierce and dedicated co-founder of my first publisher, Hera Books, who took a chance on me with my debut novel, *Someone Else's Baby*, back in 2019. Lindsey died suddenly in November 2023 aged forty-two, at the time I was writing this book.

I drew heavily on my own experience of ill health to create the character of Heather. I don't have a terminal illness, but my poor mobility due to severe scoliosis became so bad two years ago, that I could hardly walk or stand for more than a few minutes at a time. My world shrank so small that I had to reimagine my future and work out how I was going to explain to my children that I wouldn't be there for them in the way I wanted to be. (Thankfully I've since had steroid injections in my back, which are helping to keep me going along with exercise.)

I chose not to give Heather a specific illness (although I've hinted at the big C) because I didn't want one ailment to be the focus of her story. Also, I was reliably advised that not everyone's symptoms would necessarily be the same, and I didn't want to misrepresent a condition that I have no experience of, especially in the sensitive case of an end-of-life scenario.

Finally, I'd like to say a huge thank you to all the book bloggers, reviewers, librarians, bookshop owners, and most of all thank you to you, my wonderful readers.

If you or someone you know is considering having a living funeral/farewell party, I highly recommend the book, *I'm Dying... Let's Party! Saying your goodbyes – before you die* by Susan Lake-Harris, which is a practical guide and describes a variety of personal stories.

The following books also helped my research: *Dying, A Memoir* by Cory Taylor; *The Gentle Art of*

Swedish Death Cleaning by Margareta Magnusson; *With the End in Mind: How to Live and Die Well* by Kathryn Mannix.

BBC's Woman's Hour programme on Radio 4 also covered this topic on 24 August 2023: *Living funerals: What are they and why are people choosing to have them?*

The Blue Cross charity does such important work caring for pets, including rehoming them after their owners have passed away. Their **Pet Peace of Mind** service is free. Find out more about it here: Blue-cross.org.uk

ABOUT THE AUTHOR

Ruby Speechley is a bestselling psychological thriller writer, whose titles include *Someone Else's Baby*. Previously published by Hera, she has been a journalist and worked in PR and lives in Cheshire.

Sign up to the Ruby Speechley mailing list for news, competitions and updates on future books

Visit Ruby's website: www.rubyspeechley.com

Follow Ruby on social media:

f facebook.com/Ruby-Speechley-Author-
100063999185095

X x.com/rubyspeechley

O instagram.com/rubyjtspeechley

ALSO BY RUBY SPEECHLEY

Gone

Missing

Guilty

THE
Murder
LIST

THE MURDER LIST IS A NEWSLETTER DEDICATED TO ALL THINGS CRIME AND THRILLER FICTION!

SIGN UP TO MAKE SURE YOU'RE ON OUR HIT LIST FOR GRIPPING PAGE-TURNERS AND HEARTSTOPPING READS.

SIGN UP TO OUR NEWSLETTER

BIT.LY/THEMURDERLISTNEWS

Boldwood

Boldwood Books is an award-winning fiction publishing company seeking out the best stories from around the world.

Find out more at www.boldwoodbooks.com

Join our reader community for brilliant books, competitions and offers!

Follow us
@BoldwoodBooks
@TheBoldBookClub

Sign up to our weekly
deals newsletter

https://bit.ly/BoldwoodBNewsletter

Milton Keynes UK
Ingram Content Group UK Ltd.
UKHW040629250524
443096UK00003B/48